THIEF OF CAHRAMAN

FAIRYTALES OF FOLKSHORE: BOOK ONE

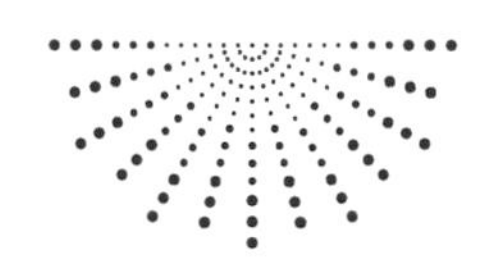

LUCY TEMPEST

THIEF OF CAHRAMAN – A RETELLING OF ALADDIN

Editors: Mary Novak, Jennifer Jansen

First edition published in 2018 by Folkshore Press

ISBN ebook: 978-1-949554-02-1

ISBN Paperback: 978-1-949554-00-7

Sign up to my VIP mailing list at www.lucytempest.com

lucytempestauthor@gmail.com

Then to the rolling Heav'n itself I cried,
Asking, "What Lamp had Destiny to guide
Her little Children stumbling in the Dark?"
And—"A blind understanding!" Heav'n replied.

The Rubaiyat, Omar Khayyam

INTRODUCTION

Welcome to the magical world of Folkshore!

Fairytales of Folkshore is a series of interconnected fairytale retellings with unique twists on much-loved, enduring themes. It starts with the *Cahraman Trilogy*, a gender-swapped reimagining of *Aladdin*.

Join each heroine on emotional, thrilling adventures full of magic, mystery, friendship and romance where true love is found in the most unexpected places and the fates of kingdoms hang in the balance.

Among the retellings will be:

Beauty & the Beast, Cinderella, Sleeping Beauty, Hades & Persephone, The Little Mermaid, Snow White...and more!

MAP

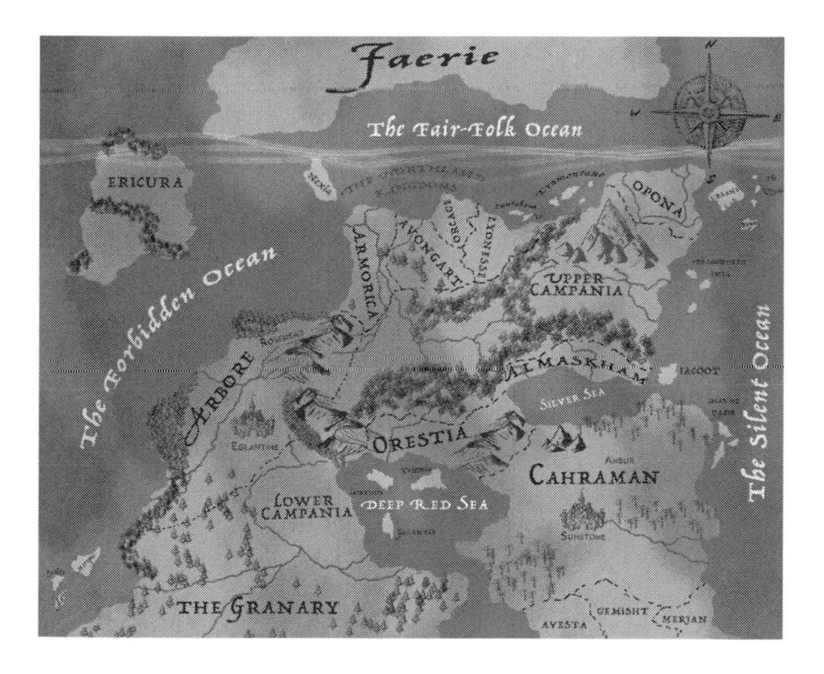
Faerie
The Fair-Folk Ocean
ERICURA
OPONA
ARMORICA
AVONGART
LYONESSE
UPPER CAMPANIA
The Forbidden Ocean
ARBORE
Silver Sea
JACOOT
The Silent Ocean
ORESTIA
EGLANTINE
CAHRAMAN
AMBUR
LOWER CAMPANIA
DEEP RED SEA
SUNSTONE
THE GRANARY
AVESTA
GEMISHT
MERJAN

CHAPTER ONE

The good part about roaming this far north in Ericura was that whenever I stole anything, its disappearance was blamed on the fairies.

At least, it was good for household items and wash-line clothes. Or whatever food I picked up from orchards and fields as I passed through towns. Anything bigger required a more sinister being to pin the blame on.

Missing livestock, children and men were blamed on the Horned God. Not that I would ever need to use him as a scapegoat. My thieving was mostly for necessities. But sometimes, I robbed those the gods weren't bothering to punish themselves. Like Lady Dufreyne, the target of today's heist.

As the wife of the resident merchant-lord of Aubenaire, Ericura's northernmost town, she lived in his mansion which was perched on a hill bordered by a stone wall that deterred both predators and thieves.

Not much could deter me. Especially when I was focused on vengeance.

My intended punishment however, would backfire if I got

caught. If the wheels scraping up the stone trail belonged to an inhabitant of the Dufreyne mansion, and I was found hanging from their second-floor window with a sack full of loot on my back, there would be no blaming the fairies. My efforts to serve justice with my sticky fingers would end in being turned over to the Horned God myself.

I shuddered at the thought, the buzz of apprehension that unfurled within me almost costing me my precarious hold on the windowsill.

Gritting my teeth, I steadied my grip, clinging to the thought that my stake-out of the Dufreyne mansion had been meticulous, that it couldn't be any of them.

I knew Lord Dufreyne himself wasn't around today. I had served him many times since I'd settled here in midwinter, the last time being yesterday, when he'd stopped by the tavern to get drunk before leaving to trade. He'd knocked back mug after mug of warm mead while slurring nonsensical rants about his late wife, his daughter, his new wife and her daughters. His drunken storytelling was always coherent compared to my usual patrons' ramblings, and along with failed bar fights, remained the most entertainment I had at work.

In contrast, most of my aggravation came from serving his new wife. She lived up to the common view of evil rich women, who believed themselves above uncouth peasants, equating themselves with royalty. And though I had never seen a real royal in my travels from the very south to the very north of Ericura, I doubted any could be as bad as her.

But what had done it for me hadn't been the many times she'd treated me, and the other tavern staff, like dirt. I was used to difficult people. It had been last week when she'd barged into the tavern, claiming that a package was supposed to be delivered there. When Miss Etheline had said that we weren't responsible for deliveries besides our own, Lady Dufreyne had gone on a rampage. She'd knocked everything off the bar and flipped tables, demolishing half of the tavern's crockery and glassware while thundering accusations at us of stealing it.

To top it all off, when Bonnie had tried to placate her as she'd stormed out—with more patience and politeness than I could have mustered—she'd pushed her aside for her troubles, knocking her down into a puddle. Bonnie's dress and book had both been ruined.

When the package had arrived a half-day later, Lady Dufreyne had made no apologies to any of us, nor had she offered to pay for the items she'd ruined.

I wasn't the type to let injustices slide, and since she'd already accused me of stealing from her, I might as well make good on that claim and replace the things she'd destroyed myself.

Now, here I was hanging out of a window, weighed down by what I stole from her home. Besides the bulging coin pouch I'd found forgotten or hidden under a bed, I'd taken two big volumes from the mansion library, two pairs of heavy leather boots, many yards of silk, and a golden, pearl-encrusted jewelry box. I'd wager none of the residents truly needed these things, and might not even miss them. But they would fill the losses Bonnie and Miss Etheline had suffered many times over. *If* I got away with stealing them.

The scrape of rough wheels on gravel was growing louder, closer, pushing the panicked immediacy to the forefront of my mind. I tried pulling myself back up and into the cluttered bedroom of either Aneira or Darla. But it was a futile and sweaty-handed struggle against the wooden sill. I had to climb down as quickly as I could without free-falling into the bushes.

A girl's voice joined the sound of crunching, getting closer up the trail faster than I could shut the window without trapping my climbing rope's hook.

"But why would I need to clean the fireplace?" complained the girl, though with a lot less displeasure and a lot more defeat than my complaints usually carried. "It's almost summer and I've already cleaned it three times last month. I breathed in so much soot, and we aren't even using it—"

She stopped abruptly, and so did the crunching noise - what I now realized was that of a bicycle. A harsher voice cut her off, indistinct like it was traveling further away from her. I resisted the urge to pause and eavesdrop, and tightened my hold on my rope to hop further down the side of the house.

A sharp sound of frustration from the girl shocked me into missing my footing on the wall. I slid down violently, drying my sweaty palms with an intense rope-burn as I held on for dear life. But my dropping weight knocked the hook off the sill and sent me crashing down the remaining feet.

I bounced off the thorny bushes and hit the lawn with a chest-rattling thump, the air escaping my lungs with a choked, throat-searing cough. It wasn't my worst fall yet, but it had been a long while since I needed to scale walls, and longer still since I was at risk of being caught.

Hissing from the flaring pain of my burnt hands, I gathered and tucked the rope into my woolen coat before scrambling up and climbing over the border wall. I landed just in time to find Ornella Dufreyne rolling up on her rickety bicycle, bags weighing down its handlebars, towing an ancient cart full of firewood.

Ella started at the sight of me, coming to complete stop.

With her crystal-clear baby blues for once void of their usual heartache, a confused frown pinched her smooth brows while stray locks of strawberry-blonde hair threatened to unfurl her messy bun.

"Adelaide?"

Despite living in Aubenaire for nearly two seasons–the longest I'd ever stayed in any town I'd roamed through–we'd barely spoken in the few times I'd seen her, always rushing. Finding me across town and at her home must be inexplicable to her.

I cracked an awkward smile and casually leaned against the wall, hoping that she couldn't hear the jewelry box and coin pouch rattling in my backpack. "Hey, Ella."

Her frown deepened as she stepped off her bicycle. "What are you doing here?"

"Oh, I was just looking for you," I said, quickly filing through all the tried and true excuses I'd used over the years. "You haven't come by the tavern in ages, so I figured the best way to talk to you was to stop by your place."

"Why? What do you want from me?" She hunched slightly, whatever curiosity she had becoming suspicion that was edged with fear.

I knew that feeling all too well, but I had never been on the receiving end of it. Which made me wonder; what did she experience inside this big, beautiful home that I had on the streets?

It made me want to clean out that house even more, sell everything down to the curtain rods and paint, and then go inform the sheriff about how bad I suspected Ella's situation was. And my suspicions were very rarely wrong.

Those instincts had been honed during my years of roaming. For more than five now, I'd hopped from town to town, skipping each one the moment I attracted too much attention. Living out of my backpack, stealing food and other things I needed, and squatting in abandoned houses was better than any 'home' the law would have placed me in. Girls with no families suffered two fates in Ericura; either becoming a godswife in a temple, or being contracted to work for women like Lady Dufreyne, who treated their maids like slaves.

From what I gathered, though she wasn't an orphan, Ella was being treated like one.

I gave her what I hoped was a reassuring smile. "Bonnie and I have been wanting to invite you over for tea, but you never appear in places we frequent. So, here I am."

It wasn't exactly a lie. Bonnie had talked about inviting Ella over. While Ella and her vicious stepsisters were barred from mingling with the rest of the town. Aneira and Darla only attended events set up by their mother and her fellow idle rich. From my stake out, I knew when the girls returned from school, when they went to events and how often their mother was with them. Ella, who seemed to be let out only to run errands, was never included in their lavish activities.

I'd been banking on their regular mid-day absences today. It was just my luck that Ella had returned earlier than usual.

Ella, now less frigid, picked up some of her shopping bags. "Why would you want to have tea with me?"

That response was word for word what I'd said to Bonnie the first time she'd invited me over. Ella probably had no friends. I didn't either until recently, but that had been because I couldn't afford to make any friends. Not when I was always going to leave them.

I adjusted my backpack and shrugged. "Why wouldn't I?"

She hunched a bit further, curling herself protectively

around the bag of produce she held, hiding half her face in the leaves of celery stalks. "I don't know."

I advanced to take the rest of the bags off her bicycle, and was met with a slight flinch and a tightening hug around the one she held. As subtle as it was, her reaction set my brain on fire. I didn't just want to take her stepmother's beloved jewels away now; I wanted to feed them to her.

I moved away gently, giving her space. After a long moment, Ella seemed to decide I wasn't about to pull any tricks or run off with her groceries, and led the way inside the house.

On my way in, I made a big show of taking in the high ceilings and the décor, just to give the impression that I had never seen this house before.

I cleared my still-burning throat to get her attention. "So, tomorrow's the bonfire."

She set her bags on the spacious kitchen's marble counter. "That it is."

"You coming? Mr. Fairborn helped build most of the wicker figures," I gushed, trying to smother the pain my raw palms felt holding the shopping bags, as I set them down. "Bonnie and I are finishing our masks tonight."

"That's great, Adelaide," she said quietly, busying herself with the groceries.

"So, you'll come over? You can make your own mask."

"No, I don't think I can..."

"Yes, you can."

She snuck a glance at the sitting room behind me. I followed her gaze, found the cement-and-stone fireplace. Why indeed would they need it cleaned when it was late spring?

This had to be petty punishment, an excuse to keep Ella busy while her step-family ran around going to events and parties. Her mousy demeanor and fearful behavior were no doubt borne out of Lady Dufreyne's capricious temper. Then another thought struck me.

Considering the baseless fury she'd unleashed on the tavern, what would her stepmother do to her if she found a whole box of expensive jewelry missing?

I couldn't bear to imagine. Which meant one thing.

I had to return the box!

There was no use in punishing her stepmother if it would lead to Ella being tortured. Helping her escape would be better. I just had to get her away from here first.

"Come to tea with us, please."

"But I have to clean the fireplace—"

I shook my head. "No, no, you really don't. It can wait."

"But—"

"If it can be my day-off from muck-work I even get paid for, then it can be your day-off too," I insisted. "If today is impossible, then meet up with Bonnie while I'm at work tomorrow. You two can come pick me up for the bonfire."

She barely blinked, seemingly stunned speechless, the pinch between her slim brows back in full force. "But I—I never…" She stopped, eyes darting around, conflicted. Then she finally exhaled. "Oh, alright. I guess an hour or two wouldn't hurt."

A thrill of relief ran through me as I started edging away from her, heading out of the kitchen. "Great! Can I use your bathroom?"

"I—I guess so, just don't use the one in Madame's bedroom."

Madame. Her stepmother had her addressing her as Madame. A servant in her own home.

Putting my anger on hold, I immediately shot up the stairs

and back into her stepmother's bedroom, placing the box back behind her boudoir's giant oval mirror. I also tossed the coin pouch back beneath one of the girls' beds. But I was keeping the silk, boots, and books for Bonnie and Mr. Fairborn. These I was sure none of them would miss.

I made sure to flush the toilet before skipping back down the carpeted staircase, backpack and guilt both much lighter.

I rushed past the kitchen, waving on my way towards the door. "Don't forget to go meet Bonnie near the tavern by noon!"

"But–"

"See you later!" I yelled as I ducked out the door and broke into a run.

Breezing past the houses that surrounded the manor, I left the richer district of town. I shortcut my way to the east by hopping the brick-and-mortar fences that divided cottages facing the crop fields, barreling down the dusty road that snaked downhill into the town square. Once on paved stone, I ran downwards towards the end of town, where the houses of business owners sat near the greenery.

My destination loomed on the horizon of the uphill road as I slowed my run to walk up the slope, panting loudly, my tongue drier than the dusty soles of my worn leather boots, and a stitch cutting into my side like a butcher had just dug his cleaver in it. Bothered and ragged as I felt from the events of the last half-hour, the sight of the Fairborn house at the end of the road soothed all my aches like a healing balm.

The Fairborn's guest room was the latest spot I'd been staying, and the first place where I had actively lived rather than squatted, in years. Not long after I had met Bonnie, she had offered—no, *insisted* that I come to stay with them. I had hesitated at first because never once had anyone offered me help without expecting a great deal in return. But over two weeks of regularly visiting my work and inviting me over, she'd worn me down, her consistent goodwill worming its way into my heart and reassuring me that she was telling the truth when she said she wanted nothing more than my company and for me to give the house some warmth. She hadn't aimed to harbor me in the servant's quarters or employ me as one. Both she and her father had me living openly among them, like I was family.

I wondered when was the last time someone had treated Ella like that.

Now in my room, I was trying to kick the overfilled backpack under the bed, when the door swung open.

Though I had been living here for over three months, old habits clung tighter than limpets. I still behaved like I was squatting in someone's summer cottage, jumping at the smallest sounds and diving into hiding spots when I heard people pass by, scared of being caught. It was hard to accept that I was wanted here, to the point that Mr. Fairborn refused to let me pay rent. As a compromise, I helped around the house and his workshop, ran most errands, and kept an eye out for Bonnie, because someone as petite and pretty as her was a prime target to get carried off by a fairy knight.

Not that I had ever seen a fairy, despite the frequent complaints about them here, and the belief that they filled the Hornswoods, riding unicorns and leaving rings of mushrooms in their wake.

"Ada?" Bonnie stuck her head into the room. Tucked under her arm was the book Lady Dufreyne had knocked into the puddle, its pages brown, bumpy and wrinkled. "Where were you?"

Breathing out a sigh of relief, I sat on the bed and took my time properly unlacing my boots. "I just left to get something."

"Get what?"

I reached into the leather backpack and took out the two books, both leather-bound tomes. One was a dusty, plain blue hardcover with no visible title, and the other was even dustier, coppery, and had gold-embossed letters proclaiming it *The Known World.*

"I found these, one to replace the one that got wet, and the other because it has all the old stuff you like to read about in it," I said. "Or at least I think it does. I don't know, I flipped through it and found a lot of maps and engravings and such. Figured you'd like it."

Bonnie took *The Known World* with gentle reverence, fascination glimmering in the depths of her large eyes like twin flames.

She carefully flipped the big, yellowed pages, eyes running back and forth over the words as she mouthed them under her breath. "Where did you get this?"

"It was personally delivered by Saint Alban himself, courtesy of his impending festival."

Her wondering expression fell into a flat-browed stare. "Ada."

"Does it matter where I got it?" I stood, busying myself with tidying my neat room.

The Fairborn house, unlike many of the ancient stone-brick houses in this part of the land, was unworn by time. It might have been a feat of construction on her ancestor's part, but Bonnie's cozy little house was in better condition than most of the affluent residences in the towns I had passed through. Those houses held heirloom furniture that creaked and buckled, walls that were hollowed out to house rats and floors that groaned like they had bellyaches.

Bonnie sat on the bed, flipping through the pages a little faster than before like she was searching for a particular chapter. "You're really not going to tell me where you found this?"

"I may or may not have found this near the Dufreyne mansion."

I hadn't had the need to steal much since moving in with her and her father. Food was available, so were old clothes of her late mother's big enough to fit me, and soaps and brushes to keep myself clean and neat.

But Bonnie knew it was hard for me to let opportunities for valuables pass me by. Even though I didn't need to take apples from someone's orchard or look through bags forgotten at the tavern, I still had that hungry, desperate impulse.

"Before you say anything," I said. "She owes you those books. And it's not like anyone in that house is using them. Their library is a mausoleum."

I stopped by the spotted mirror on the wall to tie up my hair. It was one of the few glass mirrors I had come across, and unlike the rest of the house, its age showed on its rusting iron frame and its rotting visage, littered with black spots and fogging up at the edges. But I could still see myself, and Bonnie, clearly in it.

I couldn't help comparing myself to her as I watched both our reflections.

Bonnie's hair was a glossy chestnut-brown, the kind that brushed itself and fell in glistening waves. When pulled back, it would end in one big curl, as her ponytail did now. Mine was so dark it absorbed rather than reflected light, and nothing could make it curl or wave. Aside from her enviable hair, she had a heart-shaped face with gorgeous, upturned features as petite as her frame. All this made my towering height, choppy hair, big mouth, and dark, hooded eyes hideous by comparison.

For a treacherous second, my mind wandered to my mother. My heart squeezed, making it hard to breathe as I tried to remember her face. I knew I resembled her more than anyone else in Ericura, but I couldn't recall much else. Had my mother's eyes been blue or grey? Or had they been blue-grey? I couldn't remember. Even though she'd died five years ago, my memories of her were somehow fading as fast as sunlight died at twilight.

Then my mind swerved away from her memory as it always did, turning back to Ella. I wondered what had happened to the original Lady Dufreyne, and what Ella's life had been like before she died.

Shaking off the saddening thoughts, I said, "By the way, I've invited Ella to join us tomorrow."

That made Bonnie look up, mouth half-open in shock. "And she said yes?"

"Well..." I stopped messing with my hair, meeting her eyes in the reflection. "I didn't give her the chance to say no."

Bonnie snorted fondly. "I've been trying to get her to visit me for years, or just accompany me anywhere. Yet one run in with you and you get her to accept. With me she always says she's busy, I don't know how."

"Her witch of a stepmother always keeps her busy with inane chores, like cleaning the chimney on the verge of summer," I said bitterly. "Do you think if we accuse Lady Dufreyne of being a witch Ella will be free of her?"

She looked up, her button nose, small chin, and big, upturned eyes—the same shade of cornflower-blue as her dress—all crinkled in unease. "That's a serious accusation."

"How she treats Ella is also very serious. We ought to help her out of there."

Thoughtfully, she twisted her lips from one side to the other, like she was carefully choosing her words. "You can't force someone to do something they don't want to."

"Are you telling me she likes being treated like a slave in her own home? Why is the heiress herself tending to the orders of the woman invading her space?"

Bonnie sighed, checking the nameless blue book now. "Ella won't inherit much, not unless she marries a man who will continue Lord Dufreyne's business, making him the heir. Other than that, Lady Dufreyne is still young, and could give him a son any day now."

True as that was, the thought of Ella forever being a servant in her own home stoked the raging fire in my head, feeding the headache that had begun to form at my temple.

But Bonnie was right. I couldn't force anything.

Aside from trying to make Ella's life more bearable, giving her friends who cared about her for a change, I could do nothing.

I let my shoulders slump and sighed. "Want to get started on the masks?"

As if she had been waiting for me to bring it up, Bonnie hopped to her feet and preceded me out, still focusing more on the pages rather than the hall ahead. "I have everything set up downstairs. When do you have to go help transport the mead again?"

"Tomorrow." I went down the stairs first, to prevent any possible trips. Bonnie tended to walk around with her nose in a book, which sometimes led to heart-stopping stumbles like her missing three entire steps and diving at the floor like a clumsy hawk upon its prey. "Etheline expects me at the back of the tavern by the afternoon. I'm going to be carting all the barrels of beer, mead and even wine down to the festival stands, so I need to make use of light."

"Can I come with? Perhaps we can pick up Ella ourselves and bring her back with us."

Reaching the ground floor, I turned, arms out. "That's a great idea."

As predicted, she moved to turn a page and missed the last two steps with a surprised squeak. I caught and swung her off the stairs, setting her near the sitting room.

She breathed out a relieved sigh. "*Wooh!* Thank you."

I tutted. "You really need to be careful, Bon."

"And you need to stop swiping, but, as you always say, old habits are hard to buck."

"Me not wanting to scrape by is a tad different than you falling down the stairs daily."

Her vivid blue eyes rolled up to the side in mock-thoughtfulness. "Is it really? How many times have you almost fallen off roofs?"

I was about to argue then remembered my climb down the second-floor window today, which almost ended in disaster.

"And many people die in their own beds," I said instead, which didn't do much to strengthen my initial point.

"That's what I keep telling my father, but he still won't let me travel, or stay out past sunset, or even work outside the house."

"I don't blame him. What if someone steps on you out there?" I teased.

Dropping her books on the couch by the low, polished wooden table crowded with all our needed supplies, she threw herself beside them. "I'm not that small."

I folded my legs on the floor by the redbrick fireplace,

picking up the wooden mask Mr. Fairborn had brought home for me from among the jars of paint, beads, candles, and feathers, and chuckled. "I've seen garden gnomes taller than you."

She stuck out her tongue. "And I've seen trees shorter than you. But just you watch, I'll put the fluffiest feathers on my mask and stand taller than you."

She settled on the couch, gaze flitting from the illustrations in the open book to her white porcelain mask, a scary, ghost-like thing that I recognized as an Eastern import from the strange seaport town of Galba. I had spent three months there as a waitress in a seaside restaurant, and just the memory brought back the smell of brine, fish and dirty ice.

According to common belief there, one night every year, the fog that hung over the waters there would clear up and weaken the barrier between our world and Faerie–what they called Man's Reach. On that night, the people would put on those terrifying white masks, and run around scaring each other and presumably whatever would come through the barrier.

It wasn't much unlike what we were doing now, which made me wonder...

"Bonnie?" I began, holding a candle over the lit lantern with one hand and picking up my swan feathers with the other. "What is the purpose of all this again?"

Bonnie broke her staring contest with the book's pages just long enough to give me a wide, excited grin. I was in for a passionate lecture.

"Well, you remember how I said that I want to leave, right?"

"Something I will never understand, but oh yes, I remember."

Since I had met her, she had quizzed me about my travels,

following each recount with a probing question, asking for descriptions so detailed it was like she was trying to pry the memories out from my mind and brand them in hers. She'd been compensating, since the most she could get to see beyond this town was through the pages of her prized storybooks.

But it was better that way because my journey from South to North had less adventure, romance and magic and more biting hunger, cold nights and fearful scurrying than her boundless imagination could conjure.

While I hoped to never travel again, to make this town the place I remained for the rest of my life, there was nothing she wanted more than to leave. To where? She didn't know and didn't care. And that upset me, because she couldn't comprehend that there was nothing more nerve-wracking than aimless, perilous wandering.

She dipped her brush in the gold paint bottle and began to carefully outline the mask's hollow eyes. "The origin of St. Alban's festival is lost to time, but some stories say that around that time centuries ago, Alban led the Pale Men out of their land, across the sea and onto Ericura, where they traveled north to escape the Sun until they hit Man's Reach."

"Which is the Hornswoods around here." That was the forest that covered the end of this town, marking it as the last frontier of our world. Common belief in Ericura was that beyond it lay the fairy world.

"Correct," she said with a flourish, flicking droplets of gold paint into the air. "The story goes that they wanted to go through the woods to reach Faerie, but something kept them out. They also couldn't reach it through the sea, thus naming all the points where men could go no further, Man's Reach. They were either unable or unwilling to go back to their motherland, and that made them stay and settle the North. In time, those settlers' descendants spread all over Ericura."

I nodded along, still confused. "Nice story. And you want to leave why?"

She did a little, frustrated shimmy in her seat. "Ada, don't you see? These stories prove that there are other lands out there! We aren't of Ericura, not truly. Our ancestors came from somewhere else, somewhere we, for some reason, never hear or speak of. Doesn't that make you curious?"

Unease crept up from my guts like bile, turning down my mouth in a grimace. "Not really."

She crossed her arms, pouting. "Haven't you ever wondered where you got your black hair from? It's quite a rare trait, I'm told. Even in the South."

As much as I hated being reminded of my difference, she was right. And it wasn't only my hair. I looked nothing like those in the South...or the North. I'd always wondered about that.

Southerners with dark hair were a minority. And they always grew it in big waves or curls. They also had warmer complexions than mine, but easily tanned and almost always had colorful eyes. In the North, people were like Bonnie, with very fair skin that would freckle or burn in the sun, had all hair colors but black, and vivid eyes, too.

Yet my mother, who'd looked the most like me, apart from colored eyes, had claimed to come from this part of the North.

I removed the candle from the fire, dripping the wax along the rim of the mask to quickly stick on the feathers and beads. "I'm all ears."

Bonnie abandoned her mask, picking up the book to show me the illustration of a landmass with islands and seas dubbed THE FOLKSHORE.

One of the isles on the top left was marked HERICEURRA. Right across a vast sea dubbed The Forbidden Ocean to the east was a land called ARBORIA, which she tapped for emphasis. "This! This is what I believe is our motherland."

I scanned the map skeptically. "I don't know, Bonnie, that whole book could be some bored old monk's fantasy."

"Why would it be called *The Known World* then?"

I had no good defense against that. In fact, I felt a bit cornered. "Don't you think we'd know about other lands if they existed? I mean, the story of Alban and the Pale Men sounds like a silly folktale. Why would you want to escape the sun? And we didn't escape it, it's still here, every morning without fail, shining into my eyes and burning crops in the summer."

"How about this? We go and check the Hornswoods, and if we find nothing but a dead end, we turn back."

I readily nodded, hoping that that would be the end of this idea of other lands and her obsession with leaving.

"And then I will travel south to cross the sea and search for our motherland."

Fear flared up within me like oil had been splashed onto a tiny flame, sending it roaring into a fire. "You will do no such thing. You wouldn't make it past the town limits alone."

"I won't be alone if you come with me."

Though it was a relief that she wouldn't mind my protection, and wanted me to accompany her, I didn't like this. If this was about a daytrip to another town, or even just to the South, then it wouldn't have been a problem. Even if I abhorred traveling, I would have done it gladly for her, especially if she agreed that in the end, we'd come back. But she wanted to try leaving Ericura altogether. I certainly didn't want that.

There was also the fact that no one had ever managed that before.

And since no one had, there was no harm in letting her realize the futility for herself, so we'd finally let this topic of leaving die.

I abandoned my mask, dusting the glitter from my hands. "Alright, let's go check the trees before sundown."

Faster than a startled cat, she jumped to her feet and shot out the door. I chased after her, hopping over the many mechanical parts Mr. Fairborn left strewn about the front yard, before launching into my second harsh sprint of the day. I was soon out of breath with the cleaved stitch back in my side. Even my longer legs were no match for Bonnie's eagerness. No matter how fast I ran, she remained a shrinking blue dot in the wide-open, verdant distance.

The road ended in a sea of tall, damp, grass and I had to stomp through it, the pungent scent of crushed blades and soil rivaling that of my sweat.

At the end of the field in a clearing, towering above the wildflowers was the nightmarish statue of the Horned God. It was hunched over menacingly, with a visible ribcage, huge clawed hands, a masked face and twisted reindeer antlers that cast long shadows on the ground. Seeing it up close more than unnerved me.

Steeling myself, I took the last few steps past the statue and towards the edge of the woods to tap Bonnie on the shoulder. "You could have waited for me."

She beamed up at me innocently, batting her enviable lashes. "I could have, but I also couldn't risk you changing your mind."

I huffed, turning to leave. "Well, we got here. Nothing's new. Let's go back and start on dinner before your father gets home."

She caught my elbow and pulled. She wouldn't have moved me an inch if I didn't want to, but I couldn't say no to her. Humoring her with this silly idea was the least I could do.

As soon as we moved past the first row of giant greyish trees and entered the woods, daylight was snuffed like a blown out candle. Dead leaves and twigs crunched beneath our feet and fog hung above us, thick as low-hanging clouds, creating a wet, chilly atmosphere that threw me back into dark autumn twilights.

A soft breeze followed us in, rattling the branches so the leaves whispered above us. Then I felt something shift, and I heard a loud rip, like someone tearing cloth.

My head snapped in the sound's direction.

I gripped the hand Bonnie kept on my arm and whispered, "Did you hear that?"

"What?"

"I heard...something, coming from the left."

Bonnie squinted in that direction. "What did it sound like?"

That had me stumped. What I heard didn't make sense, as it didn't sound like something walking.

But since she hadn't heard it, I might have imagined it. Or it could have been just rustling branches. Or something.

I tried to ignore the possibilities my mind kept coming up with, about what that something could be, focusing on walking further in, keeping an eye out for deer or, hopefully, unicorns.

We weren't fifty feet in when I heard the noise again, a deep, eerie whooshing noise like someone sucking in air. I snapped my head to the left again, goosebumps running like wildfire through my body. This time, I found two lights hanging between the trees.

The lights were too big to be fireflies. They quickly moved closer, getting bigger.

I froze, my heartbeats escalating into pounding, each deep thump louder and harder than the one before, until I felt them shaking my whole body. "Bonnie. *Bonnie.* Do you see that? What is that? Is that a deer?"

Unfazed, she looked back to the left. Then, when she spotted the floating lights, she stiffened up. "That's...not a deer."

The lights hovered closer soundlessly getting brighter through the fog until their precise shape became clear. They were—

Eyes!

Something taller than me, bigger than me, was watching us.

Watching me.

Throughout years of constant risk and peril, I'd known varying levels of dread and desperation. This was the first time I knew what primal, bone-deep fear was.

I now remembered this wasn't the first time I sensed this sinister presence. But I'd never felt it this close, never been caught in its terrifying stare.

Heart almost ramming out of my chest with the burst of panic, I grabbed hold of Bonnie's arm with all my strength and dragged her behind me.

But even as I ran with all the breath I had left in me, leaving the woods behind and heading back to safety, I somehow felt I couldn't escape these eyes. Not now that they had found me.

CHAPTER TWO

The glowing eyes had burned themselves behind my eyelids. I saw them in my dreams and they flashed in the brief darkness every time I blinked.

I'd barely gotten any sleep, with nightmares waking me up three times throughout the night. They all involved the hovering eyes glaring at me from the Horned God's mask as he stalked me through an endless wasteland.

The last time had been before dawn, and it had taken me three hours to fall asleep again for one dreamless round. I ended up being late for work.

It was bonfire day, the start of Saint Alban's festival, and everyone was in a hurry to get everything ready and delivered to the campsite before late afternoon. I was in charge of the alcohol, but I had come too late to call dibs on a cart, so I was stuck waiting until someone came back to hand me the reins.

I now stood outside the tavern, as skittish as a fox, jumping at the daily racket of slamming doors and shouted demands. And there came Bonnie, casually strolling towards me, oddly unbothered. I ran to meet her halfway, doing my utmost to avoid glancing at the woods in the distance.

"Good morning," she greeted cheerily, her silky hair down and crowned with a wreath of red roses, wearing her favorite green cloak and carrying a basket that had my mask peeking out of it. She dug into the basket, handed me a blueberry muffin. "I'm guessing you ran out without having breakfast."

I stared at the muffin, then at her, puzzled. "Are you alright?"

"I should be asking you that. You look like you've seen a ghost."

"That's because I have, and so did you."

When she only hummed, I grew a bit more concerned. She traded the muffin for my arm, linking our elbows as we walked uphill to where the unfortunately-named Poison Apple tavern sat. The welded sign perched on its black-tiled roof was shaped and painted like a red apple with a single green leaf, easy to spot from a mile away.

"You did see it, right? I didn't imagine that?"

"Hmm? No, no, I saw the eyes too," she said, her own intense eyes shining with wonder in the midday light. "I haven't been able to stop thinking about them."

"Me neither..."

"I can't wait to go back and see what they actually were, and try going a bit farther."

I stopped dead, yanking her back. "Wait, what?"

Now it was her turn to be confused. "We found something beyond the trees, that means there is life beyond our borders."

"I get that. Why do you want to go back?"

"Did you forget our deal? If we did find anything in the Hornswoods, you and I would explore further."

My jaw dropped and the only sound I could manage was a croak of bafflement.

"All these tales about fairies, goblins and motherlands, and we've never actually *seen* any of them," she continued, unaware of my stunned state. "But last night was the first time I had ever seen proof beyond stories. There *is* life apart from us, and if Ericura is an island, and if the Fair-Folk's shore —as Faerie is called here—" On cue, she whipped out *The Known World* from her cloak pocket. "—is across the Fair-Folk Ocean on the other side of those trees, then the rest of the Folkshore, is right across us from the South across the Forbidden Ocean. We just have to pick which end to rent a boat and travel to."

"Are you serious?"

Whatever disbelief and reluctance I had tried to get across had gone completely over her head, because, somehow, she got even more excited.

"I know, right? It would be easier if we left from here, so going to Faerie would be the shorter distance, but you never know with going to fairyland. Stories about time there concern me a little, so it'd be a safer bet to take the long route to the motherland—"

"Bonnibel." I cut her off firmly, feeling more wound up and anxious than I did before.

Her grin dimmed, shrinking into an uncertain expression. "What is it?"

That was a good question, because I had no clue how to put my many objections in order, or even in understandable sentences. All that had happened between yesterday afternoon and just this minute had my every thought running around my head, braying like a hoard of panicked donkeys.

"I don't—how—why would you—" I began, stopping to

find the rest of the words. "Those eyes were not an invitation."

She resumed her pace, tugging me along. "What do you mean?"

"I mean, how did you look at whatever that thing was and think 'this is good news'? What about it convinced you that a journey through there, to another unknown world, was a good idea?"

"If going through there is too much, then, as I said, we can go south, take a boat, and travel to Arboria, or whatever the land of the Pale Men was called."

"What part of *Forbidden Ocean* did you not understand? What makes you think crossing it would be as easy as you make it sound?"

"Why wouldn't it? Fishermen say travel by lake is a lot faster and easier than traveling by land, so, we ought to take the chance to sail while the summer tides are calm."

I couldn't help gawking at that statement. As smart as Bonnie was, she tended to speak like she had the blind bravery of a sheepdog, when she, in fact, was deeply naïve. And naivety wasn't something you could convince people out of; they needed to experience the harshness of reality themselves. To Bonnie, all her sad experiences were limited to things like burning her hand on a hot stove or barely remembering her mother.

But as much as I wanted her to understand what I was feeling—this overwhelming reluctance to move again—and why I felt it, I wouldn't wish my eye-opening experiences on her. I wanted her to remain as innocent and optimistic as she was. For while the cost of retaining both was her boredom and frustration, their loss meant becoming me—forever anxious and vulnerable from years of risk and loneliness.

Since I had no response other than a variety of frustrated noises, I decided not to answer. We could discuss this later, when my fear had subsided and her excitement had waned. Maybe I could argue for a trip to Galba and that could cure her ennui, show her that there was nothing beyond Ericura we could ever need.

She let go of my arm as we reached the tavern, looking up at me with her head cocked in concern. "Ada, are you sure you're not ill?"

"Just have a lot on my mind," I said, holding open the door for her. "We'll talk at the bonfire."

Nodding, she entered and made a beeline to her usual booth by the window. She soon had her nose in her book, just like the first day we met.

As one of the newest establishments in this whole area, the tavern didn't have the rundown appearance of all the other pubs, lodges and inns I briefly worked in over the years. It was a long and wide three-story building with whitewashed walls, a red door, and green-framed windows with shutters only on the bottom floor.

I took a deep breath and walked in, expecting the usual stench of spilled beer and pipe smoke to hit my nose along with the tone-deaf chatter of tipsy patrons, but it was surprisingly empty. The only people around were staff members and volunteers who were loading food into multi-layered carts as soon as the cooks flung them out of the kitchen, and rolling them out the double-door entrance, ready to stack the tables near the bonfire. Henny, the bartender I was meant to help today, was notably absent, and in his place, to my surprise, was Bonnie's father chatting up the owner.

Miss Etheline sat on the bar in a puffy, glossy, fuchsia dress, idly kicking her legs in the air. Her pink-rimmed, cat-eyed spectacles were perched on her curly red hair that was arranged in a towering hairstyle, her brilliant seafoam-green eyes squinting at the list she was going through. Mr. Fairborn, a sturdy, middle-aged man with a kind face, grey eyes and thick, greying hair, seemed to be trying his hardest to get her attention.

From all the stories Bonnie had mentioned about him trying to bring home replacement mothers, Etheline would be both the oddest yet safest choice. She was a charming, soft-spoken woman who always seemed to be distracted and had eyes so bright they practically glowed. Her fair skin shone like a lustrous pearl. I had figured she was a foreigner and a newcomer, like myself, but some of our patrons and staff acted like she had been here for most of their lives.

I returned Mr. Fairborn's greeting wave as I picked up my work apron.

Etheline looked up from her list, not seeming surprised or even bothered by my tardiness. "Ah, there you are. Business run a bit later than usual yesterday?"

For a moment it seemed as if she knew exactly what I'd been doing yesterday. Then my anxious thoughts came to a screeching halt, only to kick back into gear as I focused on seeming as calm as possible. "No, ma'am, I just forgot today was a half day-off, not a full day."

"Oh, well, that's what I get for employing flighty girls," she said good-naturedly, jabbing her thumb towards the storage room door, almost hitting Mr. Fairborn in the face with her writing quill.

"Is there anything else I can still do?"

She ran her bright eyes over her list. "Let me check."

In the rare emptiness of the tavern, I found myself

reflecting on the three people left around and how I had ended up here with them.

It had all started a year ago, when I'd remembered one of the few answers my mother had allowed me. Usually, my efforts to pry into her past, to find out who we were, where my father's family was and why they wouldn't house his widow and child, had all been rebuffed. But she'd once let slip where she had come from in Ericura. Somewhere near the border of Man's Reach. She had also once mentioned a woman, a cousin of sorts, named Belaina Fairborn.

Once I'd spotted Alban's Lair, now Aubenaire on a map, I'd known that had to be my mother's hometown and high-tailed it here, for the hope that I'd find her relative and maybe a new home to settle in.

When I had arrived asking for Belaina at the Poison Apple tavern, Etheline had pointed me to the cemetery where her grave sat beneath an effigy depicting her as the Field Queen, with wheat in her hands and flowers in her hair. It had been a stroke of luck that Bonnie was the spitting image of her mother's effigy, and that she'd sought me out right before I had planned to leave again.

Etheline tapped her list with the feather pen. "Henny has already taken the wine bottles down, so you have barrel duty. Four meads, two beers."

"Yes, ma'am, right away, ma'am." I rushed into the storage room, avoiding her eyes.

If I centered all my thoughts on my task, my mind wouldn't have time to wander towards scary what-ifs and theories about *those* eyes.

Before Aubenaire, my height and strong bone structure had made it easier to pass myself off as an adult. But the day I walked in here asking about the *Help Wanted* sign lodged in the grass, Etheline's only question had been, "When do you turn eighteen?"

I was nine months away at the time, but had said I was over eighteen by that much. She'd given me a look that had said she knew I was lying, but had still hired me. She'd put me to work in the bar rather than the lodging area, where most women she employed worked. I suspected that she also somehow knew if I'd taken on maid duties, I would have ended up looking through people's things or taking my tips straight from their pockets. I'd done that before with the traveling merchants who wouldn't miss a few coins, but mostly with the customers who harassed me or made lewd comments or advances towards me or other barmaids.

The way she seemed to know and see what others didn't, among many other things, could count as evidence of her being a witch. But since she was the last person I wanted to see burn with the wicker beasts tonight, I was going to keep my silly suspicions to myself.

I now pressed myself against the cold stonewall corridor leading to the cellar as other staff members rushed by me, and caught the only empty-handed man by the elbow.

"Nestor, can you help me?"

"Hmm?" He blinked at me, before his vivid blue eyes brightened even more with understanding. "Oh, sure. What do you need?"

"Can you help me take the barrels off the shelves? I'll carry them up from the cellar, get the trolleys and set them up, but I can't lift them down by myself."

He frowned. "Why did she stick you with barrel duty? Shouldn't you be, like, setting up the food or making the wreaths and crowns with the other ladies?"

"I was too late for that. I think this is her way of punishing me."

"Oh." He nodded and turned to head back downstairs. "Kay, I'll get them down for you." As I followed, he stopped a few steps down and turned to me. "But you'll have to do me a favor later tonight."

It was my mind's turn to lag, returning his earlier startled blinking. "What is it?"

Nestor stuck his hands in his pockets with an awkward shrug, a half-smile bringing out the dimples in his flushed cheeks. "Can you…would you…you know, mind helping me set up a time for an outing around town? Maybe a picnic?"

"Like one of the staff dinners?"

He chuckled, shaking his head, as he ran a hand through his sweaty auburn hair, making it stick up in an effortless, rakish look that made my heart skip a beat. "No, no, I mean like I want a one-on-one thing. And I've been meaning to ask, you live with the Fairborns, right? They're your relatives and stuff, so, do you think Mr. Fairborn would allow it or…?"

I froze on my step, forgetting how to breathe, keeping the air trapped in my chest until it burned. My answer came out as a wheezing exhale. "I guess? He doesn't mind what we do as long as it's within town limits and during the day."

"Great! If you could talk to him about that, and tell me what time and what kind of food would suit the picnic, that'd be—that'd be much appreciated." His laugh was nervous as he ran down the rest of the steps, stumbling into the cellar door before disappearing behind it.

I remained stuck on the stairs, trying to piece together what just happened.

Did he just ask to court me? It sounded like he did. Like he wanted me to go on a picnic with him in exchange for him helping me with my work.

I had nothing to compare this to because whenever I'd asked any other boy for help, I'd returned the favor by usually filling in for them if they were late or had to leave early.

Did he just seriously ask me out on a picnic?

The feeling returned to my legs once the shock wore off. I went back outside in a daze, taking the trolleys left behind by those who'd come back from transporting wine and food.

Boys had rarely paid attention to me. Most of the time I hadn't wanted anyone, anywhere to take note of me. But even if I had wanted one to notice me, there had been no point in pursuing the idea, the same way I hadn't been able to make friends. I'd always had to leave sooner or later.

But I lived here now, hopefully for good.

Was this a chance for me to be with someone? To build a life beyond this tavern and the Fairborn house? If I married Nestor I could truly become a member of the community, become part of his family, and start my own family with him.

I would never be alone again.

But I was getting *way* ahead of myself. He asked for a picnic, to return the favor with my company for an afternoon. If things went well, if he liked me that much...

I couldn't help falling back into the daydream of a true domestic life here. It would be like a full circle, becoming a part of the land my mother claimed to have come from, with my journey ending by naming my first daughter after her.

When I snapped out of it and rolled the trolleys back in, the barrels were at the top of the stairs rather than waiting for me at the bottom. A pleased flush overtook me as I fought down a giddy smile. I'd heard of boys trying to win girls' favors through help and gifts, but I had never thought I'd be on the receiving end of it myself.

Elation filled my chest like a balloon, making me light on my feet, practically floating as I rolled out the barrels, set them on the cart and rode down the hill with the horse leading the way, more focused than I was.

Though we were on the verge of summer, the last chilly remnants of spring clung in the air, breaths of wind and vapor that covered my skin like cool sweat, and hung from the biggest field flowers in fat dewdrops. Then, while traversing the vast green sea of fields on our way towards the bonfire campsite, the horse took a surprise turn and dragged the cart closer to the Hornswoods.

Near the clearing, the chill went from that of a late spring breeze to a creeping winter freeze, sending harsh shivers through my body. I hunched, tightening my grip on the reins to steer the horse back on the straight path, to avoid coming near the antlered figure that loomed over the clearing.

Just as we pulled away from the trees, I again felt something watching me. That same thing I'd felt yesterday. My marrow froze with the surge of unreasoning panic all over again. I tossed a panting glance behind me, to assure myself that it was all in my mind, that the statue hadn't come to life and begun to stalk me, its eye-slits glowing like pits of hellfire.

It hadn't. It was still where it had always been, an unsightly horror guarding the mile-high grey trees behind it. But beyond it I could see something move.

Swallowing the bile of dread, I looked back ahead, shaking all over as I prodded my horse to go faster. I tried to steel myself with the rational thought that it must be a deer or a bear, or whatever wildlife lived this far north. Or it might even be the aforementioned fairies, hunting said deer and bears with their magic arrows and unicorns. Either way, neither would be watching me.

It didn't work. I still couldn't shake the conviction that whatever it was, it had been watching me specifically.

I was still shaking when I arrived at the campsite an hour later. It took effort to unload my cart and steady myself. But it took delivering the liquor to the stone tables near the wicker figures to get me excited.

It was a setting straight out of schoolbook engravings. An ancient stone basin filled with logs, surrounded by the giant wicker effigies of a woman, a man, a cow and a reindeer, each representation standing on a cardinal direction. The Field Queen, the Pale Man, the Mother Goddess and the Horned God. Fertility, bravery, life, and death.

I couldn't wait to help burn the last one.

By the time I returned to the tavern, dusk had arrived and Bonnie was waiting for me outside, her ghost-like mask on, while her father and Etheline chatted on the porch behind her.

I parked the cart and waved at them. "Did Ella show up?"

Bonnie tilted her head, her eyes narrowed in a silent question of "Who?" before remembering with a long "Ohhh, no!"

"You mean Ornella Dufreyne?" Mr. Fairborn asked me, scratching his stubbly cheek. "She's finally joining us tonight?"

"What do you mean finally?"

Mr. Fairborn shrugged, sticking his hands in his pockets. "I've been trying to have her and Bonnie be friends ever since her mother died, but any time I asked her father to bring her over, he would always be busy, or out of town. Then that screeching harpy moved in with her foul daughters—"

"Dad." Bonnie nudged him with her book, cutting off his oncoming tirade.

"Sorry, dear." Mr. Fairborn shook his head, reaching out to stroke Bonnie's hair. "I'm afraid in my old age I have little patience left for difficult people."

"Oh, I find if anything, your patience grows as you age," said Etheline, seeming to gaze into thin air over my head. "Bothersome people like that become a source of entertainment after a while, especially if you know how to deal with them."

It was no secret that anyone here who owned a business detested Lady Dufreyne, as she treated them and their underlings like her own personal servants. Etheline had to be the only person here not to badmouth her. Even when she'd thrown her destructive tantrum in the tavern, Etheline had only offered her a slight chuckle and headshake, like the whole thing had amused her more than anything.

"So, should we go get her before it gets too dark?" I suggested.

"No," said Miss Etheline, descending the porch steps and slipping on her blue lacquered mask. "Better not to get involved with that family. Last thing we need is Dolora stomping back in here and breaking my new glassware because she thinks we kidnapped her slave."

I couldn't help cringing at that.

Mr. Fairborn reached the ground first, hand held out. "May I escort you?"

Etheline gave him a gracious tilt of her head. "You may." She then turned to me, offering me her ring of keys, seafoam eyes so vivid they appeared to be glowing behind her mask. "Adelaide, do you mind finishing up and hustling everyone else out then locking up behind you?"

Being the last one out during nightfall was the last thing I needed right now, but my job came before my knee-knocking fear.

Forcing a calm smile, I took the keys on my way in. "No, ma'am."

"Try not to take long, girls," Mr. Fairborn said as they walked away. "We're setting the wickers alight soon and I believe Adelaide claimed dibs on the reindeer."

"Yep, first light on that horned beast is ours," I murmured as I headed to draw the curtains on each barroom window.

"Don't worry, Dad, we'll be right behind you." Bonnie waved them off, before rushing to follow me in.

Once the door was shut, Bonnie hopped up onto the bar, feet kicking, eager eyes following me behind her moon-white mask. I had a feeling I was about to be cornered back into the dreaded subject and decided to move around as much as possible to avoid talking.

As I went around wiping down tables and booths with a wet rag, she cracked open that blasted book and cleared her throat. "So, have you had time to think about it?"

I made a show of scraping dried food off a table. "About what?"

"About which way you'd like to travel, through the woods or across the sea?"

"How about to the nearest lake town? You've never seen a lake, right? It's like a sea but you know where it ends."

She showed me the map of Folkshore again, tapping the darker space between HERICEURRA and ARBORIA. "We know where the sea ends. It ends where we need to go."

I held back a pathetic whine. "We don't need to go anywhere, you know. We have everything here."

"Everything but answers."

"But I don't have any questions."

"Adelaide!"

"What?"

"Why are you being so odd today?" She slid her mask up on her hair to scrutinize me with a wrinkled nose and brow. "Is it about you getting spooked yesterday?"

"Spooked is an understatement."

"Really? Years of living on your own, sleeping who knows where and eating who knows what and a deer's eyes are what does it?"

The muscle-tightening worry from earlier was now back in full-force, not just from whatever being had caught me in a staring contest yesterday, but because I couldn't find a nice or reasonable way to tell her to drop the subject.

I threw the rag onto the floor and started wiping with my foot, following a trail of drizzled beer. "You yourself said it wasn't a deer, Bonnie."

"Then what do you think it was?"

"I don't know, and I don't want to know."

She shut the book with a loud slap, the flames in her eyes extinguished, her eager impatience lingering like smoke. "Why are you being like this? How do you go from being reckless and adventurous to being so...so timid?"

I resented that. I had never claimed to be a gutsy, fearless adventurer like her folktale heroes. I was just someone who did whatever it took to survive. And right now, the best case for my survival would be staying put, not seeking out fairy creatures or rowing to an unknown land.

There was no way I could explain all I felt without her bringing up my past experiences as contradictions. It wasn't her fault that she couldn't understand me, just like I couldn't understand why anyone would want to leave a loving father and safe town for danger, or even death. I had no choice but to tell her the unadorned truth of my feelings.

"Because I don't want to leave!" I shouted. "I *never* want to leave again."

Then I ducked into the next room before she could object.

Once again, I tried to push aside the distressing situation by busying myself. I went around tidying, dialing down gaslights and shooing people out of the tavern.

In the last lit room, I collided with Nestor.

Gasping, I fell a few steps back and he caught my arms, steadying me, already offering me his endearing half-smile. "Alright there?"

I couldn't help returning his smile, before self-consciousness made me avoid his eyes in favor of my feet. "Yeah, I guess."

"You closing up?"

I nodded, chewing on my bottom lip as he walked around me, trying to think of a way to bring up the picnic. I didn't talk to boys often, and when I did it was never personal, so I had no idea what to say or what I shouldn't say, especially if I liked them.

And I did like Nestor.

To my relief, he brought it up. "So, I was wondering if you could return the favor tonight?"

The silly, giddy feeling from our first conservation was back, I felt the urge to squeal like a whistling teapot. I couldn't believe this was happening.

I inhaled deeply, going lightheaded, my headache gone and replaced with a dreamy rose-scented fog. "Do you want to sit by me tonight?" I played with my fingers to keep them from shaking. "That could be a way to get to know each other."

"That'd be great! You'll be on the same bench as the Fairborns, right?"

"Yeah, if you want Mr. Fairborn's approval for an outing or something, he'd be right there. He's very agreeable, you know. I think he'll like you."

His face lit up as he broke out a full hopeful smile that made my heart flutter. "Really?"

I nodded, tucking a lock of hair behind my ear.

He set gentle hands on my shoulders, looking me in the eye so I was the sole focus of his attention. "Thank you. I've been wanting this for years and had no idea how to bring this up."

The dreamy fog was blown out my ears, making room for the dozen question marks that popped up in its place like daisies. "Years?"

He chuckled, rolling one shoulder in a nervous motion. "Ever since I saw her in school, reading to our schoolmistress's dog by the fountain, I just knew she was something special."

Bonnie. He had meant Bonnie, not me.

Disappointment sank through me like I had swallowed a spoonful of scorching porridge.

Of course, he meant Bonnie. I was an idiot to think otherwise.

"Is there something wrong?"

"I'm fine," I croaked, coughing to clear my throat as I moved past him. "I need to finish up before we leave."

"You sure?"

I rubbed at my eyes as I turned off lamps and blew out candles, trying not to sniffle. "I'm sure. Why don't you go keep Bonnie company till I come out?"

"Wouldn't it be better if I show up later?"

"No, it's getting dark, so we'll need you to escort us down to the campsite."

"I didn't think a girl like you could be scared of the dark," he joked, oblivious to the barrage of depressing emotions I was drowning under.

"Neither did I."

This day just couldn't get any worse.

I took a longer time than needed checking and locking the last few rooms, giving myself time to steady my mood and my breathing as that thought looped around my head like a windstorm.

When I returned to the bar to hang up my apron, Nestor was unsuccessfully trying to chat up a bored Bonnie. Upon seeing me, she hopped off the counter and hugged me. "I'm sorry."

I instinctively put my arms around her, resting my cheek on her hair. "For what?"

"For being so insensitive. I know how you don't want to leave this town, let alone the whole land."

"I don't mind leaving on a trip, or even a long journey, but leaving for good is just too much."

"You're right, it's too far-fetched." She pulled back a little to face me. "Maybe we should settle for a nearby trip. Who knows, I may not even like traveling."

I let out a tired laugh. "Good idea."

If Bonnie left, I would go with her. If she stayed and married Nestor, I would be happy for her. She had given me her friendship, her support, and even her home. The least I could do was support whatever made her happy.

The moment was shattered by a slow series of knocks on the front door.

Apprehension rose up my spine as I approached it. "Who is it?"

Three more knocks followed, hard yet hollow, not made by someone's knuckles.

Chest tight, I reached out and pulled the door open.

Right on the tavern's porch, stark against the darkness of the night, were the blazing, hovering eyes.

CHAPTER THREE

Before I could scream, or stumble back, or even draw my next breath, the eyes came closer.

Their light dimmed suddenly, and the face behind them became clear.

Standing before me on the dim-lit porch was not a fairy creature, or the Horned God, or a demonic deer, but a trembling woman no taller than me.

Raised in her hand up to eye-level was a polished golden staff. The braided metal of its twisted shaft curved up to a snake-head handle with gems embedded in its eyes that reflected the light coming from behind me. *Reflected,* not glowed, and much too small to be those fearful eyes.

Relief flooded my body as I let out the air I'd been holding in and opened the door wider.

In the flickering light streaming from inside the tavern, I saw the sequined pattern of her dress clearer than her face. She didn't have the carriage of an older person, so the trembling wasn't from age.

"Are you alright?" I asked.

In answer, she limped fully into the light and—

For the first time in my life I understood what the phrase *a dazzling sight* meant.

She was swathed in a wine-red, satin gown with billowy sleeves, and sequined phoenixes embroidered on its full skirt. Her long, smooth throat was draped in an eye-popping choker of diamonds and dangling topaz, and a matching bejeweled clasp sparkled in her glossy, dark, red-tinted hair.

Draped in all that glitz, she looked like a high lord's lost wife, as out of place in this land as my black hair. My fingers twitched, itching to snatch anything off her, already calculating how much pawning them could get and how long I could live off that sum.

I shook my head, snapping myself out of it. She likely *was* some high lord's lost wife, and she seemed injured, too, making her far from my typical target. Besides, I wasn't going to steal anymore. Not unless I absolutely needed to.

Bonnie ducked under my arm, extending a hand to her. "Can we help you?"

The woman snatched her arm away from Bonnie. I was wondering if she was averse to being touched by a stranger, or if she distrusted us, but then her eyes landed back on me, and she relaxed and reached out for me instead.

It was a startling surprise, for someone to trust me over Bonnie. Her long fingers clasped my forearm, glittery nails digging in, holding on tightly. Before I could pull away myself, she put half her weight on me, almost knocking me off balance.

We ended up bent over, still on the same level, and I could see her face up close. She had flawless skin, brows filled in with a maroon pencil, full, burgundy-painted lips, and cat-like, light amber eyes framed by big, dark lashes.

Scratch the choker; I wanted her eyes.

"Yes...you can," she finally answered, trembling with nerves or cold, shaking me along with her. "My carriage...it has sustained some damage and can no longer move."

Her voice and articulation complemented her appearance, smooth, refined, making my stretched-out vowels and lilting accent seem cacophonous in comparison.

"Come in," I offered, straightening and starting to pull her with me through her painful grip on me. "We can send someone to check it over in the morning."

"No!" Her protest echoed all around us.

She straightened, too, still holding on to me. Whether it was for steadiness or for comfort, I didn't care. I wasn't fond of being touched by a stranger and her clinging just made the contact more uncomfortable.

"I need to get back home," she said urgently. "Please, I don't have much time."

Bonnie, who had stiffened at her yell, softened enough to nod. "How about I go get my father? He's the town smith, and can help with your carriage."

"Yes, yes, please," the woman said, sounding relieved.

Bonnie nodded again and tugged Nestor after her, escorting him rather than the other way around. I tried to follow them out but the woman's hold on me tightened again.

It didn't seem that any of us would be making it to the bonfire tonight. There went my chance to burn the Horned God's wicker stand-in.

"Um, madam?" I tried to move without throwing her off. "You should come in, maybe lift your legs up for a bit. I can make you some soothing mint and lemon tea."

"Oh, that would be lovely, but I was hoping you could help me with something until your friend comes back." She finally unclasped her grip from my arm, leaning her hand on her glorious cane instead. She held out her other hand to me, limp-wristed, palm facing downwards like she expected me to kiss it. "I am Lady Nariman Rostam."

The way she said "Lady" made me feel she wasn't some mere merchant-lord's wife, but a true reigning lord's consort. And she did look it. How did she end up here of all places?

Not knowing what to make of all this, I shook her hand awkwardly. "Pleasure. What can I help you with?"

"On my way here, I got lost and drove through those trees over there." She gestured aimlessly behind her, sweat suddenly gleaming on her neck and forehead. "I'm afraid a part of the carriage fell off as I rushed to find an exit."

I would have asked if she was feeling ill, but my bafflement ran over that concern. "I'm sorry, did you just say you came through the Hornswoods?"

She blinked at me. "Yes, if that's the name of the woods at the end of this town."

"And you came from the *other* end?" I strained my ears just to be sure that she meant what I thought she did. "Are you sure?"

Her maroon brows rose. "Yes. I thought there was a shortcut through it, but I got lost and the carriage ended up breaking down—and I had to walk all the way out to find help."

Her statement brought a million questions stampeding to the forefront of my mind, but only two stood out.

The first was, how had she come through the other end of Man's Reach by carriage, then limped her way out of the woods, unscathed or unbothered by whatever was in there?

The second was, if she had come from the other end, then

had she been in Faerie? Or was there an uncharted land on the other side of the woods?

The second possibility seemed more plausible as she was human. And now that I scrutinized her more, looking past the luxuriousness of her jewels and clothes and the regal posture, I saw that she shared the rare features my mother and I possessed; black hair, big, hooded eyes, a wide, strong jaw, and skin the color of milk tea.

My mother had said she was from near Man's Reach, but never specified where exactly. It had been I who'd assumed she was from here, since I'd thought there was nothing beyond Aubenaire. Could there be, and could this Nariman be from the same mysterious place my mother had hailed from?

Now that I thought of it, neither Nariman nor Rostam sounded like anything I had heard before. My own mother's name, Dorreya, was unheard of, too. She'd once told me that my name was a localized version of a goddess's name. But in my travels, I'd found that *'Adalat* was not a goddess found anywhere on Ericura.

The urge to question Nariman about her hometown and her family surged, a part of me hoping she might be a long-lost aunt brought to my doorstep by the Fates. I barely held my eager curiosity back, as I didn't want to sound like I was interrogating her, especially when she seemed so distraught.

Right on cue, she turned big, now-pleading eyes on me. "I don't know how long I was lost in there. It's why I'm in such a hurry now. Will you help me find whatever part fell out so your smith can fix my carriage in time?"

Apprehension rattled through me, the idea of returning to the Hornswoods making my nightmares flash behind my eyes. I considered telling her no, but I recognized the signs of someone on the run and knew the urgent need to split from a town all too well. If I were delaying her escape, then it would be my fault if she got caught.

But I still didn't want to go with her. Partly because she was a stranger, but mostly because of the woods themselves and my fear of what lay within and beyond them.

When I hesitated, she came closer, staring into my eyes like she was searching for something in them.

Seemingly satisfied with whatever she found, she patted my cheek and said, "Will you help me get home?"

There was something about that question, either the subdued whisper of her voice or the words themselves, that put me at instant ease. It felt like warm water had spilled over my shivering body, banishing the cold creeping in my chest and the anxiety churning in my head, making me calm and drowsy.

Against earlier reservations, I found myself saying, "Lead the way."

"Thank you, dear." She removed her warm hand from my face, leading me out of the tavern, her cane pounding rhythmically with heavy *thunks* that echoed throughout the street, as if the ground below was hollow.

I picked up the glass lantern that was to lead me to the campsite and followed her out, head void of questions or worries as the woods kept getting nearer.

Suddenly she said, "What's your name?"

Without thinking, I answered, "Adelaide."

She made an intrigued hum. "What a lovely name."

"Not really. At school, they used to call me Marmalade."

She tilted her head to one side, then the other, as if trying to look at me from all angles, amber eyes clear and gleaming in the lantern-light, their brightness unaffected by the night falling deeper around us. "Does it mean anything?"

I shrugged. "I think it's an old goddess's name, a name no one uses anymore."

Her mouth turned down in distaste. "Mine is my grandfather's. Who gives a little girl an old man's name?"

"Maybe they were expecting a boy?" I slurred slightly as a stronger wave of comforting warmth hit my body, my eyes threatening to close.

"Most likely." She sighed as she pointed ahead. "This way."

Without complaint, I continued following her. But she walked faster ahead. As the distance between us grew, the cooling mist that coated my skin started evaporating my fuzzy warmth and I became more alert with every footstep. By the time I reached the edge of the clearing where the Horned God towered in front of the woods, goosebumps of both the cold and the creeps were drenching me.

I braced myself, expecting to see the eyes again, but they weren't there. The only light came from the stars above and the pulsating lantern at my side. But then I noticed that some of the trees seemed to have silvery leaves that reflected the starlight, a sight I had never seen before.

"I think it fell somewhere around here, whatever it was," Nariman called from up ahead.

I could spot the soft glittering of her dress's sequins and beads from amongst the trees like a distant star in the night sky. Shuddering now, I felt around with my foot, crushing dead leaves and twigs with loud crunches and snaps. Lifting my foot to feel around another spot, I noticed something glimmer and I froze. The leaves and twigs I'd crushed had turned into small piles of glitter.

This wasn't a trick of the light.

"What the...?"

I heard a loud flutter and felt a sudden draft of what felt like giant wings and spun around, heart in my throat. I found myself nose-to-nose with Nariman. Her expression had gone from apparent anxiety to tense impatience as she tightened her white-knuckled grip on her raised cane's throat.

"How did you...? You were over there a second ago..." I spluttered, stumbling back.

"Tell me, Adelaide, have you ever been caught?"

"C-caught doing what?"

"Thieving," she said casually, raising her cane to our eye level.

The snake head's ruby eyes lit up with a crimson flash. I couldn't look away. And the longer I stared into them, the slower my heartbeat got, making me feel warmer and drowsier than I did in the tavern and all the way here.

"No," I answered slowly. "Never been caught. Can't tell if it's luck or skill."

Her voice was soft and distant, like I was hearing her through a pillow stuffed over my head. "How long does it take you to search a place?"

"Depends on how big it is and who lives there," I said, words flowing out thoughtlessly. "I need to have a few stake-outs, scout the doors and windows, learn the inhabitants' and neighbors' schedules, and plan how to slip in and out. Then I go in once for small items, then come back for the bigger things."

Why was I telling her all of this? I could get in big, big trouble for it, and I somehow didn't care. I was so calm.

But I was never calm. What was this?

"If you were somewhere long enough, could you find something specific that's well hidden and sneak it out?"

"I believe so, yes," I slurred, swaying.

Nariman came closer. The snake head's piercing light made my eyes water but I still failed to blink. I had become numb and lightheaded. Nothing felt or sounded bad to me anymore. I had no thoughts and no worries. It was so...nice.

Nariman smiled, pleased. I smiled back stupidly.

She tucked a lock of hair behind my ear, stroking my head softly. "I'm going to need you to steal something, Adelaide. Can you do that for me?"

I nodded mindlessly, the tears that sprang up to fill my unblinking eyes pouring down my cheeks with each bob of my head.

"Good." She aimed the cane at the thickest tree trunk near us and its red light intensified, spread, until it was seemingly burning a hole through it.

Daylight poured through the hole as it expanded beyond the tree to the ones around it, erasing the dark, foggy backdrop of the woods. In its place, a faraway outline of a walled city with a mountain scraping the sky above it materialized.

With her attention on the gap growing in the trees, I felt the earlier flight of warmth tenfold, like I had fallen into a freezing river, the temperature plummeting around and inside me, rousing me from my lulled state as sense returned to me.

But the feeling in my limbs didn't. The calmness that had swallowed me abandoned me, but I couldn't flee. I was stuck gaping at that window into this vastly different place, as it began to spin, round and round, its edges blurring.

Wind, spurred faster by the spinning vortex the hole had become, whooshed deafeningly as it blew past, blasting through my hair and into my mouth and eyes, drying them painfully. I still couldn't blink, let alone raise my arms to block it or turn my face away from it. It was like my body was paralyzed.

"Ada? Is that you?" Bonnie called, her voice so close.

"We followed the light of your lantern." Mr. Fairborn's voice joined Bonnie's as he came into view first, lugging his massive toolbox. "But we can't find the carriage. Is the woman with you?"

Panic hit me full force. I tried to wave at them, to shout, to tell them to run away. But no impulse made it past my brain to my tongue and limbs.

Then it was too late. The hole, now massive, had started reversing its spin, no longer blowing out the wind, but sucking it in like an angry weather god inhaling back the storm, and us with it.

The last thing I felt was the starburst of blinding light that engulfed me as I flew off the ground and hurtled through the screeching maw into the unknown.

CHAPTER FOUR

I knew two things as soon as I came to.

I was lying face down on sand that was almost filling my mouth. And it was pitch black.

I jerked up onto my elbows, spitting out the sand and shaking its grains out of my nose and hair. Only then did I feel the gossamer blindfold and the itchy bindings holding my feet together. My hands, curiously but thankfully, were still free.

Quickly, I reached up to tear off the blindfold. A glittery, golden scarf came off with one pull, and a yellow glare almost blinded me. I squeezed my eyes shut again and opened them gradually, until they adapted to the painful lights.

They weren't lights anymore, but big slit-pupil eyes, like those of a giant grass-snake. A layer of frost glazed over my throat, burning as I tried not to screech.

The eyes watched me, blinking calmly. The confident gaze of a predator, one that could pounce and tear me apart at any moment but was content to watch me wriggle desperately.

While maintaining eye contact, I slowly inched my trembling fingers towards my ankles. Keeping its terrifying attention on my face while I worked to free myself was a nerve-wracking effort. My arms shook so hard my fingertips kept fumbling on the knots.

"There's no point in trying to escape." Nariman's voice spread over me, echoing everywhere.

Snapping my neck in every possible direction, to figure out where her voice was coming from, I took in the vast, empty space that surrounded me in the faint light of stars, an endless sea of sand with the only sign of life distant, skinny trees with flared heads of fronds.

I froze, though my arms still vibrated with dread as realization sunk in me like a foot stomping through mud, harsh and stomach-turning.

I wasn't in Aubenaire anymore. And the lights, the eyes were *her*.

Nariman stepped forward and her eyes shrank and dulled back to a very human shape, reflecting light rather than projecting it.

"Oh! I didn't mean it like that. I'm sorry. I just meant that only I can take off your bindings. See, I made them for palace guards to use on prisoners. They're enchanted."

Palace? Prisoners? *Enchanted*?

Slowly, I dragged my eyes away from hers and toward my foreign surroundings.

Beneath the deep-blue dome of a sky filled with wispy clouds and brilliant stars, I could see settlements scattered as far as the horizon.

The closest one was the massive walled city I'd seen through the hole in the woods. From this distance and vantage point, its wall looked mile-high and made of a smooth, pale material. Half in the night's shadows and half bathed in starlight, it reflected a soft, opalescent sheen.

Peeking over the top of the wall were the spearhead tips of towers and the roofs of tall buildings and temples. But the biggest and brightest building was what sprawled along the summit of the mountain. Not a castle, but a palace, like something out of Bonnie's books about the faraway lands of sand and spices.

Bonnie!

"Where's Bonnie?" I rasped, my voice a choked, airy whisper like the wind that brushed across the dunes. "Where's her dad? *Where am I?*"

Nariman waved her hands. "Calm down, please. Oh, this was a stupid idea."

"You think?" I snapped, my voice regaining volume despite being shaky. "What did you do to them? To me? What's happening?"

She reached out then retracted her hand, fingers curling elegantly. "I need your help. At least, I think you can help me."

I edged away from her, trying to subdue my shaking. "Why would I help you?"

That got me no answer. Just wide-eyed silence as she tapped her fingers on the head of her cane in a precise beat.

"Why did you have to kidnap me, to get me to help you?" My voice shook with dread even as I found the gall to shout at her. "You could have just asked for my help."

She tucked her cane under her arm, wiped her hands on her sequined gown as she paced back and forth in front of me, with no sign of her earlier limp. "I would prefer not to call this a kidnapping, and no, I doubt asking would have done the trick."

"What is *this*?" I asked, getting dizzy keeping up with her pacing.

"This place or this situation?"

"Either, both—just tell me what you want so I can go home," I pleaded.

"Where is home, though?"

That question hit me like a punch to the throat, choking me, making it difficult to speak.

She knelt beside me, looking much younger than she did earlier, her features softened by some emotion I couldn't fathom. "Allow me to welcome you to mine in this realm."

I swallowed dryly, back to pulling on my bindings. "You... you come from the Fair-Folk's realm?"

"I'm not a fairy, I'm from the Folk's Shore, just like you," she said, turning her face so half of it was encased in shadow. Once the semi-mask of darkness hit the middle of her face, the eye encased in shadow grew big and bright as before. "But we're not exactly neighbors."

Panic resurged as her words sank in. She wasn't a fairy from beyond Man's Reach, but she was from a land beyond Ericura. The landmass dubbed Folkshore by Bonnie's book did exist. She was from somewhere there. Here. And she wasn't entirely human.

She was a witch. A real witch.

My heart boomed so violently it rattled me all over as I tried to get up, to hop away. But I hit the ground again before my knees could straighten, slamming my face into the hard sand. It scratched against my cheek as I struggled to get up, grazing my skin.

She grabbed a handful of my tunic and pulled me to my feet. "If I untie you, you have to promise not to try to escape."

It was a hard offer to consider, being freed but staying put.

But I had no other choice. After all, where could I run to?

The grudging promise escaped my spastic lips. "I won't run."

With a snap of her fingers, the bindings evaporated off my legs.

I stumbled a bit before I caught myself, regained my balance and, though I was shaking in my boots, I squared up to face her. She watched me with unwavering attention, amber eyes fixed like a hawk following its prey. I half-expected her to blink sideways.

Putting on a brave face, I asked, "What are you?"

She blinked slowly, humanly. "A woman, albeit a talented one."

So, that's what magic was called here? A talent?

I pointed to the walled city. "What is this place, and why am I here?

"This is the Kingdom of Cahraman," she said with a dramatic sweep of her arm. "Before you is Sunstone, its capital, which I can't enter. So I need your help."

"To do what?"

"I already told you what. What you do best: steal."

It was only then I remembered the conversation we'd had before that portal had opened and how I'd felt then, like I'd been in a trance. I'd been literally under her spell.

Licking bone-dry lips, I asked nervously, "Steal…what exactly?"

"A lamp."

"A lamp," I repeated dumbly.

"An oil lamp," she clarified.

I stuck my finger in my ear and rubbed. "There must be some sand in my ear, because I thought you said *oil lamp*."

"I did."

"All this for an oil lamp? Why can't you just buy a new one?"

"Sentimental value," she said quietly. "It's not just any old lamp, you see. It's a solid gold heirloom. My grandmother, Reiza, passed it down to my mother, who then gave it to me. It was the last thing she gave me."

The last thing her mother gave her, and it was gold to boot. Both a keepsake and maybe something she could sell or trade for a better situation. I knew that feeling. The only thing my mother had left me was a ring that had once belonged to her mother. I'd sold it at my lowest point, in a winter where food was hard to scavenge and no one was hiring. I'd do anything to get it back.

But given the situation, I wasn't about to pat her on the back and say something stupid, like, *"I can relate."*

I went with a question instead. "Can I ask how you ended up out here and the lamp in there?"

The temperature around us dropped a hundred degrees. Literally.

The sudden, severe chill slammed my arms to my sides and knocked my knees together as my breath curled out of my mouth in thick, smoke-like vapor.

A shudder shook me. "Guess I can't."

She snapped out of her intense trance, shaking her head, turning off the cold just like that. "I apologize. It's a bit hard to reel in my power sometimes, especially when I'm a little upset."

"A little?" A tremor wracked me at the sudden switch in temperature. "What happens when you're angry, then? A snowstorm?"

"A snow what?"

I stared at her before looking in the distance again,

noticing the bustling signs of life that peeked over the wall. If I remembered *The Known World*'s map correctly, and if snow was unheard of here, then I was farther away from Ericura than I thought. Probably on the far end of Folkshore. Much farther than Bonnie had planned to travel.

"Where's Bonnie?" I asked again, dread for my friend booming in my heart.

She dodged my question. "Can you retrieve the lamp for me or not?"

"Depends. On where it is, who has it, and how long I'd have to map out the place I'm sneaking into."

"Oh, you won't be sneaking in anywhere. You're going through the main gate."

I frowned, side-eyeing the city. "How?"

A red blast shot out of her cane and knocked me back a few feet. As I stumbled to catch myself before I fell flat on my back, light zipped around me in fast spirals. It grew ever faster and brighter until I felt it might unravel me.

Instead, it only seemed to unfurl and remake me, and all that I wore. Right before my stunned eyes, bursts of golden sparks metamorphosed every aspect of me.

My hair grew a whole two feet. My old, worn boots molded themselves into shiny, metallic shoes, my undershirt and pants spun into a gold taffeta dress with a pleated, flared skirt and shimmering gossamer sleeves, and my tunic flapped out into a flowing, white, woolen cloak.

Speechless and panting, I skimmed trembling hands over the curled ends of the glossy hair that was no longer mine, up to the thin braids that held it up. Alarm hit me full force as I ghosted my fingertips over my face, dreading finding it someone else's, too. I sagged in relief when I felt my own familiar features.

As I looked down on the palms of my hands, however, I found flecks of powder, smudges of gold eye shadow and red lipstick coming off on them; hands that were now soft, clean, and manicured, with bejeweled rings of silver and bronze adorning smooth fingers below a set of perfect, cream-painted nails. I couldn't remember the last time I had long nails, or a palm that wasn't as rough as splintered wood.

Not even my most fanciful dreams could have imagined any of that. It all went far beyond what I'd pictured when I'd heard of magic, which was always malevolent and practiced by hunchbacked crones as they sang curses over cauldrons, aiming to ruin people's lives.

But Nariman was no crone with a spellbook. As scared as I was in this unknown land, I didn't feel cursed as I reverently smoothed my fingertips over the silky feel of my skirt, the quality and softness unlike anything I had ever touched before. What added to my awe was that this had all been spun from the rags I'd been wearing.

"What...?" I gazed at her, breathless. "How did you do this?"

Nariman smiled smugly, hands pressed under her chin, cane tucked under her arm, admiring her work. "I think we've established that I have a way with magic."

"Uh-huh," I huffed, feeling my hair again, not only far longer than I could ever grow it, but far smoother and cleaner. And it curled! "So...so what do you need *me* for? Can't you just, you know?" I snapped my fingers at the walls of Sunstone. "And get back that gold lantern?"

"Lamp. And darling, I'm talented, not all-powerful," she said sadly. "And a city that spectacular was built by and is maintained with some pretty powerful magic. The same magic that banished me."

Sounds of movement burst across the dunes, fracturing the silence of the night enveloping us. I snapped my head around and saw a caravan of carriages rushing in the distance toward the gates of the city, dragged on wooden wheels by galloping horses with lanterns swinging on their sides, swathing them in fiery light.

Nariman waved her cane and a large cloth bag materialized, which she foisted on me. She then put an arm around my shoulders and shoved me forwards in the caravan's direction.

"There's your way in. Hop onto the last carriage."

I reflexively hugged the bag as I dug my heels into the sand. "Wait!"

"What now?"

Sweat popped out of every pore. The tension in my gut felt like my organs had shrunk and squeezed against my spine to take refuge there. "I... I still don't get what I'm supposed to do. Or why I should even do it."

That was a good question. Aside from the threat of being turned into a homely ice sculpture with a two-hour lifespan in this desert, what was my reason for playing along? Banished or not, she had a far better chance of getting her grandmother's clunky ornament than I did.

Nariman's maroon brows flattened into a subtle frown of impatience. "Bonnie, you said her name was, right?"

I edged away from her, wrapping my arms around the bag as if it were a shield. "Yes."

She advanced on me menacingly, cupped my cheek, her dangerously sharp thumbnail just a hairsbreadth away from my eye. "Bonnie, such a sweet, caring girl. It would be a shame to have her lovely face torn like a canvas."

Everything stopped for a good second. The contraction of

my insides, the crescendo of my pulse in my chest, stomach, and ears, and the wind whispering across the land all fell silent as I vividly pictured her imagery.

"W-what did you do to her?" I finally rasped.

"Nothing. Yet."

"Where is she?" If she was somewhere near, I could find her, then maybe I—

Nariman's next words smothered my feverish, unformed hopes. "Arbore, a kingdom not too far from your pitiful island, but a ways away from here. Quite a lovely vacation spot for those needing to escape the summer heat, but its forests are full of the most peculiar creatures. Though she only has to deal with one for now."

Despite the heartbeats clanging in my chest, I heard her ominous threat loud and clear. "Did you throw her in a cage with that creature? Is that what you're getting at?"

"Goodness, no," she said, feigning offense. "In the duchy of Rosemead, the king of the beasts lives in a hilltop fortress. But you see, the people there are always trying to find ways to appease it. I heard they were looking for a better sacrifice to offer it than a slaughtered sheep. Like a slaughtered girl, *or* a live one it can rip apart itself." She locked eyes with me, smirking. "A stranger to the land would fill the bill perfectly."

A loud hiccup jostled my heart. "Please, please don't let them—"

"I won't, if things go smoothly." Nariman tightened her hold on my face, digging her nails into my nape. The pain sank the horror of the situation deeper in my mind. "It's simple, really. Get me the lamp, and I'll give you your friend and her father back in one piece. Deal?"

"Y-yes."

Her grin bared her teeth the same way a predator would flash its fangs. "Good."

The caravan was nearing us. In the last carriage, I saw the silhouette of a girl against the lit interior.

Nariman waved her cane again, and a sealed silver envelope materialized. She extended it to me. "You better run if you want to get in."

I didn't waste a second. I snatched the envelope, slung the heavy bag on my back, and sprinted down the dune toward the caravan.

The fine clothes I'd been mesmerized by only minutes ago turned out to be a horrible disadvantage. The glittering shoes had no traction, and the billowing bottom of my skirt slipped under them a few times. To avoid rolling head over heels down the dune and sinking into that sea of sand, I hitched my skirt up. I ran so fast the smooth soles of my shoes barely touched the ground to slide or slip. I kept getting closer to the last carriage, until with a final burst of desperate speed, I jumped onto its back.

The girl inside hadn't moved since I'd first spotted her. Panting and wheezing, my arms shook hard as I knocked on the door expecting her to open it for me, or at least turn towards me. But nothing got me any reaction.

Before the carriage's violent jolting could knock me off, I managed to open the door and swung myself inside. Huffing and puffing, chest burning and legs almost buckling beneath me, I finally staggered in—and it hit me.

The girl wasn't a girl, but a paper mannequin that created a convincing silhouette. Must be Nariman's ploy for me to sneak in with the travelers. As soon as I entered, it collapsed, dropping the pink silk scarf it wore as hair and a handful of heavy jewelry to the floor of the carriage.

Stumbling forward, I picked everything up. Even if Nariman hadn't left those things with the dummy stand-in for me, as a thief, I wasn't about to leave those pretty valuables lying around unclaimed.

I stuffed the scarf in the bag, slipped on the gold armbands, anklet, and sapphire ring. Then I rested back against the side of the jostling carriage to regain my breath. I watched Nariman growing smaller from the back window, until the carriage darted through the open gates and into the brightly-lit city.

Briefly blinded by the sudden brilliance, I lost sight of her in the distance. When the burn in my eyes faded, she was gone and Sunstone was all I could see.

It was truly a dazzling sight to behold. One that would be painful to look upon in the midday sun. It sure lived up to its name. Everything seemed to be made of sun-infused materials; polished metal, reflective stone or marble and perhaps crystal. In the far-reaching illumination that lit up the night, it was—for lack of another word—magical.

We were now speeding through a bustling marketplace that sprawled below multi-floored compounds with spiraling steps on their sides. Overlooking it, a scattering of more elaborate houses and a few breathtaking mansions sat on the plateau-like shelves of the mountain towering above the city. Everything *gleamed*.

Perched on the mountaintop was the crown jewel of the land. A magnificent palace that outshone everything else, with wide towers capped with onion-shaped domes, silver spires that pierced the sky, and parapets with spade-shaped castellations in alternating shades of pewter, bronze and gold.

Entranced by the view, my every muscle went slack and I dropped the letter I'd been clutching in my hand. The seal broke on impact with the wooden floor, and a thick card fell out of the silver parchment envelope.

I stooped down to pick it up, scanning it as I did.

On cream paper, fancy handwriting in gold ink declared:

You have been summoned to Sunstone Palace to compete as one of fifty eligible young women of status, in our search for the future Queen of Cahraman.

CHAPTER FIVE

The card dangled from my numb left hand. The words I'd just read, so formal, so imperative, so unbelievable, reverberated louder in my mind with each passing second. My right hand went again to touch the dress that had materialized around me out of thin air. It still felt real. It wasn't an illusion or a vivid dream. I hadn't slipped and hit my head in the woods.

I'd slipped into what was practically another world. A distant, foreign land that I had been taught did not exist anymore, a place only Bonnie's thirst for adventure could believe in.

The enormity of it all finally hit me hard, overwhelming me, and all I could do was stare out the window as the carriage slowed down to navigate through busy streets, feeling as if I was not inside my body.

Outside, swarthy, bearded guards with red sashes around their waists and curved swords at their hips, patrolled the city on horseback. Merchants hawked products I couldn't even guess at from intricate, vibrantly painted wooden stalls to a crowd in thin, colorful clothes. Lines that looked like the web of a giant spider hung overhead, holding endless little blinking, bobbing lights that looked like fireflies, with massive lanterns at the corner of each intersection blasting light everywhere.

From the level of illumination, it felt like late afternoon. But it had been nighttime when I'd woken up, and if this place followed similar rules to Ericura, then it was probably close to midnight now as the crowds were thinning and people were leaving the market in beelines and cart trails.

We approached what looked like a train station. I made the educated guess because I could see tracks emerging from it and snaking around the city and up the mountain, diverging at different levels and heading in various directions.

So, were trains here powered by steam like in Ericura, or magic? I wouldn't be surprised if it was the latter, after everything I'd seen, and with the tracks glowing as if made from a phosphorescent metal. The brightest one led straight up to the palace.

Sunstone Palace, it had to be. That was where I was supposed to go.

The carriage stopped behind a line of others by the station. I saw my coachman hop off his seat then come around. The moment he opened the door for me I almost screamed.

It was another dummy. A mannequin animated by Nariman's magic. The sight of its featureless face made panic surge out of my gut.

I forced myself to swallow the shriek, and choked out, "Do you—uh, do you talk?"

It shook its head and offered me a papery hand. As it helped me out, my legs wobbled beneath me, and the envelope and something else fell off my lap to the gravel floor.

At first, I thought it was a baby's tiara, but at a closer look it appeared to be a bracelet or an armband made of white gold and set with a large blue opal below its pointed peak.

My coachman carried my bag and a trunk out of the carriage and led me to the platform where a crowd of girls had also disembarked with their chaperones. As far as I could tell, their ages ranged from fifteen to twenty-one, their hair and skin tones in varying textures and colors, all probably from the different regions depicted in Folkshore's map. Each had a silver envelope identical to mine. Some clutched it in their hands, some were rereading the card and others had it tucked under their arms. These were the girls I was meant to be one of, and it seemed we were all being taken to the royal palace.

It was very much like the legends and folktales I'd heard as a child. Or it would have been if it didn't involve the witch of the tale forcing me to go to the ball rather than the helpful fairy helping me get there. And the threat of my only friends being sacrificed to a woodland beast did not spell *happily ever after.*

As I approached the last girl in the queue on unsteady feet, I took out my card. I'd only read until "Queen of Cahraman" the first time and couldn't go further.

Now I read on.

You have been summoned to Sunstone Palace to compete as one of fifty eligible young women of status, in our search for the future Queen of Cahraman.

Over the course of a month, you will undergo tests, trials, and investigations in an effort to win the hand of Crown Prince Cyaxares of the House of Shamash.

Eliminations will occur in three stages by a panel of royally appointed judges. The five who remain at the end of the month will be tested by the prince himself.

I stopped reading again as I processed the words. *A prince.* And he was holding some kind of elaborate competition, gathering girls from all known corners of this world—save for mine—to find a bride. These girls were all here in the hope of becoming a princess and future queen. And supposedly, so was I.

Dread surged within me again. Nariman had said nothing about dealing with anyone, let alone getting into a competition that lasted a month. I needed to be in and out of that palace tonight!

But what if I couldn't? A palace that size could not be searched thoroughly in a few hours. The Dufreyne's mansion—now a cottage by comparison—had taken me a whole morning and part of the afternoon to scour. It seemed Nariman meant for me to enter this competition. Was I also supposed to stick around for a whole month, as they thinned out the herd every week, so I could sneak about the palace to search for that lamp?

This was far more than I'd bargained for. Not that I'd had time or mind to even think what I'd been getting myself into when I'd agreed to help Nariman.

Agreed? I'd been blackmailed then literally shoved into this.

Did Nariman not consider that I could be eliminated on the first day? Or, even in the first hour?

What was *I* thinking? Of course, she knew I wouldn't really enter the competition. This was just a pretext to enter the palace. Once inside, I would disappear and hide. With forty-nine more important girls to take note of, the judges would consider that one candidate failed to arrive. And while they were occupied with their tests, I'd search until I found that lamp, then I'd slip out to meet Nariman. I'd exchange it for Bonnie and her father and a portal back home to Aubenaire.

Shaking off the nerves, feeling a bit steadier now that I'd reached that conclusion, I continued reading:

You will be required to participate in:
Etiquette tests
Character evaluations
Skill exhibitions
Formal dinners
Diplomatic meetings

Any dishonorable activities will result in your immediate expulsion from the competition and the disgrace of your house.
Arrive at the new crescent moon and await admittance.

As I slipped the card back into the envelope, I wondered what ranked up there with theft as a dishonorable activity. Getting drunk and sliding down the palace steps on a goose-feather mattress then throwing up on the prince's shoes? And what skills did I have besides lock-picking?

Good thing I wouldn't be there long enough to be shoved into any of those pompous tests.

I tucked the letter into my cloak pocket and approached the nearest of the 'eligible young women.' A petite girl no older than myself, in a billowy cream satin gown with pleated folds and tight cuffs, stood loudly chatting with three others. She wore a necklace of alternating cream and silver pearls that complemented her tan skin. Her hair was thick, glossy dark blonde and held up in a bun by a silver coronet, showing her dangling abalone earrings. From the elaborateness of her whole outfit, she seemed to be a noble, a higher status than most of the girls.

She had a round face dotted with freckles, a small chin and cheeks heavy with baby fat that rose up to almost shut her eyes in an involuntary squint when she smiled.

The smile was seemingly for me, as she jumped up at my approach. "Hello! You were chosen for the contest, too? Well, of course, you were, or you wouldn't be here otherwise, now would you? How are you? How was your trip? Am I talking too fast?"

She did talk so fast I expected her to bite her tongue.

"Yes, I was. I'm pretty worn out. And my trip had…let's say a few bumps and unexpected turns, but I'm here now. And yeah, you kind of are," I answered her questions in descending order then held out my hand. "Hi, how are you and how was *your* trip?"

She forwent the handshake and launched herself at me in a body-slam of a hug, nearly tipping us both over. Though she was much smaller than me, I wasn't exactly steady on my feet.

"Oh, it was dreadful!" she whined with her face buried in my chest. "I'm from the other side of the mountain and I didn't know it was going to be so hot. I hope this is just a heat wave because I can't survive this weather for much longer."

Honest, enthusiastic *and* chatty. I was sticking with this one.

She released me and took my hand to shake it. "I'm Cherine! Nazaryan! Daughter of Lord Gaspar Nazaryan. I'm from Sunstone's sister city, Anbur. It's a bit smaller but even more lively." She looked up at me, interest gleaming in her big hazel eyes. "Anyway, who are you and what family and land are you from?"

As basic as those questions were, they were ones I had no answer for.

Nariman had sent me off the deep end without even a cover story.

If I wasn't so used to lying I probably would have outed myself as an unwilling tourist, or as a loon, by blurting out *"I'm Adelaide of Ericura, a land I thought to be the whole world until I got dragged into this one by a witch in the woods to get her a fancy incense burner."*

But I'd had years of practice making up stories on the fly. Now I had to come up with something that sounded convincing to someone from both The Known World and this lifestyle.

The only place I knew of, beside this city, was where Nariman had said she'd sent Bonnie. It sounded like a place too far for anyone from here to know much about. I could use that.

"I am...Lady Ada of...Rosem...Rose Isle. It's near the woodlands of Arbore."

"Ooh! Arbore! I've been there once!" I held back a panicked yelp. Cherine, giving me no time to worry, poured on. "I've heard there are roses that bloom on trees there. Is that what it's like on your isle? Is that why it's called that? I'm afraid I've never heard of Rose Isle, or else it would have been my ultimate destination. My mansion gardens could use a rose tree."

"You live in a mansion?"

"You don't?" Cherine asked, looking genuinely confused.

"I...uh, not anymore. Not for as long as I can remember. You see, my family, while noble, isn't wealthy, having lost most of its fortune to my grandfather's gambling. We had to sell all our valuables and downsize to an old summer home on Rose Isle."

When in doubt, repackage the backstory of a character from a tragedy.

"Oh, you are from an impoverished house. Is it a cadet branch of the Amarants?"

Not knowing who or what the Amarants were, I just nodded. Better for her to fill in the gaps than for me to get caught in an inconsistent lie.

Another girl approached us, diffusing Cherine's expectant silence.

Looking like she just walked out of a farmland, the girl was a tall, tanned and toned leggy blonde with waist-length, wavy, sun-streaked hair and a body that straddled the line between well-fed and sinewy. She had big leafy-green eyes, a straight nose, squared cheekbones and wide, rosy lips. All she was missing were the wreath of laurel leaves and peach blossoms and a bundle of wheat to become every depiction of the Field Queen I had seen throughout Ericura.

I couldn't tell what stunned me more about her; that she seemed to emit a soft golden glow or that she was taller than me. Never had I met a woman who towered over me, or even most men around us like this one did.

The illusion of her perfect divine glory shattered when she stumbled and crashed into Cherine, sending them both to the ground in an awkward mass of limbs.

I caught them both by the elbows and heaved them up. "Are you alright?"

The blonde girl grinned at me bashfully, tucking a stray lock of hair behind an ear with multiple empty piercings.

Upon closer inspection, this girl was kind of a mess. Her

green-and-gold dress was at least a size too small and made from rough cotton for a much shorter girl. She wore no makeup, no fancy jewelry and sweat added shine to her skin and frizz to her hair. She didn't look like she belonged in this primped line-up and it seemed she knew it.

"Sorry, I'm not used to wearing shoes, let alone these," she said, kicking out a foot to show us her heeled sandals. Why a girl her size needed heels was beyond me.

"It's fine," I said with a smile.

"It's not fine!" Cherine protested, dusting her dress. "She could have crushed me."

The girl pretended she couldn't see Cherine at first then made a show of looking *way* down to spot her. "So *that's* what I tripped over."

Cherine jumped up toward the girl, finger raised demandingly to her face. "Who are you and what land and family are you from?"

"Do you ask everyone that?" I asked her.

"But, of course. I have to know what to expect from you and if we can socialize or not."

I frowned. "What do our lands or families have to do with whether we can be friends or not?"

They both looked at me curiously.

Then Cherine patted me on the hand. "Ada, darling, I know your family is disgraced but you're still noble. There are rules within each class, especially our own. Maybe you've gotten slack in following those rules because of your situation, but if you're from a family whose ancestors fought mine, or from a land that warred with mine, or if there is any rivalry between our families, then we can't possibly be friends. Don't you think so, um...what was your name now?"

"Cora," the other girl answered. "My mother is Mistress of the Fields in the Granary."

"Oh. A farm girl," Cherine said with waning enthusiasm, looking Cora up and down with a cross between a grin and a grimace.

I gestured between us and the rest of the girls. "Aren't we all rivals now, though?"

Cora's eyebrows rose. "What do you mean?"

"Well, you know, we can't be friends since only one of us can get the prince."

Cherine tossed her head back and laughed. "Oh, that's only if you take it personally."

"And why wouldn't you?" a loud, disapproving voice cut in.

A fourth girl had arrived, this one flanked by two others.

All paled in comparison to her extravagant clothes and enviable beauty. If Cora was the glowing embodiment of my local fertility goddess, then this girl was the face in every storyteller's mind as they told of glamorous fairies whose unearthly beauty lured men to their deaths.

With dark, shiny hair that contrasted with her unblemished alabaster skin, she had deep-set eyes, a pointed nose and full archer's bow lips that were painted a dark, glossy red. Her long neck was wrapped in a necklace of brilliant greenish-blue stones that dulled in comparison to the turquoise of her eyes.

Her beauty wasn't simply enviable like Bonnie's or Cora's, it was practically intimidating. Between all three of them, I felt ugly, insignificant, a weed among flowers.

Under the newcomer's belittling gaze, Cora bristled, squaring her shoulders in a confrontational stance.

Cherine's unimpressed grimace became a full-on defensive glare. "Fairuza, fancy seeing you here."

Fairuza, slightly less statuesque than Cora, wore a flowing, glittery, silver-white dress with a long, gossamer train. Head held high, catching the light on her elegant cheekbones, she strolled leisurely towards us, hand over hand, showing off the diamond rings and a blue-opal tiara bracelet, identical to the one I found in the envelope, on her wrist.

With slight turns of her head, she eyed each of us. She tutted at Cora's dress and messy hair, wrinkled her nose disparagingly at Cherine's everything and finally raised her perfect eyebrows at me. "Gold. A bit over-confident, aren't we?"

I blinked. "Excuse me?"

Fairuza quirked her lips. "Only brides wear gold dresses in Cahraman."

Barely ten minutes here and I already committed a—what did they call it? A social grievance? Whatever it was, it was Nariman's fault. What had she been thinking, sending me here in bridal gold?

I squared my jaw and carefully picked my words. Nothing good ever came from antagonizing rich girls. "Do they? That's news to me, seeing as this is my first time here. Where I'm from, brides wear white."

Fairuza hummed interestedly. "And where is it that you're from?"

I had to give her the same story I told Cherine. "An island near Arbore."

Fairuza came closer, lowering her chin so her glittering eyes drilled into mine. "Really? I'm from Arbore and we don't have islands."

CHAPTER SIX

I stared at Fairuza, my mind stalling.

I hadn't thought I'd get caught this early.

I should have known. With my luck, the place I picked to pretend I was from—the only place I knew by name in this world—would be the one everyone knew about and could spot my lie the moment it left my mouth.

Before I could backtrack, Cora cut in, "It's an inland island, isn't it? Arbore is full of rivers, and there are a few islets in them."

Feeling like she'd thrown me a lifeline, I agreed, a bit too loudly, startling Fairuza. "Yes! That's it. My island is one of those. It's called Rose Isle."

"Isn't that in the Rosewain River?" Cora asked, drawing me another line to follow.

I nodded vigorously. "It's not that big, and a bit downstream, we were the only people of note there, which isn't saying much."

Fairuza seemed to buy the explanation, looking me up and down disdainfully. "Explains why you're here then. Because there aren't suitable girls to offer in your part of the land. But even with your obvious disadvantages, you must have been sent here with some plan in mind."

I smiled tightly. "Haven't we all?"

Fairuza's brilliant eyes hardened, becoming indistinguishable from the stones around her throat. "So what are you here for? Are you hoping to rope in some well-to-do man with a future or fortune once the prince spurns you? Or are you actually hoping to be queen?"

I shrugged. "Neither, really."

That threw her off. She didn't get to follow up on my confusing answer because the train arrived with a loud hiss of steam and a metallic screech that made us all wince and grind our teeth.

Without another glance at any of us, Fairuza turned and snapped her fingers at her coachman to lift her luggage. She was the first to hop into the front compartment, her two-girl entourage holding up the train of her skirt.

Cherine huffed loudly next to me, throwing a shawl around her shoulders and picking up a small bag. "Why? Why of all the girls linking East and West did she have to get picked?"

"Money?" I suggested, still in awe of her glittering silvery dress.

"The fact she links East and West?" Cora added, hauling up her huge, heavy-looking bag like it weighed nothing. "Wait, is this Zomoroda's daughter?"

"Sure is," Cherine said, her voice dripping venom as she hustled over to the line and shouldered a girl out of her way to cut in. "Excuse me, this isn't your local cart trail. You get in line and go in by order of rank. Cora, Ada, come!"

"I thought you said it was by order of rank?" a girl behind Cherine protested.

"Yes, and since I outrank you, I choose my companions." Cherine elbowed her again and grabbed Cora by the elbow.

Cora, in turn, clung to me and Cherine, dragging us both into the train and to a compartment. My dummy coachman followed and set our luggage above and below the seats before collapsing into a cube on the seat next to me.

This must be a land where magic was commonplace if no one blinked at it.

"Genius?" Cherine dropped on the window seat across me, her feet barely brushing the carpeted floor.

I stared at her. "Bless you?"

She made an impatient gesture as if I was being slow. "I meant is your butler a genius? Isn't that what you call a *djinni* in Arbore?"

I looked to Cora for help, hoping she'd save me like before.

Sure enough, she sat down next to Cherine and explained, "Genii and djinn—the latter commonly called genies beyond here—are quite different."

Cherine let out an "Ooh!" of realization and nodded. "Then what is that?"

"A genius, like you said, but not as you meant," Cora said. "Genii, are, you know, the living essence of every object. It's what gives everyday things like metals, waters, and oaths magical potential. I think here you would call this thing a *qarin?*"

Relieved that she'd explained, I decided to escape further interrogation despite wanting to ask about genies. Bonnie's ancient books, that held tidbits of lands I'd once thought dead or fictional, mentioned them as being lesser fairies that granted wishes once captured.

Oh, Bonnie. She would have loved to be here, blue eyes darting everywhere to take in each foreign sight, asking all possible questions and getting engrossed in this new world and all it had to offer. Nariman had seemingly sent her to the land she had wanted us to sail to, Arbore, but it wasn't in the way either of us would have wanted.

Trying to keep my heartache at bay, I patted my boxed coachman and said, "I don't know what this is. It was a...gift."

Cherine tutted. "You should always ask what something is and where it came from before you accept it. It could be cursed for all you know."

I couldn't dispute that. This magical helper was part of the curse I seemed to be sinking deeper into with each passing second. Not that I'd accepted it. I had no more will in this than it did.

The train groaned to life and moved out of the station. In a few minutes, the marketplace flew out of sight as the tracks went uphill to the inhabited levels at the base of the mountain.

As the train climbed higher, the city shrank below us, giving us a semi-aerial view of all the landmarks. Even from that distance, I could still see everything in that pervasive light that lit up the night. Colossal, weathered, russet-and-silver statues towered in squares surrounded by sprawling domed buildings. Elaborate painted shops and plazas festooned around massive fountains in shades of bronze and verdigris, shaped like open clams or flowers.

At one point, the only thing I could spot among the glittery map of reflective surfaces and twinkling lights was the line of gigantic temples splitting the city in half. If I squinted hard enough, I could still make out the designs and the figures depicting what seemed to be gods.

Soon they all blurred into the distance, then I could no longer see them at all once the train switched onto tracks that circled the mountain.

Every passing moment through the trip made the whole thing sink in harder, deeper.

I was sitting on a train winding up to a palace in a fantasy land, next to a *qarin* and two girls who might turn out to be a sprite and a sylph for all I knew.

Every time I began to accept that this wasn't a dream, something would reinforce the shock of where I was, what was happening, what I was supposed to do, and I would find myself on the verge of a panic attack. But then this distressing dream went on as if everything was normal, with my companions talking so matter-of-factly of *qarins* and genies, or palaces and princes, and I slipped back into my new role. If I could think of this as just another character I was playing for a con, I might just get by.

Trying to gather my wits again, I pressed my nose against the window as we snaked up and around the mountain. The temperature had dropped what felt like a dozen degrees, cooling my skin and turning my wet breath to fog on the glass.

Suppressing a shudder of cold and nerves, I asked, "Have you seen it before? The palace?"

"I used to live in it," Cherine said. "My father is King Darius's cousin."

Cora, disinterested in the view as she twisted and untwisted a lock of her golden hair around her fingers, asked, "Wouldn't that make you a princess?"

"I wish!" Cherine lamented. "Our family was noble beforehand but we got a slight leg-up once my great-aunt Morgana married King Xerxes, but nothing much since. I could have been a princess if the old king had married my grandmother instead of her sister. Or if King Darius married my mother like both their mothers wanted."

I listened with my eyes still aimed out the window as we winded around the mountain. I wanted to see Cherine's city of Anbur, which she'd said minutes ago would come into view. All I got from this vantage point was an obscure view of arid hills and faraway settlements, with some trees in the foreground, most of them like the ones I'd seen when I first arrived on the outskirts of Sunstone, what I'd been told were called palms.

I turned to her and Cora. "Did this happen before? A competition for the prince to find a bride?"

"Not in recent memory, I think. The last time this happened was over a century ago?" Cherine glanced at Cora questioningly.

Cora turned her calloused hands up and shrugged. "Not from here. Have no princes, either."

Cherine's irritation with Cora's nonchalance seemed to deepen as she side-eyed her while she continued talking to me. "I think there weren't many unmarried noble girls left by the time King Arsenius? Artaxias? Abraxas—Yes, King Abraxas succeeded his father without a betrothed. So, he held the bride search and picked his queen from the line-up."

"How did it become a competition then?" Cora asked.

"When Cyaxares, our current unattached crown prince, said so." Cherine huffed crankily, crossing her arms. "Can't understand why, considering that, unlike Abraxas, there are noblemen's daughters, who have the advantage of also being relatives, for him to marry."

Interesting. It sounded like Cherine and the Nazaryan family had been holding out hope for him to marry her before he sent out summons to forty-nine other prospective brides. I wondered why Prince Cyaxares had pulled something like this when he had an abundance of queen prospects roaming around his kingdom's backyard. He must be hard to please.

But if they were all entitled brats like Fairuza and Cherine, I couldn't blame him.

Cora, on the other hand—now she was interesting.

I took advantage of Cherine getting up to fetch something from her bag to lean over to Cora. "Hey, thanks for helping me out back there."

Cora blinked as if she didn't get that I was addressing her, pointing to herself.

"With Fairuza," I elaborated.

Realization entered her eyes, along with something else. I had a feeling she'd known I was lying, and this had been why she'd helped me. I wondered why.

She finally waved it off. "It was nothing."

"No, seriously, thank you."

She saluted me and said nothing more. She was the opposite of Cherine, a girl of few words, talking only when she had something important to say. It seemed I wouldn't get an explanation from her. Hopefully, I wouldn't be around long enough to worry about more slip-ups and wouldn't need her to bail me out again until I bailed out myself.

The train had climbed further up, the spiraling ascensions becoming tighter and more frequent. Anticipation tugged at my gut as glimpses of the palace appeared above us.

"You're going to like this next bit," Cherine told us, pointing around the next turn.

We rounded the corner and sheets of water instantly dropped down on us, pouring down the windows as we went through a faintly glowing waterfall.

Behind it was a cave, the ever-shifting reflection of the cascading water dancing on its walls. The train's movement set off millions of blue dots and they came to life, lighting our way as we traveled deeper inside the mountain.

It was more beautiful than anything had been so far. In such a magical place, that was saying something.

"What is this?"

With all the confidence in the world, Cherine said it was, "A natural nightlight, bits of rock that glow when they feel warmth," only to be shut down by Cora who said, "It's not the rock, it's the algae growing on them. They thrive in damp, dark areas like this and glow when disturbed."

Whatever it was, this breathtaking spectacle lasted just long enough to ready the stage for the main event as the train emerged onto the mountain plateau: the palace.

Under the bright starlight, it glittered like a colossal jewel, its silver spires piercing the sky and its blue-glass domes gleaming like they were imbued by some luminescent magic. As we approached it from a certain angle one of its entrances came into view. The most eye-catching parts of its façade were towering bronze double-doors fitted in a vast arch, worked in intricate, interlocking carvings that depicted a single scene from top to bottom. In this light, I could make out a giant bird, each wing spread on a door.

The train finally stopped about a hundred feet from the entrance, and those incredible doors swung open. The whole interior of the train was bathed in a warm light that emanated from the palace, revealing a line of silhouettes standing on the steps leading up to it.

Every compartment door of the train flew open and the girls flooded out in a stampede. They were quickly trapped in a tight mass of squirming arms, squished cheeks and stomped feet.

I held back an eager Cherine and a curious Cora after they gathered their stuff. "Better for us to be the last ones out."

Cherine, who seemed prepared to elbow her way out as she had her way in, disagreed. "We need to be at the forefront so we can be the first ones to be seen and make an impression."

I shook my head. "Trust me, if you go out now and fall into that pile, you're not going to make a good impression."

I didn't want to leave an impression at all. It was how I'd slip in and out unnoticed.

She eyed the mess outside and cringed. "I guess you're right."

We watched the dozens of girls shove at each other on their way to the entrance. Even dreading what I'd have to face once I was inside that palace, the random yelps of pain and frustrated screams that carried to us out of the hubbub made me smile, and even laugh once.

Once they were all out we followed, stepping off at our own pace. As we approached the back of the throng of girls, I saw our greeting party clearly for the first time.

Standing in two lines on each side of the wide stairs, nine imposing figures in embellished costumes stared out of impassive faces, not focusing on any of us. So much for making an impression. Which was too bad for Cherine, but great for me. I wanted to be as unnoticeable as a short stalk in a cornfield.

The oldest of our greeting party, an imposing, greying man in an embroidered beige coat that covered his white silk pants introduced himself as Master Zuhaïr, before opening up a long scroll and reading out names. The girls, at last, got the hint to shut up and listen.

Each girl who heard her name stepped out and joined a growing line by our greeting party, giving me a good look at her, her dress and her jewelry. The least impressive, and the one who drew the most gossiping whispers, was Cora.

"Cora Greenshoot!" When there was no response from her, the man called again, impatiently. "Miss Cora Greenshoot of the Granary."

Slouching, Cora moved over to the line, aiming empty stares back at everyone judging her. Whispers passed over us in a wave, all mockingly repeating "Miss!" as if it was the funniest thing they had ever heard. She was the only one without a fancy title. Her mother held a title that Cherine found beneath her. An elected not an inherited one, perhaps.

Despite the cold breeze at this elevation, sweat was drenching the back of my head and dress as I watched every name calling up a girl more glamorous than the one before. Lines of ladies, a few baronesses, and the odd duchess cropped up, then—

"Princess Fairuza of Arbore."

Princess? She was a princess?

Fairuza picked up her skirt, turned her nose up at us all and effortlessly glided over to her spot on glittering grey heels. The whispers turned into murmurs, *oohs* and *aahs* of wonder and admiration, and a few surprised gasps of "A princess!"

A satisfied smile played on her red lips, no doubt pleased with the awed comments reaching her ears.

"Is she the only princess here?" I asked Cherine.

"I can see one more at least, but *she'd* be the most special here," Cherine said bitterly, thin brows meeting in a grouchy expression. "Her father is King of Arbore and her mother was once Princess of Cahraman. They should cut out the whole show now and make it a choice between her and me."

So, that was what Cherine had meant about Fairuza uniting East and West. She was royal on both sides of her family, with her mother being from an eastern kingdom and her father being the monarch of a western one, connecting the ends of Folkshore.

I examined her again as she stopped beside Master Zuhaïr, surveyed us with all the haughtiness of her status and even more assurance in her chances than Cherine.

I had many expectations of what a princess should look and be like, thanks to hearing about Ericura's nobles, and from the many legends that feature them as unwitting heroines on quests and damsel rewards for chivalrous men. Fairuza was as beautiful as the tales promised, but as far as I could tell, she lacked every other endearing trait.

More girls followed, and the only other princess was called —an Ariane of Tritonia. The crowd was thinning and I would soon find myself standing alone. The sweat plastering my dress and hair to my body now felt more like someone had dumped saltwater down my back.

Nariman hadn't even bothered to prepare me for any of this. She'd just seen me, somehow knew I was a petty thief and had snatched me out of my land and into hers. That, and the glamorous transformation was one thing. But how had she gotten past palace scribes or clerks or whomever it was that had sent out the summons? When she was magically barred from entering the kingdom? How would I explain my presence? What would I say—

"Lady Ada of Rose Isle!"

All worries deflated out of my mouth, nose and ears like steam, cooling my heated brain, leaving me lightheaded.

Cherine put a hand flat on my back and pushed. "Go!"

"Right. Sorry. Lady Ada, that's me."

I wiped my sweaty palms on my skirt as I nearly tripped over it again, stepping on the inner hem that slipped under my foot. My mind spun with questions as I stumbled into the line.

How on earth did they get that part? I'd pulled that name and that place out of thin air.

Had Nariman somehow known what I'd said? Had that *qarin* transmitted what it heard to her? And she'd worked by its magic remotely, making it place my new identity among the others as soon as I had created it?

Why that should impress me even more than anything she'd done so far, I had no idea. But it did seem her magic was strictly long distance when it came to this place.

When every girl had been called, with Cherine being the last one, she bullied her way in front of me, not content with a position at the rear.

The greeting party ushered us into the palace, past the entrance, and into the significantly warmer interior. The floor was fitted with a lush, red, velvet carpet woven extensively with what looked like real gold thread, the parts we trod on instantly darkening and twinkling.

The curve of the ceiling held huge squares that made me feel like an ant, each dangling a crystal ball chandelier that looked like a giant soap bubble and emitted a soft, permeating light. They looked a bit too plain for their surroundings.

I craned my neck, turning my face up and, sure enough, I saw the reason for the simplicity. Instead of going all out with involved, colorful depictions like some temple walls, each square was in a different shade, depicting the sun from dawn to sunset, on a background of shifting blue. Each sun's wavy rays looked like embossed plaster painted with pearlescent shades, but at the same time seemed to be alive with energy. The chandeliers were just there to illuminate the masterpieces.

The clarity of the pattern and its range of hues depended on which angle I was viewing it from, going from faint to radiant as I passed underneath. It was mesmerizing!

If I were this captivated by one ceiling, I'd be starstruck by the rest of this palace's décor.

Past the entrance hall, we stepped inside a grand reception paved entirely in mirror-like green marble with outlines of abalone, with a matching staircase that spiraled up into two opposing flights.

Master ZuhaÏr came to stand in front of the midpoint of the first step. "You will now be separated into groups and taken to your quarters. Once you have settled in, you will be given schedules that detail what you are to prepare for and participate in during the week."

Cherine's voice rose, clearly annoyed. "Where is the prince? Why isn't he here?"

Master ZuhaÏr bowed his head to her. "I'm afraid he won't be here for some time to come, Lady Cherine. You will have to go through the filtering process at the hands of the panel of judges for the first three tests before you can be allowed audience with His Royal Highness."

And that was the best piece of news I'd had in this dreadful, maddening day.

CHAPTER SEVEN

I'd be long gone before the prince deigned to inspect the contestants vying for his hand.

The thought defused some of my tension, and made me breathe a little easier.

It clearly had the opposite effect on Cherine. She placed her hands on her hips as she advanced on Master Zuhaïr, talking at him rather than to him. "But that's not how the Bride Search is supposed to work. He's supposed to meet each one over the course of the month and pick his favorites. Then, once he's down to a handful, with a little more time with each, pick his princess. Why isn't he seeing us?"

"He has his reasons," a loud female voice answered her.

I whipped my head up and saw a regal woman slowly descending the stairs, her heels clicking on each step like a knife on a crystal glass, the echoes following each footfall like a background beat. She was wearing an emerald mermaid gown that was fully embroidered with what looked like real diamonds and hugged her statuesque, curvaceous figure to perfection. She had the same long neck and high cheekbones as Fairuza, but the cat-like eyes were more like Cherine's, and made more striking by thick kohl and lime-green eye shadow. She had a beauty mark under her right eye, eyebrows that curved at the ends and her dark hair was parted down the middle and rolled up in a thick bun, all topped with a platinum tiara set with diamonds and emeralds.

She was stunning, radiating power and confidence, though not the same way Nariman did. No, this was the assurance of status, not skills. The knowledge that you could have anyone's head with a snap of your fingers.

A third of the girls immediately bowed. Clearly, they knew who she was. The rest of us quickly caught up and followed suit.

"Princess Loujaïne, the king's most esteemed sister and advisor," Zuhaïr introduced her with a deep bow and a flourish. "Her Highness will honor you by joining those who will evaluate you before you can meet the prince. In time, if she deems you worthy, you will be among the Final Five who will be granted audience with His Highness."

Loujaïne glanced across the line, briefly pausing at two she seemed to recognize. Rubbing one hand over the other in a washing motion, catching the light in sparks on her rings, she stepped onto the floor.

"There are precisely fifty of you here today." Her voice, clear, powerful and melodious, rang off every surface, commanding undivided attention, her sweeping gaze going over the tops of our heads. "Only five can ascend to the final stage but only one can become queen. The Bride Search is an ancient tradition, going back to before the founding of this kingdom, when we were roaming tribes that lived out in the wilderness among ifrits and ghouls. A chieftain's son often found himself the only one of his generation who survived infancy or wars, and needed to establish his power with alliances. So he would send envoys to search for a bride who would fulfill all his requirements. Though the practice has rarely been used since the establishment of borders and governed relationships between different freeholds and kingdoms, it is still just as vital as it was before. If not more so."

She came up to us, towering over all save myself and Cora, the train of her green gown swishing behind her, giving us a clear view of her pointed, golden slippers. "You need to not only fill requirements of health, upbringing, and class, but prove that you can offer more; that you can be an excellent hostess to visitors and allies, a fair arbiter to the people and a firm custodian to captives. You must be capable of commanding staff, of taking charge in moments of need, and, most importantly, of being a worthy companion for your king.

"Whichever of you proves to have potential will stay to the next round. Whoever is deemed a waste of our time will not." Her voice hardened and so did her glare as she scrutinized each face before her. "And whoever dishonors the rules will be dealt with."

The fact that she left out how they would be dealt with scared me more than if she'd mentioned any specific punishment. That left us to fill in the blanks and imagine the worst.

Nariman had asked me if I'd ever been caught. I couldn't even contemplate what would happen if this was the time when my luck finally ran out.

"I assume girls with your upbringing would know what the rules are," Loujaïne continued scathingly, as if she was certain that this wasn't necessarily true. "Nonetheless, I will state them, so none of you can claim ignorance in the future." The stern look in her silvery eyes, now as brilliant as white opals as the lights from above bathed her, shifted with their color, emanating the same reprimanding displeasure that permeated her voice. "There will be no attempts to seek out the prince. You are not allowed to bribe palace staff to be shown his private quarters or be given audience with the king, or for any other favors or differential treatment. You are not allowed to have visitors, slaves or servants apart from a handmaiden. You are not to speak to any male member of the panel or staff alone or outside of evaluations. You are not allowed any outside assistance on any tests or permitted to use enchanted objects or any magic whatsoever."

She continued to list specific rules and warnings, all limitations that would get in the way of my mission. Good thing I didn't have to bother with any of that. As soon as I found the lamp I was out.

Too bad I'd be long gone when the inevitable catfight between both of the prince's cousins took place. I would have liked to witness that showdown.

"You will be divided into ten groups, each monitored by a judge," Loujaïne concluded. "Those gifted the blue opals will come with me."

Blue opals?

I glanced at my wrist as dread sank slowly throughout my guts. Had Nariman also arranged this? Making me a part of Princess Loujaïne's group of contestants? But if I was part of her group, how was I going to slip past her?

My brain overheated again as I tried to think of ways out as Loujaïne divided the other nine groups based on gemstones. Cherine halted my thoughts when she slammed into my back, pushing me right behind Fairuza and the handmaidens who held her train. The fourth girl who joined our group was a redhead who wore her hair in a complicated braid and had skin too fair for this climate. Last was Cora, who shuffled behind us like a child reluctantly tailing her mother around the market.

Loujaïne turned and climbed back up the stairs, leading us to a wing on the far end of the first floor by a ceiling-high window that overlooked one of the palace gardens. Armed guards in curly-toed slippers and red vests with scimitars hanging from their hips stood between each set of doors. Their eyes followed us as we passed.

"Is there a criminal on the loose?" I asked as we entered our quarters.

"No," answered Loujaïne. "They're here at your door and below your balconies all day, every day. For your safety."

"And for your incarceration," went unspoken but heard loud and clear.

Just like that, any plan I had or could come up with fell apart.

There was no way I could sneak out once everyone was asleep with that many guards standing out there, watchful and armed.

Feeling my anxiety spiking and my heart occupying my throat all over again, I dazedly looked around the expansive space that was to become my cage. It was all elaborately decorated in a palette of earth tones. Five brown-wood four-poster beds with deep-red canopies were spread out along the wing. A step down from the beds was a luxurious sitting area with cushions, short tables, and equally squat furniture. Wicker baskets sat open, displaying their contents, mostly balls of yarn and spools of cloth. Rolling pins and pots and pans sat in open cabinets. Flutes, lyres and some ancestor or cousin to the violin were arranged on eye-level shelves. Leather-bound books, rolls of parchment, ink vials and feathers were stacked on lower ones. There were so many other things to entertain ourselves with or to display whatever talents or skills we had.

Beyond thievery, I had none.

I'd thought I wouldn't have to worry about that. Nariman had made it sound like the hard part was getting into the palace. She'd made no mention that I'd be virtually a prisoner and there'd be no way I could get out to search for her accursed lamp.

As the other girls explored the wing, I took out the summons and reread it, looking for anything I could use as an excuse to roam around. I found nothing.

Who was I kidding? There were guards outside this giant communal bedroom. The moment I stepped out, I'd probably be shoved back inside at sword point. Whenever I'd stolen while I lived with the Fairborns, I'd at least had the privacy of the guest room and a front door I could walk out of whenever I wanted.

But this...this was going to be tough, if not impossible.

Feeling suddenly exhausted, all the bracing stress of the past hours deserting me, I stumbled deeper into the room, coming apart at the seams like a ragdoll that had been caught in a tug-o-war. Maybe in the morning I'd see a solution I was now blind to.

As I approached the bed that was closest to the door, I realized it was enchanted. The moment I touched it, the sheets turned a warm yellow and the cover and throw pillows became a satin-gossamer pattern of cream and gold. It was mimicking my dress!

There might be no privacy beyond the canopies, but this was the most unbelievable bed I'd ever sleep on. Queen-sized and dressed with silky-smooth, freshly-washed, fragrant sheets that could change color and texture. All I wanted was to curl up beneath the covers and fall into bottomless slumber under its magic spell.

But magical and all, I'd still give anything to trade it with the bed in the Fairborns' guest bedroom where I could barely fit, in a world where they were safe in adjacent rooms and none of this madness was happening.

Fairuza's handmaidens got to work emptying her bags into her bedside wardrobe while she stood by Loujaïne, surveying us and whispering out the side of her mouth, no doubt gossiping about us. Cora took the bed closest to mine, immediately kicking off her shoes and toeing them under the bed. Cherine beat the redheaded girl to the bed across from mine by pouncing on it before the other girl could set her satchel down.

I eased off my shoes to move around quietly, surreptitiously searching every nook and cranny for escape potential. Pretending to admire the décor I slid my hand over walls and other surfaces, tapping around for any hollow spots that would thump, or floorboards that would creak. And from the limited search I could make in the others' presence, I found nothing.

Unless there was some hidden trapdoor, the only way out was the front door. I wouldn't be able to sneak out. Unless...

Before the idea that burst into my mind had a chance to fully form, I took off all my jewelry, strode back to the door and held the pile up to Loujaïne.

"Excuse me, Your Highness. I can't seem to find a safe around here. Do you know where it is?" I asked innocently, slowly batting my lashes for a dumb, doe-eyed look.

"There are no personal safes here," she said, taking her first good sweeping look at me.

I hated to attract her attention, but this was my only

chance of getting out of this room to try to find out where the lamp might be. "Where am I supposed to keep my valuables?"

"Haven't you brought a jewelry box?"

I came closer, sticking my head in her personal space. "But someone can open that. Or carry it off altogether. These are very precious items! They're all that's left of my family's fortune. I can't leave them lying around here where anyone—" I jabbed my thumb towards Cora and the handmaidens, making a show of being uncomfortable. "—can take them."

Fairuza touched her earrings, my false paranoia resonating with her. "Auntie, why don't we have safes here?"

Loujaïne frowned, seeming inconvenienced rather than concerned by our questions. "The thought hadn't occurred to us."

"I have one in my chambers at home," Fairuza said. "I don't want to risk leaving anything precious out for anyone to steal."

"There's no risk of that here, I assure you."

Fairuza squinted at her. "Didn't you just tell me that the king's former advisor tried to steal—"

Loujaïne raised a hand, silencing her. "As you wish. You can all leave your belongings in the main vault and retrieve them whenever you need to use them."

Vault! Yes! Surely the most likely place a gold lamp would be!

Unconcerned with our discussion about valuables when she clearly had none, Cora climbed into her now-grass-green bed and drew her lemon-yellow canopy closed. The redheaded girl had unbound her knee-long hair and was too busy brushing the tangles out with a curved, mother-of-pearl comb to notice us. Cherine, already in her rosy nightgown and matching robe, picked up a small mahogany box and skipped over to us. "I'm coming too."

At that, Fairuza took out her earrings and necklace, stuck them in a pouch of gold coins and shoved it in her aunt's hands. "On second thought, I trust you to keep it safe for me. I need to rest so I can be at my best tomorrow."

Loujaïne watched Fairuza walk off and hold her arms out to be undressed by her handmaidens, looking like something sour had exploded on her tongue. "Does anyone else wish to burden me with her trinkets?"

Just to rub in that mood, I bowed and pretended to be clueless. "No, Your Highness, I wouldn't think of saddling you like a beast of burden. It's enough that you're agreeing to this. I don't know what I would do if my late mother's gold was stolen."

The first hint of emotion showed in Loujaïne's voice, a slight yielding of sympathy. "Your mother died?"

Bitter sadness oozed into my chest and burned the back of my throat as my mother's face flashed behind my eyelids. Or what I remembered of it. Mostly her long, dark hair, her dimpled cheeks and her big, bright smile. Yet somehow, her remembered image felt clearer than it had been for years.

I wished any of these jewels did belong to her, that I genuinely cared about losing them, in fear of losing what remained of her. But my concern was as false as my current persona.

"Yes," I said quietly, unable to keep the tremor out of my voice. "She passed a little over five years ago."

Loujaïne's eyes softened a little. "What was her name?"

"Dorreya."

Briefly, her brows twitched as recognition flashed across

her eyes, as if my mother's name reminded her of something that bothered her.

She seemed to shake whatever unpleasant memory it had brought forth off and finally nodded understandingly. "Come with me then. We all deserve our peace of mind when it comes to our departed."

I thanked her, relieved that this had worked out, but surprised that someone as powerful and seemingly as harsh as her was this agreeable. I still felt guilty for using my mother's death like that. I shook my head, shaking with it my newly long hair, reminding myself that this was all to prevent the Fairborns' deaths.

Cherine tailed us out, her short legs needing to drum up a jog to keep up with our strides.

The rest of the floor was significantly darker, with fewer windows and sconces lighting the halls. The doors of the other contestants' rooms were firmly closed and manned by unmoving guards. In the dim light, I mistook a few for statues until I heard them breathing.

I felt eyes on me in each place we passed through, even where there was no one. I made a mental note of which spots were unguarded as we descended into a darker part of the ground floor, then further down, heading to the basement.

Torches fastened to metal brackets lit the way down, their flickering, fiery light on the stone of the walls and steps shedding shadows that danced with ours. They offered little clarity and no heat and a whole lot of creepy, gooseflesh-raising atmosphere as we descended deeper into the bowels of the palace.

Cherine, clearly immune to the effects of our eerie surroundings, finally reached her limit of being silent. "Now that we're alone, can you tell me why Cyaxares isn't personally meeting the girls he picked? Why did he call all of us all the way here anyway? He doesn't have the 'lack of prospective brides' excuse other princes and kings had. What's going on?"

"Ever the nosy one, aren't you?" Loujaïne sighed.

"Well?" Cherine pressed on.

Loujaïne waved her away. "Ask him yourself if you're that impatient."

"I'd need to find him first to do that."

Loujaïne clucked her tongue. "Good luck with that. He's been hard to spot lately."

"How is that possible? He's the crown prince."

"Oh, we know he's around, just not where."

"How?" Cherine latched onto the crook of her arm, startling her stiff. "How is he getting away with all of this? He's not even king yet. Why don't you tell him where to be, what to do, who to choose and who to marry like every other —"

"If you were wondering why you weren't his first choice," Loujaïne cut her off, ripping her arm free. "*There's* your answer."

I held back a chuckle. Cherine's overzealous nature, while not enough to be a deal-breaker in princess requirements, was evidently a bit much for everyone, not just me.

In Cherine's brief, stunned silence, I heard something scurry in the darkness. I couldn't pinpoint what or where. It worryingly reminded me of my first venture into the Hornswoods with Bonnie, where the eyes I now knew as Nariman's had scared me witless.

"Did you hear that?" I whispered.

Cherine, who'd already resumed pestering the princess, turned to me. It was so dark now I could barely see her. "Hear what?"

The sound of shuffling boots on gravel seemed to skid past

me again. I spun around, right in the direction of the sound and found nothing but a stretch of dimness going all the way up to the lit doorway and the steps we descended to get here.

Cherine tugged on my skirt, looking a bit spooked. "There's no one here, Ada."

"But you did hear that, right?"

While I could barely see her, I could hear the dismissive eye roll in her voice. "No one comes down here, so it's just us."

"There are guards outside our bedrooms but not outside the palace vault?" I scoffed, though that was good news to me.

"Yes, because when we lock something in a vault there's no risk of it going out and doing something stupid," Loujaïne said pointedly, taking a torch off the wall to light her way down a much-darker section.

After numerous close calls, I finally tripped over my own skirt when a breathing sound passed over me. In a shocked jerk, I stepped on it so hard it nearly ripped. I careened off balance, crashed into Cherine and tossed us both down a few steps.

As she rose indignantly to her feet, I patted around in the darkness for the things I'd dropped. "There's something here!"

Loujaïne turned, looking up at us, her torch casting some light our way so I could pick up my rings and bracelets. "Scorpions, centipedes, a bat or two. Things that like to hide in the dark must be here. This is a mountain after all."

Everything she mentioned was preferable to that creepy, heavy breathing I'd heard. Certainly, none of those things would breathe this way. But like the shuffling earlier, I couldn't point to where it was coming from. Or was it just some strange echoing property of this place?

But why couldn't they hear it, too? Was I losing my mind? Or maybe I'd long lost it.

At the bottom of the stairs, a crack of faint light appeared.

Loujaïne dropped her torch with a gasp. "The vault! It's open!"

The princess and Cherine rushed the last steps leading to the vault. Before they reached the door Cherine was the one to stumble this time, taking the princess down with her. As they landed in a heap on the ground, the door cracked further open and something huge slipped out past them, too fast to see in the dimness.

I scrambled for the fallen torch, picking it up and swinging it around as I rose up on my knee. In the arcing flash of firelight, I saw the sources of the shuffling and wet breathing.

The first face was defined and bright-eyed, with a wide jaw and full lips accented by an expression of open-mouthed shock.

The second face…the second…

I could see its every vein mapping its severely sharp bone structure, shadowed by the long white hair scattered around it. And out of its ashen paleness, red eyes stared back at me.

A demon!

CHAPTER EIGHT

My scream as I'd dropped the torch and shot down past the demon and into the vault still reverberated in my ears.

I didn't know how long I ran inside the vault before I skidded over a pile of gold coins on the floor. I flew up in the air and fell with a clinking thud flat on my back.

Panting, my heart shaking me apart, I latched onto the first steady thing I found—a statue—and dragged myself up by its support. Then I scampered on my hands and knees and hid behind it, expecting to find the red-eyed demon chasing me.

I found nothing, and not because I couldn't see. There was ambient lighting coming from everywhere illuminating what I could see of the vault around me. I waited, breath bated, but everything remained still and silent.

Maybe it had been my recently activated imagination going haywire? And who could blame it after what I'd been through?

I heard the princess and Cherine's voices coming from the now faraway entrance. They didn't sound alarmed, and seemed to be continuing their bickering. That was more evidence supporting that I'd imagined it all. At least, I hoped I had.

But since I didn't seem to be in any danger, I had to make use of the time I had alone inside the vault. I had to find the lamp!

I stood tall on my knees, looking around. And my heart sank.

The massive stone room was *covered* in heaps and hills of haphazard treasure. Statues ranging from bejeweled idols to ten-foot-tall kings towered over the messy, shiny mounds, with gems for eyes and gilded cloaks. Open wooden chests pouring jewelry and silverware crowded around the statues' platforms. And in between, all over, unsteady piles of coins and bags of broken shards of gold with TO MELT DOWN stamped on them littered the floor.

Since Bonnie's books had turned out to tell of a world that actually existed, I bet somewhere out there a pirate ship must be avidly following a map that marked this place with an X. Or a dragon was about to move in so it could bed down and nap.

Searching for one measly lamp among the mountains of glittering clutter would be like trying to pick a single wheat grain from a bag of brown rice. But I had to try, and fast, before the others caught up with me. The faster I found it, the sooner I could get out of here and save the Fairborns.

Kicking all coins away from underfoot so I wouldn't slip again, I grabbed the statue to drag myself up. As soon as I was back on my feet, I released the cold arm, a shiver creeping down my spine. It was a bronze sculpture of a young woman with round eyes that drooped at the edges, big cheeks and wavy hair with her arms held out, hands turned up. Her accessories were not part of the sculpture, but real, removable.

Among them was a rose-gold headband encircled by conical spikes in different sizes, like the crowning halo of a sun god.

I circled it and began a frenzied search for the lamp. As I did, I found myself stashing coins, pearl rings, jingling bracelets and even a palm-sized opal in my bra. I didn't know what I was going to do with all these things in my current situation. I just knew that I needed to have them, to take them before they left my sight. I'd nearly starved and frozen enough times to learn not to pass up opportunities, no matter how perilous. I also wasn't going to come in contact with things this precious ever again. But I found nothing even resembling a lamp.

I was bending down to rummage through an overflowing chest when I spotted a lit incense bowl across from me at the feet of the statue I had steadied myself on. I found myself walking back to it, mesmerized by the glow of flickering embers among still-warm ashes. Beneath it, carved on a plaque at the front of the platform she stood on was: JUMANA MORVARID c. 532 - 552.

This must have been a queen. Or a princess. If the numbers were dates, then Jumana died at the age of twenty. What would have killed someone so young? An accident? Childbirth?

She looked so sad I half expected her moonstone eyes to start pouring out tears.

Feeling inexplicably moved, entranced, I reached up to touch her crown.

"Don't touch that!"

Loujaïne. I'd almost forgotten all about her.

I retracted my hand as if I had been burned. The offended urgency in her voice shook me almost as badly as the red eyes I'd thought I'd seen outside.

Loujaïne rushed over, slowing down just enough to steal a sad glance at Jumana before rounding on me. "You don't touch anything in here, do you understand?"

Too late for that warning. But I still nodded meekly.

Cherine reached us, holding her jewelry box on her head. "What was that about, Ada? Why did you—ah!" She dropped the box at the sight of the statue with a stunned screech. "What is that doing in here?"

Loujaïne ignored her question. "Someone left the vault door open. I'll need to report this to the chief guard and the treasurer to check if anything important was taken out of here."

Were the things I'd taken considered important? If they made an inventory would they know they were missing? And come after me?

Oh, why had I taken them? Maybe I should drop them back somehow?

"There was something in here," I said, trying to divert her, pushing aside the rising fear of being patted down later. "It's what opened the door. Didn't you see it? It ran right past you when you were on the ground!"

"I only noticed Lady Cherine squirming over my back," Loujaïne said flatly.

"That's what had you screaming?" Cherine huffed, ignoring or unaware of the princess's sarcasm, opening her box to inspect her jewelry. The crimson glint of a square-cut ruby caught my attention for a split second. "What do you mean by *something?*"

"Something long, pale and scary. It had red eyes. And that other—" I stopped as Loujaïne whirled on me, silvery eyes wide, nostrils flared for a sharp inhale. Either that description had struck her as familiar, or its unnaturalness simply unnerved her. Apart from the pale demon, the other one hadn't struck me as scary. From what I had barely seen of him, he'd been quite...pretty. Inhumanly so. My impression from that one shadowy glimpse was so vivid I could have an artist recreate his every sculpted feature on paper.

Was it possible he and his demonic companion were Fair Folk who'd ventured into Folkshore to loot a king's vault? Or was he a human thief, and had a magical being with him like I had my *qarin*? Either way, he'd probably opened the vault and was leaving when we crashed his escape. Maybe he'd been down here to get something of value to trade for a leg-up in his life or to finance an escape from it, or even to ransom a loved one. Or all of the above. Like me.

There was no way I could continue searching for the gold lamp now. I'd wasted precious time snatching up trinkets and gawking at the miserable bronze princess.

But that thief, whatever he was, clearly had access to the palace. If I could find him again, I'd ask him to show me how to come back down here. I could strike a bargain with him, to our mutual benefit. It sure would be nice to have some backup as I searched for the lamp.

"The other...?" Loujaïne asked, impatient.

"Was in the dark. It pulled on my leg," I lied, adding a scared waver to my voice. "I think it was trying to drag me away, probably to eat me."

They both looked at me as if I'd lost my mind. They clearly hadn't seen or heard a thing and thought I was a hysterical girl with an overactive imagination. That suited me fine.

I only hoped fate would let me stumble upon the mystery burglar later, because how else was I going to find him? His ghostly companion though, whatever it was, I'd rather not find again.

For the time being, as Loujaïne directed us to leave our valuables in a safe embedded in a wall before herding us back out, I knew I'd done all I could do. I was so exhausted and distraught that all I could worry about now was reaching my enchanted bed. And that Bonnie and her father had found a safe place to sleep, too.

CHAPTER NINE

I didn't remember what happened after my head hit the pillow.

All I knew was that I was rejoining the world, heart thundering, a blood-curdling scream ringing in my ears.

I leaped out of bed, snatching up my gas lamp, ready to strike as Cora burst through her canopy, fists up. It was the crack of dawn, just as the first bothersome light peeked through the slits in the curtains.

"What is it?" I yelled, squinting around, disoriented.

Cherine was pressed against the corner by one of the windows, holding her pale pink blanket up to her mouth and pointing a shaking finger to her messy bed.

Cora patted around Cherine's covers then checked under the bed, before turning her hand up. "There's nothing here."

Cherine shook her head, narrow shoulders quaking with fear, tears welling up in her eyes.

I approached, lamp still raised, asked again, "What is it?"

Her response was drowned out by a ragged exhale.

"What?"

"Ghoul," she whimpered.

"What?"

"A GHOUL!" Cherine shouted suddenly. "There was a ghoul by my bed! I saw it staring down at me in the dark!"

"Aww, did the baby have a nightmare?" Fairuza drawled, poking her head out from between the folds of her canopy, her handmaidens who slept in the sitting area already up and by her bed. "Don't tell me you wet the bed too?"

Cherine's expression hardened despite the tears flowing down her cheeks.

Smirking, Fairuza climbed out of her bed, her hair in a net and soaked in a pungent oil that reeked of sour gooseberry. "It wouldn't be the first time. At my coming-of-age party, my mother arranged a three-day sleepover with all the noble girls we knew and she wet her cot."

"Shut up! I did not!" Cherine hissed.

Fairuza chuckled. "She did. Twice."

"Well, I didn't this time!" Cherine defended with a stomp, flapping her blanket. "You would have wet yourself, too, if you found a ghoul standing over you, about to eat your face."

Fairuza's handmaidens picked up brown wicker baskets with dried sea sponges, glass bottles of soap and lavender-scented oil as she slipped on her white silk robe with peacocks printed around its bottom. She glided over to us after stepping into the white slippers set out for her, idly tying her belt. "Ghouls don't exist, Baby Cherie."

"Who's to say?" I asked her. "I didn't think witches existed until I saw one, and saw all the magic that runs through this city and this mountain."

Fairuza scowled at me. "We know witches exist because they've always lived among us, the vile, evil creatures. And magic is a part of our lives. But ghouls and ghosts? They don't exist outside your grandmother's feverish bedtime stories."

"I just saw one!" Cherine shrieked.

Fairuza, grimacing at her shrillness, snapped, "You had a nightmare, which is typical of children whenever they're suddenly far away from their mommies."

"I saw it too," I said, standing in Fairuza's way, locking eyes with her. "Actually, I saw it before she did. Yesterday. I scared it off with a torch."

Fairuza's eyes narrowed, searching my face for a tell, a hint that I was exaggerating or lying. I knew she'd find none. I was very, very good at lying, but I was also telling the truth this time. Whatever that thing I'd seen had been, it was terrifying and possibly the same thing that had scared Cherine. And then, bed-wetting nightmare or not, I would have lied on her behalf anyway, like Cora had on mine yesterday, to defend her against Fairuza.

Pursing her lips, seemingly satisfied that I at least believed what I said, Fairuza huffed. "According to the myths, ghouls would be in the nearest cemetery, eating the rotting flesh of the dead, not here, scaring gullible, *live* idiots like the both of you."

She slammed her shoulder against mine as she left the room heading for the bathroom, handmaidens hot on her heels.

I hissed a few venomous adjectives under my breath.

The fifth girl in our quarters, that so-far-silent redhead who had paid Cherine's earlier interrogation no mind, picked up her things and left as well, not looking at any of us.

Cora shut the door and pressed her back against it. "What was that about you seeing it?"

I shrugged. "Yesterday, down by the vaults, I saw something. Don't know if it was the same thing, though."

"It had white hair," Cherine said, falling back on her bed. "It was terrifying."

So, it was the same thing. I hadn't imagined it then. But what had it been doing here? Stalking me now I'd seen it? But if so, why had it appeared to Cherine and not me?

If it had followed me, maybe it would come back, and I could follow it in turn to its master or owner or whoever that handsome thief was. That might be the one way I could find him. And I needed to find him, as soon as possible.

"Tell us exactly what happened," Cora said.

Cherine sniffled. "I don't know. I was asleep when a noise disturbed me. I thought I heard a door opening. It creaked, slightly. I had just opened my eyes when I found it pulling up my covers." A sob caught in her throat as she rubbed her eyes dry with her forearm. "Probably sizing me up to see if I'd do for a quick bite."

I put the lamp at her bedside table, sat down beside her and patted her on the back. "Didn't Fairuza say that ghouls eat dead bodies?"

Cherine shook her head. "That's because they're scavenger beasts. They usually can't risk coming near live people to eat them, so they scour our cemeteries for flesh that isn't too rotten. It doesn't mean they wouldn't eat you if they got you alone."

Alright then. Scratch finding the thief from the vault through the ghoul.

I was ready to risk a lot of things to find him, but being eaten alive was not one of them.

~

After our rude awakening, our first day in Sunstone Palace officially started with our handlers hustling us out of our quarters and forming us into a line that went down the connecting hall and around the corner. They inspected us one by one, scrutinizing our clothes, cleanliness and postures in nerve-wracking silence.

As Loujaïne came closer, I smacked Cora on the back so she'd straighten up. I'd been a waitress in eight different establishments over the past two years, and each place had trained me to serve, smile and stand for hours on end with a good posture. Slouching, shuffling and swaying from fatigue or a sleepless night had not been allowed. Once you were on the clock you were *on*.

I held my head up and gave my best 'Can I take your order?' smile to the princess as she passed, my hands for once free of a pen and notepad and folded one over the other like Fairuza's.

She paid me no mind, ignored Cora, then stopped before Cherine.

After the ghoul incident, Cherine had been having trouble getting a grip, becoming progressively more twitchy and panicky. She stood there fidgeting, on the verge of a meltdown.

"What's the matter?" Loujaïne asked her.

Cherine's lower lip wobbled and she blinked back tears in a flutter of her lashes.

"I said what's the matter?" Loujaïne repeated, harsher this time.

"She has the sniffles, Your Highness," I whispered. "Think she's holding back a sneeze."

On cue, Cherine clapped her hands over her nose and mouth and sneezed.

Stepping back, disgusted, Loujaïne said, "I'll make sure you are visited by a nurse."

Inspection ended and we were hustled once again on a tour of another part of the palace. I couldn't put words to just how magnificent this place was with its high, domed ceilings, endless columns, mosaics and murals. Everywhere I looked there were detailed, vivid carpeting, marble flooring and priceless decorations, furniture and ornaments. Every inch of the architecture and interior design screamed, *"I cost a fortune!"*

Cherine, considering me her savior now, had glued herself to my side the entire time. At one point, while we passed through a dark, windowless section full of portraits and paintings, her tremors intensified so much they shook my whole arm.

Fairuza, flanked by her handmaidens, chattered the entire time in slow, hushed tones. They kept glancing back at us, the glee in their eyes only made worse by the smug giggles they pretended to hide behind their hands.

It seemed that mean girls were the same in every land. Pampered, pretty, and experts in the fine art of making you feel like trash.

DAYS TWO AND THREE, we were quarantined.

My excuse for Cherine's behavior got us segregated in our rooms with open windows and a visit from the nurse.

The nurse, a matronly woman with a lined face and sharp eyes, came with a trolley packed with corked bottles, jars and metal instruments that I found questionable. She set up a small cauldron in our fireplace and poured different oils and powders that turned into a thick, green, bubbling liquid. She scooped it into seven potbellied glasses and passed it around.

Fairuza's handmaidens, Meira and Agnë—whose names I'd learned from her demanding shouts—sniffed their glasses and gagged.

Fairuza covered her mouth with a delicate, manicured hand as she made a few unladylike noises of disgust. "What is this?"

"A prophylactic," the old nurse answered her, hunched with age, sun-beaten skin full of wrinkles sagging around her eyes, hair tinted dark red with greying roots. "If you have something, it should help kill it. If you don't, it should help ward it off."

Fairuza held her glass at arm's length, rim pinched between fingertips as if she was holding a dirty, smelly sock. "I'm not drinking this."

The nurse glared at her. "You don't drink, you stay in quarantine."

They all continued bellyaching. I was tempted to chip in on the excuses, as it looked and smelled so gross. I'd also never fallen sick while living on the streets and squatting in unheated houses for months on end, even when colds and fevers ran rampant in the town I was passing through. I'd never known if that had been some compensatory mercy from the fates, mere luck, or something else. But I believed nothing short of a plague was going to knock me off my feet.

That inexplicable immunity suddenly made me wonder. More importantly, it made me remember the thought that had formed in the back of my dazed mind during my encounter with Nariman. That she and my mother could be from the same place, that there was a closer resemblance between them than with anyone on Ericura. Which was the dumbest idea, since my mother had certainly not been a witch, and I wasn't in some form magically impervious to disease.

Before I could chime in on the complaints, Cora picked up the kettle on the breakfast table, poured warm water into her glass, thinning the murky concoction, then chugged it down like it was beer. She dropped her glass back onto the trolley, wiped her mouth with the back of her hand and looked at each of us expectantly.

Cherine and Fairuza gawked at her, trading expressions of amazement and disgust.

Now that she'd succeeded in making me feel like a wimp, I watered down my drink like hers, pinched my nose and finished it in three big gulps. It was a nauseating sensation, like I was drinking slimy tealeaves. The overpowering scents of grated lime rinds and star anise oil on my breath filled my sinuses—and those were the things added to make all the other unidentifiable ingredients palatable.

Then it was the others' turn. The nurse stood over each girl until she was forced to down it. They whined and gagged before, during and after. Then after the nurse conducted a general checkup of each of us, she left.

Stuck with nothing to do with the rest of the day, they all decided to nap. I took the chance to search our quarters again, tapping around the walls for hollow middles or camouflaged vents. A more thorough search revealed nothing. The only windows that opened were ten feet up and had no handles, needing a hooked pole to pull them apart, something servants brought with them, and took away afterward.

The windows within reach were wide and set into the wall, with glass set in place by cement, ending in a marble ledges to be used as seats, which Fairuza had used as shelves for all her perfumes, lotions and oils. The combined aroma wafting from them reminded me of the few times I cooked food in taverns and restaurants rather than served it. Alone, the scents were mouthwatering, but nauseating once combined.

Anyway, the only way out of a window was up to another part of the palace, not down, for the same reason the balcony wasn't an option either. I might have been able to navigate the fifty-foot drop to the palace gardens, but not the forest of sentries posted below day and night.

There truly was no way out but through the front door.

But if that was the case, how did the ghoul get in?

DAYS three through seven blurred together in my increasingly feverish efforts to find a way back to the vault.

The constant scrutiny we were subjected to—the so-called initial evaluation—made it impossible to do anything and not be caught. In the times we were allowed out, it was to yet another part of the palace, one that was always so frustratingly far away I couldn't even try breaking from the group and sneaking back down to the vault. Not just because of the guards stacked everywhere, but because Cherine had a tight hold on my arm the entire time, keeping me right by her, and dragging attention to us by her hyper behavior.

Today's new section of the palace was a series of rooms on the extensive second floor, filled with every article and instrument needed for every hobby, skill and talent. Those who survived to the first elimination were meant to use this space to practice for the next stage.

The structure of the competition consisted of a major test every nine days. The ones who failed each test would be sent home on the tenth day, what was not-so-fondly known as

Elimination Day. The first one would see us decrease from fifty to forty, the second from forty to twenty-five, and the third from twenty-five to five. After every round of eliminations, the "survivors" had to adapt with whatever was thrown at them next so they wouldn't be among the next bunch to be chopped, until only five remained at the end of the month.

I was undoubtedly going to be cut on the first Elimination Day.

That meant I had three days max left in this palace. Time was running out for me. And if it did, it meant life would run out for Bonnie and her father.

I couldn't let myself dwell on that too much or I'd be a mess and useless to them. Impossible as it felt, I had to keep my wits about me. I'd fought my way out of dire situations before—none that involved tests or magic, but I always came up with something. I would this time, too.

I *had* to.

As I felt the timer in my head ticking down to the inevitable explosion of Elimination Day, the palace rumor mill picked up speed like a fan in a windstorm.

While there'd been no sign of the ghoul again, gossip about it in a hall full of girls had traveled faster than a lit fuse. News of Cherine's nightmare had been met with either ridicule or superstitious fear. Our quarantine had also been a source of malicious amusement or increasing aversion. Both incidents spawned more packs mocking Cherine for being a giant baby and Cora for being an unfashionable mess who had no sense of taste or smell.

The gossip didn't stay focused on us though. Defensive strategies kicked in and soon each quintet closed in on themselves and started gossiping about every other girl in the rival groups. Apart from a passing mention of my association with

Cherine and Cora, no one talked about me, which was good. The less of an impression I made, the less memorable I was.

Not that being unnoticeable had helped. The one good thing to come of it so far was that it made them leave me alone.

I now picked up bits and pieces of conversations as we headed to the practice rooms. According to the Sapphire group ahead of us, a girl from the Ruby one behind us was from the land of Orcage and had a witch for a mother. Another from the same group was supposedly half-demon because her eyes were a hazel that was almost yellow. From there, the gossip only got progressively more outrageous.

We were passing by a room full of mirrors when Fairuza loudly broadcasted her own contribution to the slandering speculations. "You might have heard that the Queen of Tritonia consorted with an animal? She did, most likely a centaur. And that's not the worst of it. It's said she gave birth to a beast—"

The line stopped dead and we all knocked into each other.

Ariane —the Princess of Tritonia—stepped out from the White Opal group at the front of the line. Her fair, round face was almost as red as her hair as she seethed, "What was that?"

Instantly, everyone stepped back in a circle, giving a wide berth to the princesses, leaving the space between them empty so Ariane could glare holes directly into Fairuza's head.

Though her smile dimmed, Fairuza didn't buckle. "I believe you heard me."

Ariane stalked closer, the dead silence of anticipation in the massive corridor making the footfalls of her heeled shoes echo menacingly.

"Careful, Fay-Fay, I'm not the only one here with rumors of

beastly brothers," Ariane taunted coldly, head tilted slightly, pale green eyes sharp like daggers. "What happened to Leander again? Didn't your parents trap him in a tower once he started to get a little toothy? I hear he's gotten quite hairy, too."

Fairuza's mouth dropped open, accentuating her glazed deer-in-the-lamplights look. That reaction made me wish I could sketch, so I could immortalize the one moment someone managed to not just upstage her, but to shock her silent.

"What? You didn't think we'd hear about you as much as you've heard about us?" Ariane sneered. "People talk, honey, even if you pay them not to." With a toss of her hip-long, dark red hair, Ariane linked arms with Belinda—the always-silent, fifth girl from our Blue Opal group—and they both marched off, noses in the air.

"What was that about?" I asked once the line resumed its sluggish pace, my mind racing.

In contrast to the excitement buzzing around us in the aftermath of this dramatic confrontation, Cora seemed to find twisting a lock of her hair the only entertainment to be had around here. "Mostly how Fairuza's brother, the former Crown Prince of Arbore, pretty much vanished two years ago."

I leaned in closer, ears perked for the intriguing insider information she always provided. "Former?"

"They made his baby brother heir instead," she said disinterestedly. "No one's seen or heard of him since, but we know he's not dead, or they would have said so. So, there are tons of stories about what happened to him." Distaste wrinkled her nose. "He used to oversee the shipments of grain and potatoes from our fields and farms, would actually come himself."

"What was he like?"

Cora cringed as if she had just tasted something sour.

"Worse than his sister?"

Cora grimaced again. "So far, his sister hasn't cornered me in a shed and demanded a 'roll in the hay' because according to him, '*who else is going to give me any attention*?"

I goggled at her, appalled. "Are you serious?"

"Very. The only way I could get him away from me without spearing him with a hayfork was to head-butt him so hard he hit the ground."

I let out an amazed laugh. "You are awesome. Really. Don't let anyone tell you different."

"I don't." She sighed. "They tell me anyway."

I reached up and mussed her hair affectionately. "Well, next time slam that hard head of yours into *their* faces."

She grinned, leafy eyes a bit brighter. "Will do."

Cherine popped up, this time on Cora's side, reasserting her presence. "And what happened with Leander after that?"

"I don't know. He disappeared right after that incident."

"Is this why you don't want to be here?" I asked.

Cora smirked bitterly. "Because I don't want to deal with an impossibly rich and entitled monster of a boy? Yes."

"My prince is not like that," Cherine protested.

"His name literally sounds like a demon out of a summoning book," Cora argued. "Who names their child Cyaxares?"

"Sigh-ak-sa-reez." With each syllable, Cherine pointedly jabbed Cora's arm. "And it was the name of five great kings before him."

Cora, still unimpressed, stressed her point. "Think I once read a play with an evil witch called Cyaxares."

"Sycorax," I corrected automatically, flashing back to a cold night spent by the Fairborn's fireplace, when Bonnie had read a play aloud while I'd helped her father fix a broken clock. A rainy night in like any other, but one I would give my right arm to experience again. Then I realized what I'd said, and quickly amended, "Uh, I mean, it could have been Cyaxares. Probably not the same play."

Cora raised a blonde eyebrow at me, an unreadable expression in her green eyes. Then she only said, "Probably."

Sometimes, somehow, I felt she was onto me.

DAY EIGHT, we were kept mostly inside our wings to practice and review anything we felt could come up in tomorrow's test. I had no idea what tomorrow's test even was. It was only important to me because failing it meant I'd be kicked out of the palace empty-handed. Unlike the first night, when a simple ruse had had Loujaïne leading me into the vault, nothing worked now. I couldn't take two steps without being seen and questioned by palace guards and personnel.

Needless to say, I was going stir crazy with anxiety.

I was going to fail the dreaded test tomorrow, and then it would be all over.

"It's a character evaluation and etiquette survey," Cherine repeated for the fifth time, practicing her walk in five-inch pumps with a heavy, hardcover book on her head.

Feeling like pulling my enchanted hair out, I shut *Noblewomen of the Modern Age*, the book I had slipped out from under Belinda's mattress. Belinda would only miss the book at night, as its sole use to her was raising the end of the mattress, apparently to keep her ankles slim and feet dainty.

I tucked my own big feet under me on the armchair by our largest window to stop the nervous bouncing of my legs. "Yes,

I know the scroll of instructions said so. But what does that even mean?"

Cherine stopped her prowl, hands on her waist. "Darling, your family may be disgraced but I can't imagine they didn't bother teaching you to *have* grace, either."

For a moment, I had forgotten my cover story and was about to retort that, unlike her, I had no family, let alone anyone to teach me the refined graces of womanhood. But I bit my tongue in good time and just stared at her in frustrated silence.

With a heavy sigh, she stepped out of her shoes. "Character evaluations are tests they give you to see if you have the right personality to be queen."

I continued biting my tongue to block the first retort that came to mind. I knew what job interviews were; I'd done many of them in my travels. Most of my answers were lies—white lies that would get me hired, and secure me the leftover food at the end of the day. But I'd gotten it down to an art only because I knew what people in my land and social sphere expected to hear.

What was I going to do here? Go up to a palace official, who trained girls to be fancy, flouncy ladies from infancy and tell them that I was punctual and didn't mind lock-up duty? What would that even entail in a palace the width of a mountain?

This was a completely foreign society that I knew nothing about beyond what I'd learned in the past week through observation and Cora's insights.

"What would you do?" I asked Cherine, hoping to pick her brain for ways to avoid being kicked out on the first test. I needed more time in this palace. I had to find that lamp! "To show you have the right character and etiquette?"

Cherine, always happy to talk about herself, daintily spread out her arms with a delicate upturn of hands as she bowed, then held out the sides of her skirt and tucked one leg behind her as she smoothly curtsied. "There's this for a start. A good, quiet impression that you know the rules and that you bow to your superiors."

I rolled my eyes. "Which is everyone."

She wagged a finger at me. "Not everyone, only nobles and royalty who outrank you as a lady. You don't bow to palace staff of any kind."

"And then?"

"You smile, or you don't smile, depending on your rank compared to theirs. For you, you'd need to smile a lot. If you're a high lady like me, or a countess or princess, you don't need to. You'd just need to keep your head high and survey everyone with an air of importance."

Fairuza had that down to an art. Then again, she *was* important.

Not that it had saved her from being here, competing against forty-nine other noble ladies for that prince's hand.

Make that forty-seven. I wasn't competing and Cora couldn't care less. She had scarfed down a plate of cakes and grapes and hit the sheets early today. There was nothing I wanted more than to join her and escape in slumber until tomorrow. But I couldn't.

I'd done *nothing* the whole week.

Eight days here and nothing to show for it. No new information, no second sighting of the beautiful thief or his demon, and no way to get back into the vault.

"Are you even listening to me?" Cherine pouted, each word punctuated with frustration.

I nodded and she continued her lesson.

But there was no use to any of her advice. She did those things as easily as she breathed. If I did them, they'd come across as fake and grating if not downright pathetic.

There were no two ways about it. I was getting bundled up and chucked out on Elimination Day. My last chance to get back into the vault would be when I would ask for my jewelry back. I then had to do everything I could to find that lamp and carry it out with me.

Only then could Bonnie, her dad and I get back to Ericura.

Dusk seemed to be falling faster every day. It now painted our room in dim orange and purple rays through the thick glass windows, casting the squared shadows of their pane linings, making it feel like the luxurious prison cell it was.

After Cherine finished imparting her copious but useless advice, I gave up and turned in. I took the book with me to flip through until lights-out, then I forced myself to sleep, sinking into a series of anxiety-ridden dreams.

During another harrowing shift in my dreams—a scene involving Bonnie as a rabbit being devoured by a wolf—another blood-curdling scream woke me up.

CHAPTER TEN

Cherine's ghoul proved himself to be the ultimate escape artist.

This time he'd disappeared in the instants between her scream and my jump to action. That or it really was just a nightmare this time. I hoped it was, since I couldn't bear the thought that I'd missed yet another chance to follow it to my fellow thief.

Fairuza used up nearly all the hot water in our joint bathroom by having Meira and Agnë run her a bath. She returned reeking of lavender and sat in our living area on a stool while Meira brushed, dried and styled her hair with a hot metal rod that curled its ends. All through, Agnë quizzed her on an array of facts, statements, beliefs and cultural etiquette.

To keep an ear out for information that might come in handy, I showered last. By then the water in the pipes had reheated and I had gotten a good idea on what our tests were today.

Basically, elitist, judgmental interviews.

My *qarin* had worked its magic, filling my trunk with

folded, beaded and sequined dresses and their matching glittery shoes. All were different shades of blue, gold and bluish-green. If I wasn't wracked with worry, I would have tried them all on and asked if it could materialize any changes and requests I made.

For today, I picked a turquoise dress just to remind myself that this was a competition, and to annoy Fairuza. All of her dresses were either pearly white, glittery grey or vivid turquoise, and she seemed to think she had exclusive rights to those colors.

Cora sidled up to me, comb in hand, wearing a grass-green, floor-length, chiffon and silk dress with her hair braided in three sections from crown to nape. "Want me to do your hair?"

I grabbed at her offer. "Oh, yes, please. I braid like a drunkard would roll a cigarette while holding up his pants."

Cora stifled a snort. Belinda gave me a searing look of disapproval.

Cherine, scandalized, dropped the hand mirror she was using to apply her makeup. "Who talked like that around you?"

"I—uh, my parents couldn't afford a well-learned governess," I supplied the fabrication quickly. "Mine was an aggressive lady, usually drunk, too."

She and the other girls glared at me before returning to their chores.

Cora started combing my hair and leaned down to whisper, "Careful, Ada, you don't want Her Highness to feed you a soap bar."

"Sorry I'm not as educated or pedigreed as some people here," I grumbled.

"Same here. I'm not even noble at all, though the post my

mother holds is heritable, passed from woman to woman in our bloodline. I'm meant to be next once I get sent home."

"What makes you so sure you'll be sent home?"

She aimed her comb at Cherine and Fairuza. "Look who we're rooming with."

I nodded dejectedly, thinking of my impending elimination. "Don't know who this prince thinks he's kidding with this so-called contest. He'll end up picking the one who makes the most sense."

Cora started parting my hair. "Meaning, the richest and most well-connected."

"Might as well hand Princess Fay-Fay the crown she's panting for now, and be done with it."

Cora bowed her head to bury her snort in the chunk of hair she held. "True."

Then as she braided a crown from my temples, bringing both ends together down the rest of my hair, I questioned her about where she came from and she supplied more details. The Granary was a vast, independent region at the southwest of Lower Campania on the Forbidden Ocean, and was the breadbasket of Folkshore. Her mother, Mistress Cerelia, managed the region's largest farms, all its fields, orchards and some of its vineyards, and controlled most of this world's edible exports.

As the whole picture became clearer in my mind, I thought that making Cora a princess would be a far smarter move on the Prince's part than marrying Fairuza. If a war broke out between Cahraman and another kingdom—say, Arbore for not picking Fairuza—all they'd have left were prickly pears and dried figs and dates. So, having Cora as queen would ensure an alliance with the desert kingdom's major food source.

My heart suddenly squeezed as I remembered my mother

had loved dried fruit. *Especially* figs and dates. One thing that had once slipped past her tight lips about the father I didn't know was a mention that he'd wooed her with barrels of the stuff. Apart from that, she'd never even mentioned his name, just that the fates had torn them apart before I was born.

"I never knew my father," Cora said casually. I started. That wasn't the first time she'd said something as if she'd read my mind. "My mother likes to claim that the children of all Greenshoot women are fathered by gods. She says my father was a minor field god."

"Seriously? That's amazing."

She put down her comb and moved in front of me, a case of brushes and powders balanced on her arm. She started painting my face in soft, careful strokes high on my cheekbones, over my eyelids and under them in shades of pink, green and beige respectively. It reminded me of being twelve, the last time my mother had brushed my hair or painted my face for a local celebration. She had rarely let me join other children outside of schooling hours, and had declined most invitations to temples, festivals and dinners. I never understood why she'd been so guarded and now I never would.

And for the first time, I began to wonder if it had been out of fear, that like me now, she'd been trying to remain inconspicuous, in an effort to avoid exposure. But though I couldn't imagine exposure to what, that was still no explanation for why and how she'd left me. One night, she'd disappeared without saying a word to me, leaving me wracked with worry until a sheriff had knocked on my door to deliver the life-destroying news that she had died, miles and miles away from our town.

The vividness of the memory, exacerbated by Cora

grooming me like my mother used to, had my tears pricking my eyes and surging to fill them.

"I don't believe we're sired by gods, though," Cora said quietly, noticing my filling eyes but making no comment. "I believe it's just an excuse all the women in my family used, because had they gotten married to men who did sire us, then the ownership of our lands would have transferred to the husbands. This is the only way they could keep their trade, lands and names along with having daughters who can inherit them. You can't dispute the will of the gods."

"I don't know," I mused. "We just had a ghoul in our room. Why not a god in yours in a couple of years?"

She blushed furiously, ducking her head as she refocused on finishing up my makeup.

A clap like the crack of a whip made me start and whirl around.

Loujaïne was standing at our door, looking as regal and as impatient as she always did. "Girls, time to go."

Fairuza, Meira and Agnë beat us out of the room. Belinda followed them to meet with Princess Ariane outside, who we'd learned turned out to be her cousin. Cherine hooked her arm through mine, leaning half her weight on me. Cora linked hers with my other arm just in time for us to be dragged out by Cherine.

Once in the corridor, I withdrew myself from the two girls and ran up to Princess Loujaïne. "Your Highness, can I please head down to the vaults to retrieve my things? I need just the earrings for now."

Loujaïne shook her elegant head. "There is no time for that now. But we will return all your jewelry and we will be moving safes into all of your rooms while you're out today."

My heart sank to my guts with a painful thud.

There went my one chance to get back to the vault.

But I had to say something, after I'd made such a fuss over the lack of safes in our rooms.

"Oh! That's great." My voice cracked over the fake relief. "Thank you for that, Your Highness. Really puts my mind at ease."

She scowled at me for a moment then said, "About ease... what was this I heard about your group waking up so early and making such noise you disturbed your neighbors?"

"Cherine rolled out of her bed and woke us all up," I lied immediately. "She screamed so loudly we were afraid she broke something."

"That sounds like her." Loujaïne sighed, speeding up her pace to be ahead of the group.

"What's that supposed to mean?" Cherine called after her. Getting no answer, she turned to me. "Why didn't you tell her about the ghoul?"

"We're about to go get evaluated. Fairuza says ghouls aren't real, I figured Loujaïne might not think they're real either. If you keep insisting there was one in our room today they'll think you're crazy. If you're crazy, you get disqualified. I think."

"Oh!" She breathed in wide-eyed realization, before she grumbled, "But I'm not crazy."

"Not saying you are, just telling you what it might look like."

"You do remember that we are competition, right?"

"Don't worry about that," I said, scrambling for a new plan that led back to the vault now that Loujaïne had crushed the one I'd banked on. "Believe me, I can't wait to get home."

~

THE TEST WAS TAKING place in a vast room with paneled walls, a soaring ceiling, minimalist décor and a wide set of windows at its far end.

Silhouetted before the windows was a long table with our ten judges in heavy cloaks, the men in moss green, the women in pale pink. Each examiner had a stool set in front of them across the table, and a set of articles on it which included a book, three metal containers of gold, silver and lead, a cane, an hourglass, a crystal tea set and a bronze kettle.

Lines of five were organized in front of each examiner, with all servants, handmaidens and handlers hanging back.

In my line, Belinda went first. With me at the back of the line, I only heard incomprehensible snippets of her exchange with our examiner, but Cora blocked most of my view. I settled for watching the lines on both sides to get a clearer idea of what was going on. They didn't prove any help either, and my eyes strayed to the rest of the room and—

I did a double-take, my jaw going slack, my heart nearly firing out of my ribs.

Him. It was *him*! The thief from the vault!

He was standing by one of the doors, as if sticking close to the exit in case he needed to make a run for it.

And if I had found him pretty in the dark, I found him stunning in broad daylight.

I didn't know where that adjective came from. Where men were concerned, I never thought in terms stronger than "handsome." But *stunning* was the first word that struck me as I examined him, the only one to do him justice.

His jaw-length, wavy hair that parted at the middle was a rich, chestnut brown that accentuated his golden skin tone. His face was centered by a sharp nose and ended with a strong, square jaw. His mouth was an archer's bow, the lower lip plumper than the top. It curved into a smirk that could be construed in so many ways as he crossed his arms over his broad chest and leaned on the wall, watching the whole spectacle.

I couldn't help but wonder what a real smile from him would be like. Going by the rest of him, his smile could probably melt iron. But the crown jewels of his face were his eyes.

Under a prominent brow and thick, arched eyebrows were deep-set eyes the icy-green color of northern lights.

Nobody else seemed to notice him. And he didn't seem to notice me, which was a relief considering how hard I was staring. But I couldn't believe he was really here, just like that, after I'd given up hope of finding him.

Now I had to find a way to approach him…

A movement ahead roused me from my trance. I swung around and found Belinda leaving and the line moving.

Fairuza tossed back her curled hair as she moved ahead to take Belinda's place, hitting Cora in the nose with it. I tossed the thief a conflicted glance before I rolled up on my toes to peek over Cora's shoulder. It was my chance to see and hear something now I was closer.

Our examiner was a trim and handsome mustachioed man with intense, slanted, dark eyes and close-cropped silky black hair. He wore a fez and a coppery brooch of a chimera—a creature with the head, front claws, wings and tail of a hawk and the body of a lion.

"Good morning, Your Highness," he said, offering her his hand, his dark gaze leaving her to focus where Loujaïne sat two judges from him, then back to her, as if he was comparing the two. "I am Master Farouk, Minister of Treasury and Commerce here in Cahraman."

Fairuza curtsied lightly, not taking his hand as she sat down. "Shall we begin?"

His friendly smile twitched. He retracted his hand and flipped his hourglass, starting the countdown of her allotted time. "Introduce yourself."

"Fairuza of House Silverthorn, Princess of Arbore, Duchess of Eglantine, second-born and eldest daughter of the former princess of Cahraman, Queen Zomoroda, and King Florent of Arbore."

That was quite the list. No wonder she was always on the verge of exploding with pride.

"And why are you here?"

"To become the queen I am meant to be."

Farouk nodded as he took down notes with his fountain pen. "Which is?"

"The best queen this kingdom has seen since Queen Amanita the Gentle."

"And how do you plan on doing that?"

"By recreating her effect on court and society, reviving her causes, building up their importance and implementing new, protective laws, while enriching social prosperity by attending to emergent needs with charity projects and functions."

She continued to hit each question Master Farouk asked with a practiced and confident response. If I hadn't felt dismally unprepared before, I sure did now.

The questions moved on to requests. He handed her the book, asked her if she had read it, to which she replied "Yes," then he asked her to demonstrate its use to her. Fairuza set it on her head, circled us and returned to her spot without the book having moved a hairbreadth off her glossy hair. I snatched another look back at the thief, wanting to see his reaction to Fairuza, my mind crowding with a hundred theories why and how he was in here. I couldn't come up with a logical reason. His smirk remained the same.

Master Farouk received the book with a congratulatory "Good job" as Fairuza resumed her seat in front of him.

"Pour the tea," he instructed, gesturing to the small bronze kettle on her left. It rested on a burner with hot coals spitting out fiery sparks.

He watched her closely, hand still held out over the glass teapot and the short, vase-shaped glasses.

She shook her head calmly, crossing her ankles, straightening her back and setting her folded hands on her lap. "After you, my lord."

He gave her a curt nod and scribbled something on his notepad.

"What was that about?" I whispered in Cora's ear.

"High-born ladies don't serve people they outrank, but are served by them, or both are served by a servant."

During that moment, I missed what he asked her to do with the cane. They were now having a weird discussion, one that sounded rehearsed as well. With more focus, I realized that they weren't having a real discussion, but *quoting* one.

There was something I should have memorized?

I was doomed.

Barely keeping an anxiety attack at bay, I stole another glance at the man by the door.

He was gone!

I frantically searched the room for him and noticed the guards scattered around for the first time. Speaking of guards, I'd discovered they stood outside and below our quarters whether we were inside or not. So how did Cherine's ghoul keep getting past them?

Then I spotted *him* again. He had moved to the window

closest to Master Farouk, half-concealed by the curtain's shadow and holding a tray of opaque orange and translucent burgundy drinks.

Unobtrusive, he stood there, subtly turning his head as if to catch as much as he could of the conversations. His gorgeous face was very hard to read, not because it displayed no emotion, but because of the quick succession of reactions flashing across it.

Just as a girl in the adjacent line asked loudly enough to be heard across the room, "What does this have to do with being queen?" he grimaced as if something heavy had been dropped on his foot. When another shrieked and dropped the kettle he seemed to be suppressing his laughter.

He found this amusing?

Come to think about it, if this weren't a matter of life and death to me, I'd probably see the funny side in all this too.

I resumed watching him as Fairuza left the judge and Cherine took her place, noticing more details about him now I wasn't just staring at his face. He was tall. Taller than Cora. A knee-length, white kaftan overlaid with a light pattern of green vines and leaves hugged his strong shoulders and chest, displaying their breadth and power, and a reflective, pewter sash wound around his trim waist. He had solid white pants underneath and his tan shoes were not polished like the guards', with a layer of dust on them. From this angle, I could see inside the sleeve of the arm holding up the tray. A thin gold bracelet peeked out of it.

So he had made it out of the vault with loot.

He *was* my one ticket back there. I needed to catch him.

I kept running scenarios in my mind of how I'd do that until Cherine left the judge and Cora took her spot, playing nervously with her hands.

Master Farouk asked her the same questions and made the same requests. I didn't pay enough attention to her responses but I could hear the lack of investment in her tone. The one thing I was invested in was watching the eavesdropping servant, feverishly thinking up ways to approach him.

"Introduce yourself."

I jumped around at the loud demand, stumbling. "Sorry, what?"

"Introduce yourself," Master Farouk repeated, his gaze mildly annoyed. "It's your turn."

I swallowed the jagged lump in my throat.

My turn. To be exposed for the fraud I was.

CHAPTER ELEVEN

I bowed before I remembered Cherine's mini-lesson and curtsied. My sweaty, slippery feet twisted in my high-heeled shoes, turning the attempt into a clumsy stagger.

I barely caught myself and mumbled, "I'm Ada. Of Rose Isle."

"Is that it?" Farouk asked, sounding bored. I would be, too, after repeating the same tedious questions over and over and getting a variety of rehearsed answers.

I shrugged. "So far it is."

He raised a thick eyebrow as he set down his fountain pen, folding his arms on the table to give me his full attention. "Why are you here?"

"Opportunity."

He raised both brows now. "Which opportunity?"

Since I couldn't tell him the one I was here for involved the palace vault, I decided to say as much truth as I could to make my answer somewhat plausible. "Anything to better my situation and through that, the situation of a friend and her father."

"What about the reason you're all here, isn't that the real opportunity?"

"It's a one-in-fifty chance and I'm not one to put all my eggs in one basket unless I absolutely need to, or I'm sure it's going to work," I rambled on. "Might as well have plans for if and when I get eliminated."

"What plans?"

I should shut up. I couldn't. I had to respond. And I couldn't include any truths anymore. Back to on-the-fly lies. "Uh…leaving with new information, experience and helpful connections? Or anything else really that I might be able to use to my advantage in the future."

He nodded, sneaking a glance to the side, likely at Loujaïne. "Sounds like you've given much thought to the many paths your future can take. But what if it leads to becoming the princess and future queen, how do you see that opportunity?"

As hypothetical questions went, this was a difficult one. But I figured that the best way was to approach it as a real one. What did a princess and future queen do?

What would I do if *I* were one?

I cleared my throat. "I'd need about a year of research and schooling on what it really means to be in such a position. I'd need to learn everything about this kingdom, and how this palace works. I'd want to explore this city for myself, to see the people and the society in action and to learn the history and social norms before I could start fulfilling my duties. In the meantime, I'd do things that don't need too much information, but just power."

He leaned in, eyes intent on my face. "Like?"

I gulped. I kept backing myself into a corner.

But why was I even stressing it? I had no hope of passing this test. Might as well speak from experience, from the heart, say what I believed in, what I'd do if I were to have power.

"I'd start with building orphanages and staffing them with the best caretakers and teachers. I'd have a special brigade supervising the treatment of orphans and foster children. I'd make sure they're not taken advantage of and, when the time comes, are helped in transitioning into independence. I'd do something about the unemployed, maybe have the palace commissioning more from locals instead of relying on imports or court-approved suppliers, to make more jobs. And I'd send children and youths to apprenticeships. I'd also build more public housing so no one has to live on the streets. Actually, on the way through the city, I think I saw many abandoned houses. Those should not be left unused and deteriorating. I'd have those fixed up and given to people who need places to live."

A long moment after I'd fallen silent, he said, "Interesting answers."

Interesting as in good, or as in weird?

Before I could decide from his expression, he sat up. "Now, we shall move to the next part of our exam." He shoved the book toward me. "Here, show me what you can do with this."

I took the book and ran my hands over the tough, embellished cover. I compared it to the dusty tomes I had seen in libraries, the time-worn volumes of my schoolmistresses, and the variety Bonnie displayed in her room, from the first book her father had gotten her, to the book I'd stolen for her, starting this snowballing disaster.

With a meticulously made dark-green, leather cover and gold engravings in Cahraman's traditional script, twisted around in fancy calligraphy, this book was in a league of its own.

The first page declared it as *The Anthology of Dunes.*

I skimmed through the first story called *The Silent City of Alabasta.* It was about a desert civilization that thrived thousands of years ago, before half of its land fell into the Silent Ocean and its people vanished. Nothing was left behind in the remaining land but monuments, and idols of nameless deities with the heads of animals, most of a cat or a lioness goddess.

The story was told from the perspective of a man called Esfandiar of Gypsum, who was sent by a Queen Zafira to explore the silent city. He managed to decipher the language written on the walls and at the feet of idols. Once he vocalized a few words, a magical barrier rose around Alabasta. A statue of a bird-like creature came to life, blocked the gates and demanded an answer to riddles in exchange for admittance. In Esfandiar's case, he needed to be let out.

I examined the illustration of the creature. It was the same as the pin on Master Farouk's chest. Esfandiar called it a *simurgh.*

It asked him three riddles, decreeing that if he failed to answer any, it would eat him. If he answered them all, it would let him go.

The first was *"What flies without wings?"* to which he answered: *"time."*

The second was *"You heard me before, you'll hear me again, then I die 'till you call me again"* to which he answered: *"echo."*

And the last was:

"Made of fire and trapped in a hold
That won't expire until I am told
Bestowing riches and miracles untold

But one must be wary of wishes within
My prison that glistens
And the mischief I bring"

To which, after much thought, he answered *"Djinni."*

The *simurgh* flew off, leaving behind three feathers, to burn if he ever needed its help.

I flipped through more pages, found a collection of stories about the places and creatures Esfandiar encountered. Some were by other explorers. Each story had a few ink illustrations.

I stopped at one in particular. It had a man with long fair hair standing before the massive chimera, holding up one of its feathers with the subtitle: *The White Shadow of Avesta and the Simurgh.*

That man reminded me very much of Cherine's ghoul.

I closed the book and put it back on the table, only one thing on my mind: I wanted this book.

But since I couldn't shove it down my dress and slip away with it, I might as well ask.

"Is there another copy of this somewhere around here?"

Master Farouk's thick brows rose, adding to his wide-eyed confusion. "There is. Why?"

"I want to borrow it."

He pushed the book back into my hands. "You can keep this one. I have others."

Wow. This was easier than I imagined. "Are you sure?"

"Quite sure." He gestured before him. "Have a seat."

I looked sideways as I sat down, and found the green-eyed thief was now closer, stealing sips from one of the glasses on his tray. I thought he looked…excited?

Hoping he'd remain there for me to catch after I was finished, I checked everyone else in the room. Cora and

Cherine stood by the doors we'd come through, the size difference between them even more apparent at this distance and slightly comical.

Not so was the way Cherine was darting restless glances around with her arms folded tightly against her chest. Did she think the ghoul would appear to her even here? Or was she, like me, starting to question her sanity?

"Pour the tea," Farouk ordered.

Without hesitation, I got up and started arranging everything like I did back at the Poison Apple tavern. I opened a box full of loose tealeaves and measured two scoops into the teapot. Then using the skirt of my dress to pick up the hot kettle, I poured the steaming water over them. I waited until the water was stained a rich, dark red, then picked up the cups, placing one in front of each of us. I tapped around for the sugar and he offered me a footed metal container packed with sugar cubes. I asked if he took sugar, and he said two, so I scooped two cubes in each glass, then set a hand on the teapot's lid as I poured the tea, his cup first, then mine.

I stirred the sugar then sat back down and pulled the chair in closer. Only then did I realize that I had committed a grave mistake. Highborn ladies didn't serve those they outranked.

Master Farouk's face was unreadable, telling me nothing about his judgment as he blew the steam off his cup. He took a tentative sip, again showing no reaction.

Then he set the cup down and said, "Next task."

He handed me the cane. It was a literal cane, a hollow, yellowed sugar cane that was attached to a hooked handle.

"What do I do with this?"

"Break it."

I noticed the nine other girls currently being tested trying to snap their canes. One was banging it on the floor. Another seemed to have twisted her wrist in an attempt to snap it and was crying in obvious pain as the cane slipped from her hands to the floor.

I tried breaking it against my knee. It didn't work. That meant brute force wouldn't cut it. I mulled over the problem for moments before I got another idea.

I held the middle of the cane over the coals, rotating it until it burned on all sides. Then I banged the charred part against the edge of the table and the bottom half snapped off.

I raised my eyes only to find the thief had moved straight behind the examiners, holding his tray, but still serving no one.

I fought hard against my straying attention, trying to keep it on the task and away from how divine he was in every type of lighting.

"What's the point of this?" I asked, raising the broken cane.

"You'll find out soon enough. Now—" Farouk slid the three boxes to his right to the space between us, swept his hand above them. "Choose a box."

On each box a note was written in an elaborate script.

Over the gold box the note said: *Whoever chooses me will get what they most desire.*

On the silver: *Whoever chooses me will get what they truly deserve.*

And on the lead box: *Whoever chooses me must gamble all they have.*

Unless it had a key to the vault and an invisibility cloak along with it, then the gold box did not have what I most desired. And unless the silver had a way of getting us out of here and back to the life the Fairborns and I had, then it wasn't what I truly deserved.

I was already gambling my life to get out of this mess. Might as well pick the last one.

I flipped open the lid of the lead box.

It was empty.

I raised my eyes to Farouk, confused.

He only nodded, shutting the box. "That's all we have for you today. You can go now."

As if taking the dismissal as an order to himself, the thief rushed towards the closest door.

I erupted to my feet, barely curtsying to Master Farouk before I chased after him.

"Wait!"

He stopped and turned, looking surprised for a moment, before he bowed his head. "Yes, my lady?"

Checking to see if anyone was watching, I found many eyes on us. I took a glass off his tray, to pretend this was why I'd stopped him.

I sipped the drink that smelled of apricots and almost choked. "Gah, what's that taste?"

"I reckon that's the rosewater. Awfully strong, isn't it?"

"Kind of is."

He bowed again then turned to leave. I rushed after him.

At the door, I yanked him back by the collar, almost making him spill his drinks. "Hey!"

He didn't seem to mind, balancing the tray expertly and turning back to me with a smile. "Yes?"

I was right about the melting iron part. I could feel my bones turning to jelly at the simple spread of his lips. But this wasn't the time for me to ogle and swoon. And I wasn't a waitress anymore, invisible to all I watched and eavesdropped on.

It seemed he was, though. It seemed people ignored those

who served them in every world. Thankfully, those who'd turned to investigate my actions were once again watching the main event. I had to make this quick before I attracted their attention again.

"You were in the vault last week, weren't you?" I asked urgently.

His eyes widened a fraction before avoiding mine. "No."

"I saw you."

His eyes returned to mine, narrowed to wicked slits. "You sure it was me?"

"I'd recognize your face anywhere."

His smile grew smug, not bothering to deny my claim. "I'm that memorable, huh?"

"You'll be pretty easy to spot once I report you to the guards."

His brows furrowed in mock shock. "You'd do that?" Then he relaxed into that teasing smile again. "What do you care if I was in the vault?"

"So, you admit you were inside it?"

He leaned closer, whispering, "Yes, I was. And?"

My voice lowered to match his. "What did you steal?"

He shrugged nonchalantly. "Nothing the king would miss."

"How many times have you been in there?"

A perfect eyebrow rose. "What is this, an interrogation? Are you angling to become a palace guard once you're disqualified?"

"Is that allowed?"

He laughed lightly, shaking his head. That messed up his parted fringe, scattering the wavy brown locks that hung over his eyes. "No, not really. The most you could aim for is becoming the lady-in-waiting to a princess."

The idea of waiting on Fairuza made being eaten by the beast of Rosemead sound appealing.

"Have you been down there more than once or not?" I said between gritted teeth.

"What's it to you? I doubt you'd have much use for a few daggers."

I frowned. "Planning an assassination?"

His smile became lopsided, an amused smirk that made my blood fizz. "I just found that silver blades are required for certain potions, or at least that's what the apothecary texts claim. *Crush the moonseeds with the tip of a silver blade,*" he pontificated, waving his free hand to mime the ritual. "Then use the blunt side to squeeze out the juice."

I smacked his hand. "Can you quit it? I'm trying to be serious here."

His grin widened as he shook the sting out. "Why would you ever do that? Being serious gives you frown lines."

"Not the point." I almost stomped my foot in frustration but I involuntarily felt for bumps on my forehead, forcibly relaxing my brow muscles as I realized they were actually sore. I must have been frowning a lot lately. I persisted, "How many times have you been down there?"

"My answer depends on why you're asking," he teased as he held out the tray toward me, pointing to the glasses on the other side of it, the ones filled with the dark burgundy drink. "I think you need to calm down. Try the hibiscus. You'll like it better, since I take it you're not fond of rosewater."

"Or apricots," I shuddered as I took the glass he was offering me.

His nod was sympathetic. "I've found that I can't stand the taste of anything orange. Apricots, carrots, and, well, oranges."

"That's nice," I hissed. "But you really need to stop dodging my questions."

The corners of his bright eyes crinkled and heart-melting dimples formed in his cheeks as he chuckled. "You're focused, I like that."

"Well?"

"Shouldn't I have the honor of knowing who's threatening to report me first?"

I mock curtsied. "Call me Ada."

He bowed fully this time, tucking his free arm under his chest. "Call me Cyrus."

"Nice to meet you, Cyrus." I glared at him impatiently. "How did you get into the vault?"

"Nothing is going to shake you off, is it?"

"No."

He straightened, again making me aware how much taller he was than me, appearing amused and intrigued. "I have a... friend who knows how to sneak around undetected. He's taught me a few tricks."

Could he mean the ghoul? He might, since that creature got around unseen by everyone. So far, only Cherine and I had seen him.

But maybe I was assuming too much. Maybe this friend was just a normal but equally useful person. "Is your 'friend' a guard here?"

"In a manner of speaking, yes. He is a guardian."

"Can you bring me your friend? To take me into the vault?"

"I could," he said coyly. "But you complain about me dodging your questions when you've hopped over mine. What are you looking for and why do you want it?"

"It's kind of an I'll-know-it-when-I-see-it situation. I need to get back into that vault as soon as possible and have enough time to look around for it."

"Odd," he mused. "Thieves usually have a clear idea of what they're after."

"I'm a bit of a rebel," I said sarcastically.

He looked me square in the eye, a mischievous glint in his. "Oh, I bet you are."

His voice had dipped to a low, velvety timbre that made my fingers spasm and my heart stumble.

But this wasn't the time to get flustered. I needed to pin him down, not the other way around.

"So, when can I meet your friend?" I persisted.

"Seeing as *somebody* exposed our trips to the vault..." His emphatic glance left me in no doubt who he blamed for that. "...patrols have been checking there every night. I'd say the first chance we have at getting there undetected again is when the stationed guards get reassigned, which should be tomorrow."

Tomorrow. Also known as Elimination Day.

That would be too late.

But...maybe it wouldn't be. I'd expected to be cut for sure, but after seeing most of the contestants bumbling their way through the test, maybe I wouldn't be.

I squared my shoulders, clinging to this new hope. "Fine. If I survive Elimination Day, you're taking me down to the vaults."

He held out a hand to me. "Deal!"

Without thinking, I put my hand in his.

He had a wide palm and long fingers, a powerful yet sensitive hand, made to grip a sword or the bow of a violin. My hand looked tiny and delicate in his, though I'd never thought of myself as either.

With a flick of his wrist, he turned our handshake into a light grasp on my fingers as he raised my hand to meet his kiss.

The moment his lips touched my hand, something overwhelming surged inside me.

I barely fought back the most idiotic, ridiculous urge to blurt out, "Rob the vault and run away with me."

CHAPTER TWELVE

"What does he think he's playing at?"

The yell made me jump and whirl around. By the time I realized it was only Cherine stomping towards another door and turned back to Cyrus, he'd given me the slip.

Sighing, feeling at least relieved to have finally found and talked to him, even cut a deal with him, I turned my attention back to Cherine and Cora, strode to catch up with them.

Cherine was loudly expressing her displeasure at the crumpled note in her fist. "What is this *nonsense*?"

"Did Farouk write you reports?" I asked as I came up behind her.

With a startled shriek, she jumped around, arms raised protectively. "Where did you pop up from? Where have you been?"

I raised my glass. "Getting a drink. When are we going to eat?"

"Should be now." Cora looked back to check the clock

behind the examiners. "They're probably going to test if our eating habits are worthy, too."

The clock was made of pinewood, carved into a two-headed, claw-footed bird. It said eleven o'clock. And they hadn't let us have breakfast yet. Most establishments I've worked in were ready to serve by eight. I realized with a start that my appetite had returned for the first time since I'd Nariman had stolen me into this world. My stomach even grumbled.

What I'd give for a greasy pub breakfast right now.

"Forget food. What did you get?" Cherine tried snatching Cora's note but she held it up way out of her reach.

"You first," Cora insisted.

"I asked first!"

"And I have longer arms."

Shimmying in a frustrated little dance, Cherine finally gave in, holding out her note.

Cora and I moved in to read it.

All that is gilded might be precious or of no matter
A golden casket is as worthwhile as a noble name,
The body within the first and wielding the latter
Will fill with maggots all the same.

I tried hard not to laugh. "Ouch. Farouk wrote this?"

"No, Prince Cyaxares did." Cherine pouted, hugging herself. "It's his handwriting."

Our prince was a snarky poet. I was impressed.

"You don't know what he looks like but you know his handwriting?" Cora asked, amazed.

"We corresponded occasionally, but I haven't actually seen him since I was five."

"What about you?" I asked Cora.

Cora shrugged, handing me her note. It was an equally poetic yet more caustic reply.

The median choice is well and good, but often a silly mistake.
Picking silver to conceal greed is the empty gesture of a vacant head.
Forgoing gold but avoiding lead is an uncertain stance to take,
One indulgent, the other humbling, picking neither is pitiful instead.
Even if covetous fools and wavering cowards are equally fake
Fools might have their use, but cowards have none till they're dead.

Cherine's note was a jab but Cora's was an insult. Just reading it made me feel like I had been slapped. Indecisiveness seemed to be a bigger problem to the prince than plain avarice, predictability and superficiality. That painted a clearer picture of him in my mind, of what kind of person he was.

"This is..." I tried to commiserate, but I was kind of lost for words. I just shrugged and took a sip of my burgundy drink.

It was rich, sweet and less sour than it smelled. But from its flowery undertones, I could tell this hibiscus was made from petals rather than a fruit. And Cyrus had been right; I did like it better. I hoped he was right about everything else.

Cora nodded. "I don't get it."

"That's because you're a farm girl," Cherine said meanly, bordering on a childish whine. "It's a wonder you can read."

I suppressed the urge to kick her for that.

"My mother is the leader of the farming valley, of course I can read," Cora retorted, offended, cheeks turning pink with anger. "What do you have against farmers, anyway?"

"You're all sunburnt and dirty and sound funny and have

no class," Cherine hissed, wild-eyed, looking even more hyper than she usually was. "And you don't wear shoes indoors."

"Work-boots track dirt and mud all over the place," Cora exclaimed. "That's why we take our shoes off outside the house!"

"Girls. Breakfast," I reminded them, trying to put an end to this spat.

Cherine glared at me. "Forget your stupid breakfast. I think I just failed this test!"

I was too tired and hungry for this.

I bent down, almost pressing my nose against hers. "If you think you're that much more important than food, I guess I could always chomp a few bites off your arm."

She stiffened, edging away from me. "You can't do that."

Since she was actually taking it seriously, I decided to capitalize on her naiveté. "Some days I was so hungry I could have eaten the next person I saw, so, yes, I would."

The incident with the ghoul this morning probably brought her some unwelcome visuals. She seemed to wilt as she scooted out the door. We followed.

"That was a bit much," Cora said.

"It got her to shut up and move, didn't it?"

"Still, something did try to eat her this morning..." Suddenly the compassion on her face drained as her eyes shot daggers at Cherine's back. "Shame it didn't, though."

"What were those notes about, anyway?" I asked.

Cora checked her note again, raising a brow at me. "They're our responses."

"I get that." I gestured impatiently. "Where did you get them?"

"The boxes," Cora said confusedly. "Which box did you pick?"

"The lead one," I said.

After answering her, the realization hit me in a rush of dread. "I didn't get a note. My box was empty!"

Cora's eyes widened. "Maybe Master Farouk forgot to replace the note after the last girl?"

"No one else in our line picked lead. Fairuza, Belinda and Cherine picked gold and you picked silver."

"Maybe it was empty by accident? Did the minister say anything?"

I shook my head, rethinking every one of my choices and answers, trying to figure out what I did wrong.

The box had claimed that "*Whoever chooses me must gamble all they have*" and it had nothing inside. Why didn't my choice get any kind of response, even one more denigrating than Cora's? Or was that choice so bad it didn't even warrant a response?

That seemed to be the likeliest possibility. Who in her right mind would choose lead?

But I had. Because I wasn't in my right mind. I was still as clueless as I had been the first day I'd been tossed into this game with no rules and no plan. Like I had been tossed out into the cold, unforgiving world after my mother died.

I'd survived the world. But there was no surviving losing the prince's game before I found the lamp, and therefore losing Nariman's.

I had gambled all I had, like that note had said. And I had come out with a big, empty nothing, like the lead box I'd chosen.

CHAPTER THIRTEEN

Next morning, a fancy send-off breakfast was held for us in the gigantic theatre room.

The feast was spread on long tables before the low stage and podium. It was a nice gesture, I suppose.

To me, it felt like a last meal before execution.

The optimism that had assailed me yesterday after meeting Cyrus and the thought that I might not get eliminated had long evaporated. I was torn between being too nauseous to eat and wanting to stuff myself in case I didn't get to see food ever again. Nariman would probably kill me along with the Fairborns. Or worse, she could leave me stranded in the desert. Either way, I'd end up dead.

Cora, being the least stressed of us all, had two plates piled the highest and had dragged a round coffee table before our seats to accommodate them. Encouraged by her example, I kept myself off the edge by gorging myself as I listened to Cherine's idle chatter.

Finally, feeling about to burst, I pushed my plate away, and anxiety swamped me all over again.

I cut through Cherine's rambling. "I still don't get what all those silly tasks were for!"

"Me, neither," Cora agreed through a mouthful of flat-bread, spraying crumbs onto her plate. "Was that the etiquette test or the character evaluation? I couldn't tell."

"Don't talk with your mouth full," Cherine snapped, shoving a napkin in Cora's face, before pouring coffee for herself into a two-inch-high glass. At least I thought it was coffee. It was a suspicious shade of turbid yellow. The coffeepot—a *dallah*—looked like some kind of exotic bird. Long, bulbous body, spire-like cap and a spout shaped like a crescent-shaped beak.

Plucking the pot from her, I poured three cups and put one of the offered additives in each—cardamom, saffron, and a mixture of cloves and cinnamon. Might as well try everything I could while I could.

"Why did we spend most of our time here doing nothing just to get tested for an hour on the last day?" I grumbled as I tasted the first one, grimacing at the bitterness rivaling my own right now. "Why not give us more tests, more chances?"

"To be fair," said Cherine with a sigh, "we were supposed to spend our time preparing for the test, so we have no excuses if we were unprepared."

Cherine being fair and reasonable? Now I'd heard it all.

But if she was done whining, and had found wisdom overnight, I'd pick up where she'd left off. "But they didn't exactly tell us what to expect."

"They're not supposed to," she said matter-of-factly, a wave of her tiny hand rattling her circular, gold bracelets. "We're meant to be prepared from birth to impress the noblemen and their families with our mastery of many subjects, skills and fine arts, which we were mildly quizzed on yesterday. If you fail a test this easy, then you must be as clueless as a commoner."

So if I fail it would be because I was a pleb, not because of unfair rules or bad luck.

That just made everything *so* much better.

I let out a ragged exhalation to suppress my rising anxiety. "Right. Where's the sugar?"

Cherine quirked an eyebrow at me as she sipped from her tiny glass. "You don't put sugar in coffee."

"Or milk?"

"You put milk in your coffee?" Cherine nearly shouted. She wouldn't have looked more horrified if I'd revealed I put fresh baby blood in it.

"Then what do you put milk in?"

"Tea!"

"I put milk on pearl barley," Cora piped up. "Actually I put the barley in the milk. Boil it in milk, really."

After a period of silence, Cherine declared, "You're both animals."

"Why do people use animals as insults?" Cora frowned as she curiously sniffed her coffee. "All the animals I've met were much better company than most people. Or when they compare someone's looks to animals as an insult. Have you seen cats and birds and horses?"

"Send her back to the henhouse, please," Cherine moaned dramatically. "If you compare someone to a cow here, you'll be out of court before you can say *moo!*"

"Excuse you, have you seen cows?" Cora's voice sharpened. "Cows are lovely and beautiful creatures. Our mother goddess Gera is associated with cows, and being said to have cow-eyes is a huge compliment."

Cherine cast a sweeping arm to encompass the whole

room. "See? This is why a foreigner can't be the princess. You don't know anything about the people here. They should really just call this ruse off and tell Cyaxares to quit horsing around."

"Again with the animal analogies," I pointed out. "Though the note you got from the gold box was a kick in the face, huh?"

She glared at me and popped a grape in her mouth. "Not as bad as yours, which was nothing. Something is always better than nothing."

I had to taunt her when I was in a far worse position, didn't I? I *would* have preferred being kicked in the face by a horse to the nothing I got.

"If you say so," I mumbled.

She jerked her head back and forth between Cora and me, her hair flailing around her bejeweled neck in a blur. "What is the matter with you two? Why aren't you taking this more seriously?"

If I took it more seriously, I'd have a heart attack.

"Meh," I replied.

Cherine frowned. "Meaning?"

"Just what it sounds like."

Cora dropped her cheek in her palm with a groan. "Ugh, by the time I get home I'll be too late for the summer equinox preparations and I'll have to do the leftover work."

"What's that?" I asked.

"It's a festival we hold in The Granary. People come from all over the region to witness the shift from spring to summer around the Great House on Starset Hill. We have to make a lot of food, weave new baskets and make men out of wicker and burn them. "

Like the celebrations the Fairborns and I were going to

partake in before Nariman came and ruined everything. If our ancestors who settled in Ericura—what I now realized was an island—mostly came from Arbore, then some had to have come from Campania as well. Those in the South did share Cora's sun-infused coloring more than Bonnie's roses and cream one.

"I always help with the weaving..." Cora continued. "...but now I'm going to be stuck picking the fruits that are hardest to gather."

Someone her size should be able to easily reach most fruit trees, except for those native to the desert here. "Let me guess, dates?"

She shook her head listlessly, cheek still cupped in her palm, squishing it further to shut her left eye. "Pomegranates."

Before I could ask how plucking pomegranates was harder than climbing palm trees, a velvet pouch hit our table with a rattling crash. It burst open, catapulting colorful glass pebbles that splashed into our cups.

The shock wore off quickly, anger replacing it, elevating my sluggish with despondence heartbeat.

Fairuza appeared in a satin grape-grey gown with a half-sleeve overlay. Complementing cream pearls adorned her fingers, earlobes and throat. I could also count her perfect teeth, as they were on full display today.

"Souvenirs." She set one hand on the back of my seat, the other on her hip, swaying gently from side to side. "To entertain each of you on the long trip home today."

Cherine fished a pebble out of her coffee, flicked it off with her thumb, hitting Fairuza's chin. "What makes you so sure we're going home and you're not?"

Rubbing her chin, now less gleeful and more subtly aggressive, Fairuza flung her glossy curls back. "Because it was a waste of time for you to haul yourselves over here at all. There's only ever been a princess for a prince, which makes Ariane my only true rival, not any of you."

Cherine gaped at her, offended beyond expression. Of course, the only thing that could make her speechless had to be Fairuza.

"What?" Fairuza smirked. "Did you think the prince was going to pick you, Lady Bed Wetter, over me? Or Ariane's lesser copy, or the gargantuan farm girl? You must be delusional as well as stupid."

"You forgot me," I chimed in, standing, pushing back my chair to unbalance her weight on it. "What's my epithet?"

"You?" Fairuza scoffed. "You're not important enough to warrant one."

I wanted to feed her each of those ugly glass pebbles, or just smash the whole bag against her mouth and break all her pearly teeth. It would be hard to laugh at us then.

All the judges filed into the room at that moment, stifling my wrath but spiking my bone-rattling dread.

The greying Master Zuhaïr and his waxed mustache stepped up on the podium before us, unfolding a scroll. "Ten names are on this list. If you are called, you are to thank your host, bid goodbye to your friends and exit the room quietly. Do not argue, protest or make any attempts to obtain a second chance. Am I clear?"

A clang of metal hitting the floor came from our left. A waiter had bumped into a table near the door, knocking an empty tray onto the carpet.

Cyrus!

He patted around the carpet as if he had dropped something. "Apologies, Master."

Dismissing him, everyone turned their heads back to Zuhaïr, who was less than pleased with the interruption. Cyrus rose to his feet. He was wearing a knee-length, embroidered black kaftan this time, and had his pants tucked into laced leather boots. I didn't think it possible, but he looked ever more stunning—there was that word again—today. He quickly became busy with several tasks with another servant.

There was no discreet way for me to get his attention as he rushed around the room, opening curtains and refilling glasses of water. As he passed by the judges' platform, he was stopped by Princess Loujaïne. She yanked him back by the elbow, whether to order or reprimand him, I couldn't tell. He smiled and nodded. I knew that smile, the customer service one. Looked like he'd done a lot of faking to please people in his life and the practiced niceties and placations had long become a reflex.

He and the other servant ducked out and my nerves cranked up higher. Either Zuhaïr was prolonging the wait on purpose or he liked to wax poetic about the honor of being here.

Master Farouk was staring into space behind him and Mistress Asena and Princess Loujaïne had brought their heads together to trade hushed whispers.

"As you know, it is a great privilege and honor for you to be here," Master Zuhaïr rambled on. "So don't take your time here lightly. But don't regret it, either. Being even considered as an option made you all better than every other girl in the kingdoms. That's what we want you to take home with you, as well as a few other things."

On cue, Cyrus and the other boy came back, each with five gift bags hanging off their arms.

As he passed by my side to reach Zuhaïr's, I did the only

thing I could to catch his attention without being noticed. I pinched his backside.

He jumped into an alarmed halt and checked behind him. Instant recognition eased his posture as he smirked cockily. "I assume you…stopped me to ply me with another threat?"

"Just making sure you remember our deal because I'm going to need your help a lot sooner than we agreed. Like, right after this."

"What makes you think that?"

"I'm going to get disqualified with nine others. Keep up!"

"Don't be too sure about that, you might have more time than you think." With that, he headed off, winking at me over his shoulder.

"When I call your name, stand and receive your gift pack, then our guards will escort you out." Zuhaïr cleared his throat and called out, louder than before. "From the cities of Cahraman itself— Lady Merve of Gül, Lady Lara of Sunstone and Lady Marihan of Anbur."

One stood immediately, angry. The second had to be pushed up by others, unwilling. The third took her time slumping up and around the seats, rubbing at her eyes sadly.

Each took a gift bag off Cyrus's arm and headed out. He smiled awkwardly at them and tried gently patting the sad Marihan of Anbur on the arm.

"From the islands of Orestia, Miss Marissa of Lorthos and Duchess Belinda of Tritonia."

"There goes the first of them," I heard Fairuza comment smugly.

Belinda made sure to pass by Princess Ariane so they could hug one last time. "Write to me every week."

"I will," Ariane promised fervently.

Miss Marissa—whose name was the start of a tongue

twister—was either doing her best to keep a blank face, or she had flat eyebrows and dead eyes. She followed Belinda out without acknowledging anyone or the gift bag that Cyrus tried to hand her.

"From the Northland kingdoms, Lady Mariliese of Armorica, Countess Guenelle of Ursane and Baroness Crisela of Orcage."

Lady Mariliese was among the oldest at twenty-one. She didn't seem surprised to hear her name, taking the path of the sad but graceful loser along with her gift bag, and even returning Cyrus's uneasy smile as she passed him.

Countess Guenelle, on the other hand, was big, blonde and cranky. She stomped up, making it well-known that she was not happy, and ripped her bag and Marissa's from the boys, and slammed into Fairuza on her way out.

Baroness Crisela was among the youngest, with her face mostly made of rosy cheeks and watery-blue eyes. She rose, curtsied to us, then to the table of elites, and took her bag without a word. Fairuza's handmaiden, Agnë, tried to trip her on her way out.

That made eight, which now left two.

Fairuza turned, staring at us quizzically, eight of her fingers raised. She had expected all four of us to be out today, but only Belinda had left so far.

That left room for—

"From the Kingdom of Arbore, Baroness Cordelia of Briarfell and Lady Kiersa of Guelder City."

My jaw dropped.

I was stunned speechless but Cora reacted for me when she yelled, "I'm *staying?*"

Between the overwhelming shock and the debilitating relief, I missed seeing who Cordelia and Kiersa were.

I wasn't eliminated.

I was staying for another ten days.

I had more time to save the day!

Master Zuhaïr's voice rang in my swimming head again. "Congratulations. You have made it into the next round. Tomorrow, the preparations for the harder tests, not just of character..." He took a dramatic pause before elaborating. "... but of quality, begin."

I sought out Cyrus's gaze and found him already looking directly at my face, searching it as if it held an elusive answer. The corners of his bowed lips quirked up in a small, close-mouthed smile rather than his usual smirk. He waved discreetly at me.

Though my body had cooled, nerves and worries having evaporated in sagging relief, I felt my face burning in an embarrassing blush.

I cautiously raised a shaky hand and wiggled my fingers back at him.

"How did you know?" I mouthed.

I could tell he'd read my lips, but he didn't answer. He just gestured for me to wait and slipped out the back of the room.

Cherine's loud voice burst past my daze. "We're all still here."

"For now." Cora sounded so disappointed as she rose, pulling us both up with her. "Shame, I could have used one of those goodie-bags."

"Don't worry, you'll be on your way out soon enough," Fairuza called over the heads of the forty murmuring girls squeezing out the hall.

"Why do you care so much?" I called back. "What's the matter, Fay-Fay? Feeling a little threatened?"

She didn't get the chance to retort, the sea of girls carrying her out with them.

"Cow," Cherine spat.

"Don't call her a cow," Cora reminded her.

Cherine rolled her eyes. "Yes, yes, I know. Because your mother cow goddess will get offended."

"No, because she's a rat."

"I thought animal insults made no sense to you?" I pointed out as we followed everyone.

"Yes, good animals, like cows and dogs. Rats are the worst, no one likes them. They're vicious, destructive and carry diseases."

"Imagine if the animal her brother turned into was a giant rat!" Cherine seemed giddy with the thought.

"What's the story behind that again?" I asked.

"No one knows anything for sure." Cherine frowned her displeasure at not knowing. "But I intend to find out within the coming weeks!"

Still shaky with the release of tension, I leaned on her as we walked. She was the perfect height to collapse upon. "Speaking of next week in particular, what did he mean by our *quality?*"

"You know, how cultured we are."

"But we just did the etiquette thing."

Cherine waved my protest away. "Oh, that was barely a proper test of etiquette, and by cultured I meant our hobbies and talents." Stopping in the now empty hall, she faced Cora and me. "By the way, what are your talents? We need to start practicing tomorrow."

"I can weave, cloth and baskets." Cora acted out the motions of weaving. "I can also sew and sketch—and cook, in a sense, too."

Cherine threw her hands up and shimmied. "I am going to choreograph a dance."

Cora nodded at her, uninterested. "What about you, Ada? What can you do?"

Steal. Which was what I needed to do with my borrowed time.

Apart from that, what could I do?

Nothing, that was what. Absolutely nothing.

CHAPTER FOURTEEN

"What do you mean you can't do anything?" Cherine's voice was loud enough to carry to the whole floor.

I sighed, feeling far worse than I had before the first round of eliminations, if that was possible. "Exactly what I said."

It was day eight, a day before our second test. I had spent the first day after Elimination Day unwinding. The other seven had been consumed in waiting for Cyrus to show up, then in searching for him, and for anything to give me more time if I didn't fulfill my mission before the second test. I had found neither him, nor anything that could pass off as a talent.

What was I supposed to do? Go up to Loujaïne and say, "Hey, want me to give a demonstration on the arts of lock-picking and pick-pocketing?"

But I wouldn't be in this desperate state if Cyrus hadn't vanished since our first exam.

I'd been stupid to pin all my hopes on his help. He'd just told me what I'd wanted to hear to get me off his back.

What if Nariman had done the same thing? She'd told me the Fairborns were safe for now, but what if she'd been lying? What if they were already dead and buried beneath the dunes we'd made our deal upon? What reason did I have to believe she'd been telling me the truth?

I had none. But I could do nothing but cling to the hope. If I started thinking they might be dead…

I shook those thoughts out of my head before I hyperventilated.

I looked around, trying to escape Cherine's interrogation. We were now in one part of the room of mirrors in the hobby hall—a dance studio. Cherine had intimidated four girls out of the room earlier, shouting at them and bouncing around until they fled her sight. She now practiced barefoot in loose pants and a sleeveless blouse, humming notes and mumbling words to a song under her breath as she danced.

I'd been watching her as I sat on a high-backed chair in the corner, flipping through the book Master Farouk had given me. Mostly the sections on the travels of Esfandiar of Gypsum and the adventures of the White Shadow.

Why couldn't Nariman have sent me to do something like this? Why did that stupid lamp have to be here and involve this ridiculous competition? Couldn't she have sent me into death-trap ruins so I could at least use my skills and have fun pretending to be an adventurer?

"Nothing? Nothing at all?" Cherine's disbelieving shout rang out as she pirouetted.

I shook my head, reluctantly looking back at her. "None."

"No singing or dancing?"

"None at all."

"No painting or sculpting, either?"

"I can't even draw a straight line."

"What about playing an instrument? Any at all?" she squeaked, appearing at her wit's end as she made a graceful leap.

"Does the triangle count?"

She palmed her face in frustration as she came to a perfect halt.

I sighed. "Guess not."

"How do you not know any of those things? These are the hallmarks of a gentlewoman's upbringing and education."

"What part of 'we were and still are poor' have you missed?"

"Cora's not that much better off, and she can do stuff."

"Is that a compliment?" Cora asked from her corner where she was making a wicker basket with dried sugarcane strips.

Cherine looked over at her as if she'd never heard anything so ridiculous. "It's an *observation*."

As they continued to bicker, forgetting about me, I slouched further in my chair and redirected all my focus towards the book.

The illustrations were incredible, setting the scene of the events. I had to wonder if all of these were real stories, or if the White Shadow of Avesta was a mythical figure.

In some of the illustrations his companions or his wife, Princess Nesrine of Zaranga, were added for contrast. While they were colorful, he was monotone with his long white hair, pale skin and brows and light eyes. He was also the only one not properly shaded, with just enough grey to differentiate between his face, hair and cape. But apart from the stark difference in his coloring, his features were drawn similarly to the other men. It might have been the illustrator's style, but I felt that there was a reason for that.

Like every time I saw him, I thought of Cherine's ghoul.

He hadn't revisited since Belinda had left our quarters. Which was how long it had been since I'd seen Cyrus.

I turned the page to the start of another chapter, chronicling the tasks the Shadow had had to perform to win Princess Nesrine's hand. I flipped further in and found another illustration with him giving us his back, his white hair flying in the air as a storm of smoke and sand spiraled out the mouth of a bottle.

"Are you listening to me?"

I blinked, jerked my head up, found Cherine leaning over me, bare arms firmly crossed over her chest, her slender fingers tapping them grouchily.

I closed the book. "Yes, dear."

"Then what did I just say?"

"Er...something about me being incompetent as a lady?" She took a swipe at my head. I ducked. "Hey! What was that for?"

"I was saying that I still feel like that ghoul is following me. Watching me."

Cora flapped a sheet of cane at her. "For the last time, you had a stupid nightmare."

Cherine stomped. "I did not!"

Cora set down her things with a long-suffering groan, no doubt knowing Cherine wouldn't let us focus on anything but her. "What would a flesh-eating monster even be doing way up here? How would it survive without exposing itself? If it was picking off the living then the guards would have noticed people going missing."

"The guards didn't notice it was in our room!"

"That's because it never was! And before you scream me deaf again, even if it was there, why target only you?"

"I don't *know,*" Cherine shrieked. "It might..."

A loud knock on the double door cut their argument short.

They both beat me to yelling, "Come in!"

No one entered.

Another knock followed.

"I said come in!" Cherine shouted.

Silence. Then another knock.

Giving up, she shooed me. "Go see what that's about, we have stuff to do."

"Stuff that includes you taking hour-long breaks to obsess over your ghoul or needle me about my lack of talents?"

The unimpressed stare was back, rendering her hazel eyes beady. With an effortless spin on one foot, she dance-marched to the door, posture exaggerated, arms flowing behind her.

She had barely cracked open the door when she squealed and slammed it shut and flattened her back against it, panting.

Tucking the book under my arm, I rushed over to her. "See a ghost?"

Judging by her aghast face that was exactly what she'd seen.

"I-it's outside," she choked.

My heart jumped in my chest, and not with fright. "Really?"

She nodded vigorously, messing up her hair.

Cora appeared over us. "It's still light out. Don't these things go bump in the night?"

"I'm t-telling you...i-it's outside the door," Cherine whimpered, clutching at me. "White hair, red eyes and veins. S-so many veins."

Nudging her out of the way, I opened the door wide enough to stick my nose out.

The veiny, red-eyed ghoul had been replaced by a golden, green-eyed man.

"Cyrus!" I breathed.

"I got the right room then." He brushed a lock of hair off his bewitching eyes. "Do you have a minute?"

I checked the others over my shoulder. Cherine had split to the other end of the room to squeeze herself by Cora who was back to working on her basket, weaving hands unaided by her rolling eyes.

I slipped out of the room and joined him in the hallway, scowling up. "I had a week's worth of minutes, mister."

All the other doors were thankfully closed, muffling the cacophony of misplayed instruments, off-key singing and thumping choreography. The arts and crafts rooms were dead silent in comparison.

He seemed to be examining the sea-green carpet beneath us, as if its geometric pattern was more interesting than me.

Every anxious moment of the past week crashed down on me, making me want to grab and shake him. "I've been waiting for you to make good on our deal. What took you so long?"

He rolled his shoulders in an easygoing shrug, the picture of unhurried ease. "Patrol never left their post at the vault, still paranoid that thieves were lurking. Rummaging around in the treasure would have been impossible, so I had to wait until I was sure they were gone. That, and I do a lot of odd jobs around the palace. I've also had to take up managing an entire project after the original manager up and left it all to me."

My fury suddenly drained at his explanations, especially when I realized he did look very tired. "Don't know about shouldering a whole task, but I know what it's like to fill in someone else's shift when I'm dead-tired, so…you're excused."

"Your mercy is much appreciated." That was clearly his 'the-customer-is-always-right' mode, of biting his tongue and reciting insincere thanks.

He didn't appear that much older than I was, but it seemed he'd been in the business far longer. His grip on his tone and emotions was seamless, no doubt ingrained from years of learning how to avoid conflict or even appease those who started it.

"I tried to come to you as soon as I had time off," he assured me, this time looking earnest and sincere. "But I couldn't find a way to get you alone until now."

So, he was a fellow thief and server who upheld his promises, with a bonus sense of humor and one-of-a-kind good looks?

I dragged my wandering thoughts back to the literal life-and-death situation at hand. "So…any news about the vault?"

He hummed, clasping his hands behind his back. "Yes, about that. My friend, the one I mentioned before, he has a way in that could bypass the guards. You wouldn't even need to walk through the palace itself."

"That's great!" I jumped up in excitement before I forced myself to lower my voice. I couldn't afford anyone coming out to investigate. "How do we get there? Are we going now? Please tell me it's now."

"It could be now. Could be later. It all depends." Cyrus mused as he started to circle me with slow strides. I could feel his eyes on me, sizing up every inch and angle. His engrossed gaze was like a caress, like he wanted to reach out and touch me but settled for watching me as if he was afraid to blink. As if he wanted to commit every part of me to memory.

It was the first time anyone had ever looked at me like I was something worth remembering.

"Depends on—" My voice cracked with a surge of throat-sealing emotion. My heart rammed my ribs hard enough to bruise them. I coughed, tried again. "Depends on what?"

He brought his face closer to mine, whispered, "Why do you want to get there so badly."

I felt my face burn. "Uh. Um. I—um, told you. I'm hoping something in there might help me."

He tilted his head, amplifying the scrutiny in his eyes. "Help you how?"

It was hard to keep steady with him looking at me like that. Or just looking at me in general. What I had intended to be a cool, confident deflection came out as a stumbling stutter. "What's it to you?"

"Funny, I said the same thing to you before and you called it dodging."

I *hated* it when my own arguments were used against me.

I exhaled, conceding. "That I did. And I answered you the first time, too. That I'll know it when I see it."

"Alright." He stepped back, hands up in surrender. "Say I sneak you in now, you get what you're looking for. They're going to notice you were gone by the time we slip you back to your chambers."

"I'll come up with an excuse. I can't afford to keep putting it off or I'll become as forgettable as Fairuza says I am."

At the mention of Fairuza, his features twitched. "How come whatever you want doesn't seem important enough for you to actually know what it is?"

"No, no, it is important. And I'm running out of time. I'm definitely going to get kicked out this round. I need to do this now."

"You were wrong last time," he reminded me, looking pleased with himself.

"This is different. Last week ten other girls actually did worse than me. That won't happen this time. This is talent week. I have none. None I can show to get points with, anyway."

"Talent? Is that what you think it is?"

"What else could 'quality' mean? Quality to these types of people, these types of girls, is how they've been trained to be special—or cultured, that's their word."

He paused, mulling it over before saying, "I see your point."

"So?"

"So?"

"What are we going to do?"

"Ah. That, again, depends," he said, stepping back. "Do you want to get caught wandering around alone, or worse, with me? Or do you want to be sneaky about all this, go in and out and be back before anyone notices?"

"Definitely that second option. It will need to be tonight, after they've already seen me as part of the headcount, so everyone can agree that I did enter our room and stayed there. I'd do it myself if you give me your friend's secret to roaming around unseen. But if that vault door is closed even I might not be able to open it. Unfortunately, I need you for that."

"Unfortunately?" he echoed with mock-offense, hand over his heart. "And here I thought you liked me."

The protest that I did like him almost flew off my tongue. I barely caught it back. It wasn't wise to let him know how much I did.

Instead I said, "I'll like you even better when you help me."

"In that case, I'll pick you up after bedtime."

Before I could ask a hundred questions about how he planned to get me out of my room, he had sped off in the other direction. He paused only to speak to someone unseen in the shadowy corners and then he was gone.

CHAPTER FIFTEEN

Long past lights-out, I was wide-awake, staring at the roof of my four-poster bed.

I had been counting the fifteen visible loose threads in my canopy for what felt like hours now.

Cyrus had left me hanging. Again. He hadn't given me a time, or a sign to use as a heads-up or even an idea how he was going to get in.

This was a terrible idea.

Shame it was my only one.

My feverish thoughts wandered, as they always did, back to Bonnie.

What had happened to her in all this time I'd been languishing in this palace? Where were she and her father being kept until my time ran out? Had they been stashed in some kind of dungeon in Rosemead? What did Rosemead even look like? All I got from the word Arbore was that it was very wet and very green. Kind of like Northern Ericura, whose settlers most likely came from Arbore.

What kind of monster lived there and did it really eat girls like Bonnie?

If so, I wished they'd feed it Fairuza instead.

Finally, after an interminable stretch of dead silence, I heard something. The scrape of marble on marble. It was followed by the smooth slide of fabric on the floor, then a tread too heavy to be any of the girls.

I hopped out of bed, bag in hand, ready to follow Cyrus out. Then I stopped dead.

Because it wasn't Cyrus.

It was the ghoul.

And he was again standing over Cherine. Who was wide-awake.

Scared speechless, she stared up at him, trembling mouth half-open, holding the covers tight up to her chin and shivering in terror.

The ghoul held out a hand to her and I panicked. I zoomed toward him, clasped my hands and swung them with all my strength at his back. It was as if my blow had the impact of air.

He turned his red eyes on me, all I could see of his head beneath the scarf that wrapped it.

"If you're trying to defend her, there's no point." He sounded calm, his voice soft and raspy, as if he hadn't spoken in ages. "I'm here for you."

Cherine finally let out a choking squeak and hopped out of her bed to run for the door. The ghoul instantly caught her back. His big hand clamped over her mouth and nose as she struggled wildly.

He was going to kill her!

I attacked again, rabidly trying to loosen his grip on her. He only put his other hand on my face and shoved me away.

As I stumbled back, he rumbled, “If I wanted to kill her, I’d have snapped her neck in an instant.”

He removed his hand from her face and she fell limp in his arms, still breathing.

He’d just knocked her out.

Instead of setting her back on her bed, he started pushing her under it.

“What are you *doing*?”

“I can’t leave her here. If she wakes up she’ll wake everyone up and they’ll discover you’re gone. If she doesn’t until I bring you back, she’ll tell everyone I was here, and would demand that you back up her claim, as usual.”

As usual?

“Have you been here every night?”

He stopped tucking her under, leaving her arm sticking out, looking back at me. “Not every night.”

“That’s creepy.”

In the faint moonlight seeping in between the curtains, his eyes glinted the color of blood as he looked back at me. “In case you haven’t noticed, I *am* creepy.”

That he was. He really, really was. It just made me all the more hesitant to follow him under her bed to wherever the other nightmare monsters came from.

“Are you coming or not?” Cherine had been tucked out of sight and he joined her under her bed, only an arm and his pale head visible. “Hurry up, I don’t have all night.”

This was a bad idea. Terrible.

And since it was, I, of course, crawled in after him.

Under Cherine’s bed, I found a square floor tile moved out of place, exposing the hollow mouth of a dimly lit, vertical tunnel. So this was how he entered our room, through a secret passage I had failed to find despite extensively searching under all the beds.

Sliding down after him as he held the unconscious Cherine against him, I found steps hewn into the wall, barely deep enough to accommodate half my foot. But I was used to worse footholds in my career as a thief. I started climbing down as I silently prayed that I wasn't making us this thing's live dinner.

Once I was on his same level, he reached above me and pulled the tile back into place, sealing the floor seamlessly. I doubted—if we never came back and they investigated our disappearance—that anyone would ever find this masterfully hidden outlet. It would really be the perfect crime.

"Don't scream."

Before another thought fired in my brain in response to the raspy whisper that abraded my every nerve, he seemed to be swallowed by the darkness below. Just as I lost sight of him, one of his hands shot up, caught my ankle and pulled me down.

I screamed at the top of my lungs the instant I started falling.

I flailed at thin air as I plummeted. Kicking and clawing to catch on to anything, I only managed to bump and scrape against the rough, rocky walls hard enough to spawn a thousand bruises.

I landed with a teeth-rattling thud on my feet on a flat surface, before stumbling forwards to fall on my face right beside Cherine. She was on her side, still out. The ghoul was towering over both of us.

Had he thrown her down, too? Maybe it had all been a ruse to get me away from the safety of our dorm, to cripple me, so he could devour us both at his leisure and in peace.

I struggled to turn over, looking around feverishly in the

dimness for a rock or anything else to use as a weapon against him. Finding nothing, I scrambled into a crouch, ready to pounce and fight him to my last breath with my bare hands as he bent towards Cherine.

Just as I was about to leap forwards, tackle him, everything inside me stalled.

It was the care in his movements as he stood up with Cherine in his arms, the gentleness with which he hauled her over his shoulder. It forced to conclude that he hadn't thrown her down, had placed her on the ground only to adjust her position before he picked her up again.

Finally deciding he wasn't about to eat either of us, my observations turned inward, to the aches all over body, the ringing in my head. Groaning as I checked I was still in one piece, I took in my surroundings.

The tunnel was wide enough to accommodate three people walking side by side and just a foot higher than his head. Torches were lit on both sides, their flames fighting against a sourceless wind to stay alight.

A figure with a satchel on his back and a scarf wrapped around his head approached holding a torch of blue flames. "Had a nice trip?"

At hearing Cyrus's joking voice, I picked up a handful of dirt and chucked it at him. "I could have broken something!"

"Regretfully, there's no easier way down here. The hewn steps go only partway, and you have to jump down the rest of the way. The good news is that climbing up will be much easier with me holding you up."

I huffed as I dusted myself off. "What a relief. But I didn't jump down. Your 'friend' pulled me down, with no warning about what to expect."

Cyrus tossed an irritated glance over my head at said

friend before looking back at me. “I apologize on his behalf. He always forgets that everyone doesn’t have his strength and agility. He’s also not used to dealing with others, let alone ladies.”

“I’m no breakable lady, but I could have used a heads up. It would have saved me the one huge bruise I feel I’m becoming.”

“I should have come for you myself, but he insisted it was safer for him to do it. I apologize again.” To his credit, he did look and sound truly sorry. That doused my chagrin as I rose to my knees, grimacing at the aches all over my body. He came to bend over me, his eyes blazing with concern in the torch’s light. “Are you injured?” At my headshake he pressed, “Are you certain?” I nodded and this time he reached a gallant hand down to me. “On to what I promised, then. Our grand yet vague heist.”

I took his hand and let him haul me up. His one strong pull took me straight up into him.

For a moment, I remained there, plastered against him from chest to calf, feeling every inch of his warm strength through the roughness of his clothes and the flimsiness of mine.

Flushing, I jerked back, composing myself, making a show of dusting off my robe and nightgown again. “You didn’t mention your ‘guardian’ friend was the ghoul!”

“The what now?” He unwrapped the scarf, letting it fall around his neck so he could show me the extent of his confusion. “You mean Ayman?”

“A what?”

Cherine’s supposed ghoul stepped into the light, now carrying her over his shoulder like a sack of laundry. He still had the scarf hiding all but his eyes.

He raised his free hand in acknowledgment. "I'm Ayman."

Still wary of him, I stepped back, half-behind Cyrus. "What is he?"

"Not a ghoul, that's for sure. Ready?"

Embarrassed, I lowered my gaze, nodded.

Ayman, decidedly not the monster I'd thought him to be, led the way.

Cyrus offered me his arm with a bow and a grin. "Shall we, my lady?"

Holding in my urge to squeal with relief and excitement, I curtsied badly and linked my arm with his. "We shall."

It was so easy for me to get lost in this moment; just the simple pleasure of walking arm-in-arm with a handsome young man, one who was charming, witty, dimpled and had great hair. It was something I had thought more impossible than magic. If, by some miracle, a boy at school or work had liked me, there hadn't been anything I could do about it.

Looking back, I felt that all those incidents had been like Nestor, that I had misread the situation and imagined their interest. But miscommunication aside, the pursuit of any real interest would have been pointless when I'd kept moving. That natural desire to be liked, admired, to have a connection had had no place in my life. I'd always had more vital worries to focus on.

Like I currently did.

Still, it didn't mean I couldn't enjoy whatever attention I got now. I could still pretend to be in any of the dozen romantic situations I had imagined while watching street-fair plays or browsing Bonnie's novels.

For at least a few minutes, I was not in a dark, dusty tunnel heading to a risky mission that might lead to being caught and thrown into a dungeon for the rest of my life. For now, I was walking arm-in-arm with a handsome stranger, around a duck pond in a park, and instead of the torch, he held an umbrella to keep the rain at bay. Something straight out of a chivalric romance rather than whatever tragedy I had fallen into.

"Is that Cherine Nazaryan?" Cyrus suddenly asked, a belated realization narrowing his gaze at her dangling form.

I nodded. "The one, the only."

I felt him stiffen against me. "Why is Ayman taking her with us?"

"To eat later, I presume," I quipped.

He relaxed as he chuckled. "She's more of an on-the-go snack. Besides a tongue, there's not much of her to eat, is there?"

I covered my mouth, smothering my snort. "You know her?"

"I had a few run-ins with her years ago. Can't say she's changed much."

"Hasn't grown an inch since you mean?"

"Or grown in general, by the looks of things."

Fascinated, I couldn't help pelting him with my intrigued questions. "How long have you been here?"

"Long. I came to officially reside in Sunstone when I was nine."

"Where were you before that?"

"Almaskham. It's a principality in the north, across the gulf of the Silver Sea."

"Why did you move here then?"

"My father. He works here. Once he got promoted he decided it was about time I joined him and got used to the place so I could one day take his position."

We reached the top of a staircase that led down to a platform and then split up into branches, some going up and some down, in every direction. The tunnel that had become a cavern was lit, not by flames, but by smooth stones embedded in the walls, emitting an eerie, permeating white light.

When we reached the center of the platform, it was like being surrounded by stars.

Ayman led us up the stairs to the right. As we ascended the lights got brighter and the air felt thinner. At the top, we entered a better-constructed pathway, the ground beneath us smoothing out, with the walls made of polished stone.

"How did you find this place?" I asked Cyrus.

"I had a lot of free time when I was younger and studying the palace became one of my pastimes. Then while searching the archives for information, I found a map of tunnels and passageways that were used by the builders to get from place to place, and maybe for the inhabitants to escape during attacks or sieges. We've made great use of them ever since."

The pathway ended with a wooden door. Ayman kicked it open, Cherine's limp arms flapping on his back.

Cyrus held open the door for me as we passed through. "Honestly though, why is she here?"

"He said she could blow my cover if she woke up."

"Good point. Watch your step."

I missed the start of the surprise staircase. I would have landed on my teeth had he not caught my arm.

"Thanks," I gasped as I grabbed him back.

Grinning down at me, seeming as reluctant to let go of me as I was of him, he led the way.

The spiral staircase snaked almost a mile downward to a lit doorway. I held my gown with one hand and the wall with the other as I carefully followed him down.

I still slipped off a shorter step on the curve of the spiral.

These fancy slippers weren't made with heists in mind. He rushed up and caught me again, this time by the waist.

"You're falling a lot tonight," he remarked teasingly as he clasped me to his hard body. "If I didn't know any better I'd say you liked having me pick you up."

"Or I'm just falling for you," I blurted out stupidly.

He blinked. "You—what?"

Thank heaven it was dark. Besides seeming to have no control over my tongue, I could do nothing about the blush I felt burning my cheeks.

"Falling for you...to remind you how much I need your full attention in this mission?"

That was one of the silliest things I'd ever said. His crinkling eyes as he set me back upright told me he thought so too.

"It's a mission now, is it?" he finally drawled as his arm remained around my waist, not in a hold but in a cautious prop, to catch me if I were to fall again.

Phew. Glad he decided to let me off the hook and changed the subject. I couldn't handle teasing right now.

"When was it not one?" I mumbled.

His only response was a probing glance, before he invited me to climb down the rest of the way. He remained close in front of me this time, an arm propping me, cautious, protective.

He cared. Or he was just that nice. A very nice, sneaky thief.

Which was what I was. So, no judgment.

He actually checked all the boxes on the Ideal Man traits list I didn't even know I had. I now also remembered my mother telling me to pick someone I had major things in common with; that the foundation of every relationship was shared interests. We had lots of those.

Unfortunately, it all made no difference to how improbable my chances with him were.

I was just passing through his land. And if this mission succeeded, I'd be gone two days from now, and I'd never see him again.

The idea felt like a fist had closed around my heart.

Ten minutes later, at the bottom of the stairs, Ayman ducked past the doorway with Cherine still snoozing over his shoulder. It didn't lead directly into the vault as I'd thought, but to a vast, dome-shaped stone chamber.

It was empty.

At least, it looked empty at first. Only at the halfway-point of the chamber did the etchings on the walls become clear. Like the panels of a picture book, each square foot held a smoothly etched scene. I couldn't figure out which wall I was supposed to start reading from, but the one across from the doorway held the biggest image of them all.

It was just like one of the illustrations in the White Shadow's stories. A smoky whirlwind coming out of a bottle. Once I came closer and the perspective I was viewing it from shifted, I saw finer etchings within the lines of the vortex, revealing the form of a giant being with clawed hands and pointed ears.

A shiver ran down my spine even in the warmth of the cavern.

This place sure wasn't where Loujaïne had taken us on our first night in the palace. A pathway that was unknown or forgotten, like those secret tunnels. But Cyrus knew about it. I'd been right when I'd thought only he could lead me back to the vault.

I continued to gape around as Ayman went up to the etching of a door and pressed it.

With a heavy, scraping noise, a part of the wall moved aside to let in blinding light. I swung my arms against my eyes. I didn't remember the vault being so bright.

After my eyes adjusted, I could see the shimmering masses of treasure, with its scattered reflections dancing on the floor and the walls.

Cyrus stopped by the doorway and held out his arm, presenting the room to me. "After you, my lady."

Bracing myself, feeling I was on the threshold of so many possibilities, I entered the vault.

CHAPTER SIXTEEN

The first thing that came to mind as I stepped into the vault again was that I could swim in that sea of gold coins.

Though I'd seen it before, I still couldn't believe my eyes. It was even more fantastic than the first time I'd been here, as if my memory could not retain the enormity of its dazzling reality.

Sacks upon urns upon chests of cut and uncut gemstones and elaborate jewelry that could cover the whole population of the palace or even of Sunstone from head to toe stretched from wall to wall. In their midst, the priceless sculptures soared, and an array of precious objects, no two alike, gleamed. Filling the space between all of them, were the piles of loose golden coins I could drown in.

This place was the ultimate fantasy and temptation, especially for a thief like me.

I desperately wanted to haul off one of those sacks. If I could just get them back home, it would mean that I could start a business and help expand Mr. Fairborn's. In fact, just a handful of these things could make our lives so much easier.

Yet, the people who owned all this did nothing with it. None of the treasures served any purpose around here, not even a decorative one. It was a useless abundance of invaluable items, collecting dust, and reminding me just how unfair life was.

Ayman carefully placed Cherine on the massive pedestal of an oxidized bronze statue and unwrapped his scarf. Long, thick white hair fell past his shoulders and down his back. The warm light bounced off his impossibly pale skin, mapping out the blood vessels under his skin like the black veins on white marble. He had no claws, no fangs, no scales or anything demonic. And now my shock over how different he looked had passed, I thought that he was actually beautiful, in a unique way. Made of a far more interesting material than common human flesh.

As I scrutinized him, he got visibly uncomfortable, squirming under my gaze. It seemed he was unused to anyone looking at him for any length of time. He remained kneeling with his shoulders hunched, winding his scarf around his hands. Then he looked up straight at me.

I could now see that his eyes weren't red, but an intense purple. It was reflecting the flames brightness at certain angles that gave them that bloody hue. In the early morning light, with those eyes and coloring, he'd be enchanting.

I could have thought he was a platinum blond from a region where the sun rarely shone. Like the Pale Men of the North—or Arbore. But his features didn't add up. With his sharp nose, that started from between his thick, arched, silver brows, his hooded eyes, his chiseled lips and prominent cheekbones, his facial structure seemed native to this land.

The only difference was that everything in him was almost white...

"You're an albino!" I suddenly realized. "Like Saint Alban!"

The side of his mouth twitched. "I am a *zāl*."

"I told you to stop calling yourself that," Cyrus snapped, his voice a bite of anger.

Ayman slumped down by Cherine in a defeated sag. "Everyone but you calls me a *zāl*. What's the point of denying it?"

"Apparently our guests have been calling you a ghoul," Cyrus growled, kicking things out of his way. "Does that make you one as well?"

Their argument ended with that.

Ayman focused his attention on our unconscious company, gently moving her head onto his lap and covering her body with his cloak, tucking her in it. This sweet gesture was something I wouldn't have expected from the man who haunted her nightmares.

He watched her with soft fascination, his hand hesitantly hovering above her, seemingly itching to stroke her hair or pet her face. The sight of them tugged at my heartstrings. I didn't know if it was on his behalf, for his clear desire to express affection, or for mine, because I wanted to give and receive it, too.

It was probably for both of us.

How strange to find such a commonality with someone I'd thought a monster not an hour ago.

Feeling Cyrus coming closer, my attention was dragged back to him. Like a weak pile of iron filings eager to stick to a magnet, I followed as he passed by me.

As I shadowed him, looking around for the lamp, he pushed coins away with his feet, creating a narrow but clear path for me. At least, I believed it was for me. I was grateful anyway, remembering how I'd slipped on them the first time I'd been here.

He came to a halt at a statue, that of the sad-eyed princess.

I stopped beside him, unable to take my eyes off him. He ran a hand through his hair, pushing it back, effortlessly styling it to bring out more of his perfect profile. In that moment, before the statue of Jumana Morvarid, his skin pale gold, his hair bronze and his eyes emeralds, Cyrus was another one of the timeless statues that towered over the treasure.

He took out a flower—a pink rose—from the depth of his cloak.

For a foolish moment, I thought it was for me.

In silence, he bowed to Jumana's miserable likeness and set the rose at her feet. Then he picked up the incense bowl I'd seen still burning during my first time here.

He placed the silver bowl in one of her upturned hands and produced a lighter and sparked a flame into it. A trail of warm and woody aromatic smoke puffed to life. Myrrh.

I approached him carefully. "Who was she?"

He sighed. "I'm not sure exactly. I've heard different stories from different people, so my idea of her makes very little sense."

"Do you know how she died?"

He wrapped his arms around his middle as he gazed up at her. "No one would tell me. But her statue being here, away from where people could see her and pay their respects to her, means hers was a dishonorable death."

"Childbirth is dishonorable?"

He tore his eyes away from Jumana to quirk his eyebrow at me. "Childbirth?"

"I assumed it was the reason, seeing that she's so young."

"If she had died bringing someone into the world, she would be out in the hanging gardens." He lowered his head, plunging his face in shadow. "If she's in here, that means she killed herself."

A jolt of shock went through me, making me lurch.

It was strange how with just one statement, my entire view of someone I didn't know and would never know tilted. I went from pitying a young mother who'd never met her child to being mortified by the tragic end of a girl barely older than me. What had her life been like? Who had she been? How long ago had she died and why had she ended it all?

In my darkest hours, especially in the early days after my mother had been taken from me, I had considered following her. I'd no longer had anyone to lean on or have an emotional connection with. Without her, I'd felt I'd had nothing left to live for.

Who or what had Jumana lost to push her over the edge?

After I lost my mother, what had made me climb out of the pit of despair and cling to life, had been the hope that I'd one day find someone to live for and with. Someone to be my safety and support, my family and home. Then I'd found Bonnie and her father and had pinned all that hope on them. But they might be taken away from me, too.

Except, if it came to pass, their loss wouldn't be like my mother's, who had died in an accident miles away from home and had been buried before the sheriff had even informed me of her death. It would be gruesome murder. And it would be my fault.

I needed to find that lamp now.

"Are you alright?" Cyrus asked, concern hushing his voice and softening his eyes.

I wiped away the tear I hadn't realized had trickled down my cheek. "Are you?"

"As I'll ever be." His gaze still probed my face as he turned away from Jumana. Then he rubbed his hands together, seemingly to drum up heat and excitement, and change the melancholy subject. "So, what is it we're looking for?"

"I told you I'm not—"

"Not sure what it is but you'll know it when you see it," he filled in impatiently, rolling his eyes. "That's the vague answer you give to strangers, and I should hope we're friends by now. After all, I did set up this heist for you."

My shoulders slumped. He was right. I had to tell him what I was after. Maybe he'd help me find it, too, once he knew.

"A lamp."

His brows fell flat in a bewildered stare. "A lamp?"

"Indeed."

"As in a lamp?" He pointed to one of the lanterns hanging off the walls.

"No, an oil lamp."

His confusion deepened to a confounded stare. "You asked me to sneak you out of your dorm, risking being caught and punished, caused us to accidentally kidnap a nobleman's daughter, and made us take you through the secret tunnels into the richest part of the entire kingdom—so you could get a worthless oil lamp?"

Embarrassment buzzed under my skin, making me squirm. "When you say it like that—"

"What do you even need it for? Lamps like that haven't been in use for decades."

"Then me taking a useless antique shouldn't be a problem."

Cyrus gawked at me like I was crazy. Then he shook his head. "You're mocking me, aren't you? This is an elaborate joke to teach us a lesson, for scaring you that first night, isn't it?"

"It's really not."

His gaze lengthened, as if he was deciding whether to believe me or not.

His next words told me he did. "Why a lamp, though? Why not a sack of coins or a jewel-tipped staff or an enchanted idol?"

My eyes snapped wider. "There are enchanted things in here?"

His grin emerged at my involuntary excitement as he turned his head around. "There should be."

I couldn't help my eagerness as I stepped closer. "Like what?"

"Among other things, I heard that there's a ring that can grant wishes and a carpet that can fly. But I have yet to find either."

Though a flying carpet and a wish-fulfilling ring sounded fantastic, I couldn't think of wasting time looking for either. All I needed now was that lamp.

"If it's a lamp you need, I can get you one," Cyrus said. "We might have some ornate silver ones in the pantry, used in ancient, symbolic ceremonies."

"It's not just any lamp, it's a gold one."

His lips twisted. "So, you do know what you're looking for?"

"I have no idea what it looks like," I insisted. "I just know that it's gold and that it's here."

"Now you've disclosed that much, won't you tell me why you need it?"

"Is it really important why she needs it?" Ayman appeared a few feet away, sounding impatient. "We wasted enough time doing nothing. Help her find the blasted antique then ask what it's for when we're safely out of here."

Cyrus seemed about to protest before changing his mind. "Fine. Let's find your outdated lantern."

All the trapped air left my tight chest in a trembling sigh of relief. "Thank you. Really. Thanks."

He bowed with an arm extended towards the nearest pile of treasure. "After you."

As I passed him, I let my hand linger lightly on his shoulder, a gesture of gratitude and acknowledgment. He put his hand over mine, kept it there as I got further away, until my hand slipped out from under his. His touch set me aflame like his lighter had lit the incense.

Wrestling with my thundering heart and trembling limbs, I hid my burning face in my hair as I dove into the search.

Hours passed with me chasing my own tail among the hills of treasure. Both Cyrus and Ayman helped me with total commitment. They implemented my plan to canvas the vast vault, dividing it into a grid using ropes. Then we searched each section, thoroughly digging through each pile, emptying every bag and checking every chest.

But we found nothing that could function as a lamp or even remotely looked like one. I got more desperate until I was reduced to debating if a white-gold *dallah* could count as a 'gold oil lamp.' I was getting to the point where I dreaded having to admit the possibility.

That there was no lamp in the vault.

CHAPTER SEVENTEEN

"It has to be here."

My desperate groan slurred even as my gaze blurred. It had been hours and we had combed through every inch of the vault. We had unearthed diamond rings, inventoried loose gems, matched scattered earring pairs, but we couldn't find one bulky gold lamp.

But if it wasn't in the vault, where could it be?

Cyrus's hand gently curled around my arm, tugging at me. "We need to go. The palace will be waking up soon."

"I can't." My lament came out half-yawn, half-sob. "I need to find it."

He stroked my arm soothingly. "We can commission one for you if you need it that much. I'll pick some gold from here and send it to be melted down and fashioned into a lamp."

I shook my head, eyes burning with frustration, sleeplessness and the long, fruitless search. "No, it needs to be this specific old one. It's an heirloom with a value you can't even imagine."

"Then explain it to me."

Where could I even begin to explain this whole situation to him? That I was from a forgotten land and needed to trade a stupid, misshapen teapot full of oil for the lives of my friends, and probably mine, too? That for some reason, the king had stolen it from Nariman? And that she'd stop at nothing to get it back? How was that supposed to make any sense to—

"There are sounds inside!"

"Someone is in the vault!"

The yells came from outside the other door at the far end of the vault. Footsteps stomped down the steps we'd used the first time down here.

"We must go." Ayman appeared again with Cherine in his arms. "Now!"

He turned and streaked toward the door we'd come in through. Cyrus pulled me after him by the arm. I dug my heels in, kept reaching back for any space I felt hadn't been searched thoroughly enough, just in case we had missed something, anything!

"Ada, we have to go!"

"I can't! You go. I'll hide until they're gone. I have to keep looking!"

"Ada, I can't leave you here. There is no place to hide. You'd be caught, then disqualified and punished—"

"I don't care. I'm getting kicked out, anyway!"

"The punishment would not be sending you home, but throwing you in prison."

The word *prison* exploded inside my head.

If I were in prison, I'd be no good to anyone. Starting with myself.

The vault door began to screech open, scraping the floor loudly, drowning the guards' shouts.

With a growl, Cyrus pulled me with all his strength behind him and rushed me through the domed hall then to the stairwell we came from.

In seconds, we caught up with Ayman, who reached back and pulled me after him by my robe. “Hurry!”

Cyrus pushed me ahead of him and I ran up along the spiral of stairs, my lungs burning, my every muscle quivering as I slammed into walls at each bend. I only checked behind me when we reached the last flight before the secret pathway, and—

Cyrus wasn’t there.

I stopped dead, panicking, panting. “Where is he?”

“He’ll catch up,” Ayman grumbled as he tugged on my sleeve so I’d continue moving.

“He’ll get caught!”

“That’s his problem!” He pulled harder.

I wouldn’t budge. My lungs were almost bursting with the urge to scream as the etched stonewall started to seal itself behind us, blocking the pathway.

“CYRUS!”

“You’ll wake her up!” Ayman hissed at me, gesturing at Cherine as she dangled over his shoulder.

Sure enough, her eyes cracked open as she started to stir with a confused, sleepy snort.

If she woke up now…

I didn’t know what to do but stroke her hair softly and whisper, “Shhh, you’re dreaming. Just go back to sleep.”

“Alright,” she said, and thankfully closed her eyes once more.

I tore my eyes away from her, stared helplessly at the now-fused wall, feeling sick to my stomach with anxiety. “W-what happens if they catch him?”

Ayman slowed his pace now that he considered we were home free, tossing me an unreadable glance over his shoulder. "I don't know. I've never been caught."

He didn't sound too concerned. Or concerned at all. Was that a sign for me not to worry either, or was he just a lousy friend?

Knowing that I couldn't open that wall again without Ayman's help, and that all I'd do if I went back for Cyrus was get caught myself, or even cause him to get caught if he hadn't been, I dragged my feet behind Ayman as we returned through the path we came through, still lit by torches and the field of glowing gemstones.

If Cyrus got caught and punished—or worse—then it would be three lives instead of two that were ended by my failings.

"He'll be fine," Ayman said suddenly. "You, on the other hand, I can't tell."

"How do you know he'll be fine?"

"Because I do."

I got no further explanations from him. But I somehow felt that he was telling me the truth, and Cyrus was in no danger. The tension squeezing my every cell drained.

But with fear for Cyrus subsiding, it only rushed back to Bonnie and her father, and my current dilemma.

"Are there no other treasure vaults?" I asked. "No safes I can search?"

Ayman shrugged his free shoulder. "Since old oil lamps were mostly used for holy ceremonies, there might be some at shrines."

"Then maybe I'll find it at a shrine in the palace or even in the city?"

"Not a gold one you won't. The most you will find is one made of silver, sometimes not even pure silver, but an alloy."

"How come?"

"It's not worth the precious metal, not like coins and jewelry are."

"Oh."

This whole mess made no sense. If people didn't waste precious metals on stupid items like lamps then who would have made a gold one so his descendants would consider it an heirloom to pass down? Why did no one melt it down into something more worthy, like a necklace or a dagger? And why had King Darius taken a lamp of all things from Nariman before booting her out of the kingdom? Had he too considered it invaluable and coveted it? But for what reason? If lamps were for ceremonial use, holy by association, did that make a gold one the ultimate offering to their patron god…or something?

It was either that, or she had lied about its purpose. Or this was just the most absurd part of a never-ending dream.

Heaven knows I'd had my share of outlandish ones. And if this was a dream within a dream, all I'd have to do was wake up, and everything would disappear like the night terrors always had, tendrils of darkness evaporating in the light of day.

But I knew I wasn't that lucky, and this was real. And reality would turn to tragedy if I didn't find answers and concoct an alternative plan.

"How do you avoid getting caught?" I asked Ayman as we climbed another set of stairs. "Do you just use the tunnels? Do they go through the city, too?"

"They can lead out, yes, but I don't leave the palace. I just can't go outside."

"Because of the way you look?"

He exhaled loudly. "And because of the sun. It *burns*."

"Your skin?"

"Everything. Once, when I was nine, I went out at high noon and nearly went blind."

I winced as I imagined his pain and terror at the terrible experience. I also realized something else. That this was what the story of Saint Alban and the Pale Men meant when it mentioned "fleeing the sun." Though most of his followers had been extremely fair-skinned and haired rather than practically colorless like Ayman, they'd followed him to Ericura, a land that had longer, colder winters and milder summers than the rest of the Known World. The Northern Ericurans I'd known must have once been Arboreans like Fairuza and the Southerners Campanians like Cora.

"What about going out here in the palace?"

"Only at night when we don't have too many guests. Only among the people who know me, and are used to my..." He waved a hand around his head. "...ghostly pallor."

"So, the staff here knows you?"

"Some do."

"Cyrus said you were a guardian of sorts?"

"I'm sort of a personal bodyguard and a night watchman if need be. During the day, I hide."

There were so many questions I wanted to ask, about his life and about Cyrus's. About what they did here with all the knowledge of the palace and what they hoped to do in the future.

Did they expect to live here for the rest of their lives or were there other alternatives for them? Life couldn't be easy for either of them here, as it wouldn't be for me. Not that I had any kind of future here. Nothing beyond the blasting end of Nariman's magic staff.

But they could be saving enough stolen goods to one day up and run. If so, they could come with me, help me find Arbore myself and save Bonnie from the beast and—

And I would still be stuck in this land.

Whether I liked it or not, I needed that witch to get home just as much as I needed her for all three of us to stay alive.

No matter which path I tried to take, it all led back to that lamp.

The lamp that didn't seem to exist.

I waited until we reached the darkest part of the tunnel to burst into bitter, silent tears.

After long minutes of pure, suffocating hopelessness, I finally brought myself under control. Soon enough, we were back below the shaft leading up to the false tile below Cherine's bed. My heart squeezed again at Cyrus's absence as his earlier promise to lift me up reverberated in my ears.

Ayman said he'd help me instead after he got Cherine up, but I stopped him as he started climbing. "Are you going to be at the test today?"

He adjusted Cherine over his shoulder as he looked down at me. "I can't. Cyrus might be there if he gets out in time and can find work around the hall."

"When I get disqualified—" I stopped, sniffling, even when my burning eyes had run out of tears. "—can you sneak me out again? Keep me with you?"

"For what purpose? To find your teapot?"

"Lamp."

He rolled his peculiar eyes. "Even more pointless."

"Can you or can't you?"

"I can't. We can't."

"Why?"

"You haven't given us a good enough reason. You'd need to have something all-important for me to risk harboring you beyond your elimination. That and you're not like me. You're a lady. You can't disappear without causing an uproar. The last thing I need is for some nobleman to think I ate his daughter."

Our eyes flicked to Cherine.

I let out a ragged breath. "What do I do then?"

"Not fail today's test?" he suggested unhelpfully.

"Ayman, I have no quality of any value to offer in that stupid talent show today."

He said nothing as he climbed up nimbly even without a single foothold up to the halfway point of the deep shaft. It was only when he moved the loose marble slab, revealing the bottom of Cherine's bed that he looked down at me and said, "Then it's been nice knowing you."

His nonchalance made my temperature shoot up until I almost felt steam blowing out of my ears. If I'd had anything at hand, I would have hurled it at him.

But then…he'd already risked so much for me, and he'd owed me nothing to begin with.

After he got Cherine out, he climbed down, jumped the rest of the way to my side, and helped me up until I latched onto the first step. Using all my skills in climbing walls, I hauled myself up, then all the way out. He effortlessly came up after me and slipped quietly out of the hole in the floor. He carefully dragged Cherine from under the bed and set her back on it. He tucked her in, and before he walked away, he brushed her hair out of her eyes. My throat closed again at the sheer sweetness of his gesture.

Tearing my eyes away, I got into my bed. By the time I

drew my canopy closed, he was gone without a sound. Just as he'd always done.

Closing my eyes, I wished I were like Ayman. Able to disappear, to roam freely in the dark with no fear of ever getting caught.

Getting caught. That had always been my worst fear as a small-time thief. I'd just thought if it ever came to pass, it would involve being caught in the act of stealing my loot, not in a failed attempt to find it.

But that was what would probably happen when I was forced to search for the lamp tomorrow, without Cyrus's and Ayman's help.

Which meant these might be my last hours of freedom.

CHAPTER EIGHTEEN

Keeping a cool exterior proved to be harder to pull off when I was perpetually on the verge of hyperventilating.

Cyrus was nowhere to be seen.

All I had was Ayman's word, or rather, his opinion, that he was fine. I had no idea if he was or not. And it was driving me insane with worry.

On top of that, fifteen girls were going home today.

I was going to be among them.

But though I felt like the world was ending, it went on unconcerned, with a spectacular day outside. Despite the approaching summer, it was a calm, balmy morning with thick, cottony clouds gliding on the tranquil breeze against a brilliant-blue backdrop, with exotic birds bathing in fountains or twittering a medley of joy in hedges and trees. All in all, the view of the palace gardens from above the pavilion was nothing short of breathtaking.

Or it would have been if I had much breath left to take.

This was where the talent show of day twenty was being held.

A marble-paved stage was in the center of the hedges and a few feet beneath it was the judges' table. The forty of us stood in a line that winded up the balcony steps and down the side of the pavilion. One after another the girls were being called down to demonstrate their quality, or whatever made them valuable.

Our Blue Opal group was seventh in line. This gave me more chance to watch the demonstrations...and to sink deeper into despair.

Some girls sang, some played instruments and some danced, while others claimed to have created their own songs, pieces or routines to one-up the others. A few recited difficult poems, some flubbing their order of stanzas or forgetting the words entirely. A couple presented handmade objects and explained their design and process in detail, just in case the judges suspected they had commissioned work to pass off as theirs.

Even if their handiwork was inferior to any professionally made counterpart, it was far superior to what I had, which was nothing.

And I was the only one with nothing to offer. Behind me, Cora had her contribution balanced on her head, the sugar cane wicker basket. She had used melted resin to bind it and filled it with fruit she'd picked from the orchard. Before me, Cherine went through the steps of her dance, humming the tune of her accompanying music as she warmed up. Fairuza was wearing another flowing gown today, so her presentation didn't involve a dance.

"What are you going to do?" Cora asked me as our line moved down the pavilion steps.

I winced. "Weep and hope they take pity on me?"

"That would certainly be something different."

"How much leeway do you think I can have with *different?*" I groaned. "Think I can flail around and pass it off as an interpretive dance? Or just rant and call it freeform poetry?"

"What's freeform poetry?" she asked.

"Ranting that you pass off as poetry. Common in pubs."

Cora nodded, clearly giving up. "Uh-huh."

Our line moved again and Cherine hopped down the last few steps like an excitable child. "On the topic of different, I had the strangest dream yesterday."

"We know," Cora said dully. "You tossed, turned and talked in your sleep for like an hour."

"Yes, but after that was when the dream got strange. The ghoul was back—"

"So, you admit the ghoul is a nightmare?" Cora smirked at her.

Cherine hopped off the final step with a spin in the air, facing us with her hands on her hips. "No, I'm saying I had a nightmare *about* the ghoul."

I didn't need to look at Cora to know that she was palming her face.

Cherine spun again and skipped ahead of us. "Anyway, the ghoul appeared and attacked me, but someone stopped him and carried me off to safety."

I stumbled. Did she remember anything else from last night?

"He held me in his arms the entire time. I've never felt so secure in my life," she continued babbling. "I think at one point I had my head in his lap and he talked to me softly as he stroked my hair. Oh, it was just the loveliest dream I've ever had."

That was a relief. If she remembered anything else, it would be part of the dream to her. I wondered how she'd feel if she realized her ghoul and savior were one and the same.

"Do you remember what he looked like?" I pried gently while also looking around for escape routes. This place was too wide open and there weren't enough people for me to disappear among. I needed to leave right after my turn so I could have time to go back to our chambers and through the tunnel under Cherine's bed for one last look inside the vault. Perhaps even find the shrines Ayman talked about.

Looking suddenly elated, Cherine jumped abruptly and bumped into Princess Ariane, who shot her a quick glare from over her shoulder and clutched her offering closer to her chest.

"Foreign," Cherine said, in dreamy fascination. "He was certainly foreign. Very fair, silver-haired, like a prince come alive from a storybook."

More like from the illustrations of the White Shadow...

Of course! The White Shadow must have been an albino, too. It sure gave some sense to his tragic backstory, since his father, the King of Avesta, left him out to die of exposure as a baby and had his wife killed for bearing him a demon.

Poor Ayman.

It was a good thing I wasn't actually a part of this land or this royal lifestyle. If I had to deal with a prince, or even a king, I wouldn't have been able to tolerate their level of entitled superiority. People who were raised to believe they were better than everyone from birth were guaranteed to be insufferable at best, and sociopathic at worst. Fairuza and the prince were going to make quite a pair.

Not that my current situation was any better. Not when I

still had to deal with the witch and her murderous obsession with elusive antiques.

Cyrus had mentioned a ring that granted wishes. I could use it right now. Maybe that was what I should be looking for later.

Sure. That sounded simple enough. I'd try on every ring and make demands at it until one told me where Cyrus was, made sure he was okay, undid this whole mess and took us all back home before I was—

"NEXT!"

A girl with shiny, black hair held up in a bun, wearing wooden sandals and a floral pink silk robe, stepped onto the stage with a harp. She introduced herself as Princess Misa of Yukimura Island and sang a tranquil tune as she plucked the harp strings. It was so soothing I started nodding off where I stood.

The judges were less than impressed. Whatever ease Misa's song gave me evaporated like a splash on a hot stove. If this bored them, then what chance did anyone else have?

"Next!" Loujaïne sighed, not even bothering to feign courteousness or interest.

Another girl was stepping forward when Fairuza cut to the front of the line.

"Hey!" the girl protested. "Go back to your spot."

Fairuza flapped the bottom of her glittering skirt to smooth out imaginary wrinkles and pretend to be too busy to hear her. She stepped onto the stage and curtsied to the judges with her arms extended to her sides, fingers arranged in a delicate gesture. She sparkled brightly all over, catching whatever rays made it through the clouds on the crystal beads adorning the gossamer overlay of her magnificent turquoise gown and her silver and diamond tiara.

When she straightened up, she hooked the fingers of one hand into those of the other. "I hope you don't mind me moving things along. I could tell the mediocrity was dampening your moods on such a lovely day."

The judges traded looks among themselves before facing her.

"Present yourself and show us your quality," Master Farouk said, his deep voice as expressionless as his face.

She bowed her head slightly. "I am Princess Fairuza of Arbore and since an early age I have delighted all, family, guests and servants alike, with the enchantment of my voice."

"Proceed," Farouk ordered, setting his chin in his palm, dark eyes watchful.

Fairuza took a deep breath and opened her mouth. The vibrato that burst out of it filled the whole square and turned every head, blowing the energy back into the judges and nearly knocking me off my feet.

After the impossibly sustained opening note, she smiled broadly, pleased with herself, and continued singing, projecting her voice in a powerful soprano that could crack glass and shake mountains.

This wasn't how this was supposed to go. She was supposed to prance up, cocky and self-assured, and make a fool of herself. To shriek and bray off-key like every obnoxious girl in a festival talent show who'd thought tackling a temple chorus song was a good idea.

But she didn't. Fairuza sang assuredly, perfectly in-tune, and far, far better than every celebrated singer I had ever heard.

She owned the stage and the rapt attention of everyone who watched her. In that moment, eyes closed with immersion in the aria, cheeks flushed with effort and pleasure, she was passionate, mesmerizing and truly beautiful.

I felt my eyes and throat burn. Not just with anxiety but with unwilling admiration, and mounting anger. I hated this. I hated her. I hated myself for feeling so useless and inferior.

Why was I even here? I should just walk out of the line and save myself the time.

"Overkill much?" Cora deadpanned.

Sure, if you thought being the prime pick for *The Fairy Queen* in a high-end production overkill. My mother had loved that play and I couldn't stand it, but now I was nostalgic for it. Springtime theatre productions in our town had been one of the few public activities she'd partaken in, the only thing she'd indulged in. If only she were here to defend her undying love for them and critique Fairuza's performance. If only she were here at all.

Fairuza finished with a masterful falsetto that she controlled to the last trill and bowed.

The garden erupted in applause from everyone, the judges, the staff and even the other girls. I would have clapped too, but the risk of missing and slapping my own cheeks over and over in despair was too high.

With a flourish, she turned and walked off stage like a true performer, exuding enough confidence to fill a hundred girls. She knew that after that performance, no one had a chance to stand out. Every girl after her would be held to her standard and come up woefully short in the comparison.

That—harpy. That magnificent, glamorous, talented, royal harpy.

I wished I was her.

The girl she had cut off went on next and read out a poem

she'd written, immensely underwhelming compared to the storm of perfection that had come before her.

After her, Princess Ariane went up and unfolded a tapestry wider than her body. She described in great detail how she'd created it, why she'd picked the subject and how she would weave tapestries of the lives of notable ancestors on both the prince's and her side to hang in their children's chambers, to teach them their history and traditions and for inspiration.

Surprisingly, most of the judges were impressed, nodding approvingly or commenting on the artistry of her craftsmanship.

Master Farouk though, made the best comment of the day. "It's heartening to see someone your age prioritizing a useful talent rather than a superficial one, and thinking how it can affect the future generations. Performance arts are all well and good but practical skills will always trump entertainment and outlive our voices."

In the sidelines, Fairuza, as well as every girl who sang, looked downright offended.

I felt a bit better. If I had to root for someone in this mess, it would be Ariane. Mostly because she was the only one with enough personal and political clout to knock Fairuza back.

They called for the next one but Cherine didn't move. She had stiffened up, hands clasped tightly, shoulders narrowed and heaving with her labored breathing.

I poked her. "Move."

"I can't," she whimpered.

If this were any other day, I would empathize with her cold feet. But today, regardless of how she did, Cherine was still a nobleman's daughter heading towards a cushy future in a mansion, to have another nobleman's daughters. My trajectory involved no such safety nets, only the sharp rocks of capricious fate to bust my head on.

"Between the two of us," I hissed at her. "I'm the one who should be paralyzed with dread. So move it already."

She didn't budge. I shoved her but only made her glide along the floor on the heels of her dance shoes.

"Now is not the time to lose all your obnoxiousness," I snapped. "In fact, this is the best time for you to be as loud and attention-seeking as possible."

"But Fairuza—"

"Screamed at us for five minutes, big whoop. But you keep saying the competition would come down to the two of you. Prove it. Prove you're the only one besides her who's worth all this fuss."

She looked up at me in wonder. "You may be poor and uncouth, but you sometimes say the best things."

I huffed. "Thanks. Now dance your little feet off!"

She stood up straight, steadying herself for one last moment before she scuttled to the center of the stage and made an exaggerated curtsey that looked more like a sideways lunge.

After Cherine introduced herself, Mistress Asena, the elite in charge of the White Opal group, and the only blonde at the table, asked, "How will you present your quality to us today?"

"I will present to you a dance I choreographed myself combining the traditional dances of our ancestors and the classical dance of Anbur." Cherine snapped her fingers at the orchestral section and struck a pose.

The music, a vivacious blend of string arrangements and tribal drumbeats rolled into a blood-firing intro. After the first few beats, a dramatic drumroll introduced the main melody and Cherine sprung into a dizzying, spectacular dance that combined swift, complex movements with smooth transitions in between spins and mid-air pirouettes.

I gaped at her, wondering how anyone could be so agile, how she didn't slip and break a limb. I bet anyone else would have. I could tell Fairuza was thinking it too, her expression hovering between burning envy and malicious anticipation.

But Cherine built her routine in difficulty instead, until she was spinning round and round, smoothly, masterfully, like a perfect, glittering top as the music built to a crescendo. Then in the same beat it came to a sudden, towering end, she abruptly fell into a pause, recreating the tranquil pose she'd started with, panting, face and arms shiny with sweat.

Applause as loud as what Fairuza had garnered thundered, turning Cherine's reserved smile into a massive, smug grin. She skipped off the stage, swinging the sides of her skirt as she bounced past both princesses to take her spot in the line of those who'd finished performing.

"What was that about?" Cora asked me.

I blinked at her. "Which part?"

"You egging her on like you're her instructor. She's competition, remember?" she said, even though it didn't sound like she meant her own statements. Not where she was concerned.

"Maybe I wanted her to put her money where her mouth is?" I said, exhaling the breath I hadn't realized I'd been bating. "She's been bragging for days about how she's the best, it would have been a real letdown if she botched her routine like that girl from Shimmerhale."

Cora cringed, hand flying to her chin. The last girl to present a dance had attempted moves beyond her abilities for extra points and had paid for her gamble, dearly, by landing on her face and cracking her jaw.

"NEXT!"

I clung to Cora's free arm and begged, "Trade places with me?"

"I'll be up there for a few minutes at most, and the delay won't make any difference," she said honestly, eyes softening with pity. "But I will if you want."

I was really going to miss her.

I gulped down the spiked rock in my throat. "No, you're right. I'll go."

She cupped my cheek affectionately. I again had a feeling Cora realized how afraid I was of being eliminated, and for a reason other than caring about the competition itself. She had no empty words or white lies to give me, but this quiet, empathizing gesture meant far more than any variation of "You can do it!" could have.

"NEXT!" The yell from Master Zuhaïr came again, impatient now.

I smoothed my gold dress, the one I had arrived in, and stepped up. As if I was stepping up before my executioners.

CHAPTER NINETEEN

"Present yourself and your quality," Mistress Asena recited emotionlessly.

I could only answer the first part of the demand. "Lady Ada of Rose Isle."

Master Farouk livened up instantly, recognizing me. "Ah, Lady Ada, what have you got for us today?"

The lump expanded again in my throat, choking me with its nauseating pressure, making the world before me sway as fresh tears burned behind my eyes. "Nothing."

A puzzled crease pulled his thick brows together. "I take it you're telling jokes today?"

The tears I tried to blink away stuck to my lashes and blurred my eyesight. I sniffled and forced my wobbling lips into a smile. "No jokes, sir. I have nothing to show."

Loujaïne's grey eyes were like cold silver in the daylight. "What does that even mean?"

I turned up my hands in a shrug, a guileless move reserved for whenever I delivered a convincing lie to an adult. Except, for once, I really was clueless and couldn't lie my way out of this situation. "It means I never learned a skill."

"None at all?" Farouk asked, sounding disappointed.

"I can't sing or dance. I can't paint or draw or sculpt or sew, neither can I tell one end of a flute from the other or remember more than two lines of poetry." My voice cracked on pitchy squeaks as I smothered sobs. "If there's anything else I can do in this test, *please* tell me."

"You had ten days to prepare for this." Mistress Asena scowled. "You could have learned something, *anything* to present to us, in that time. Why didn't you?"

I'd tried. I really had. But in such a short time I couldn't learn to work with my hands, sing or dance well-enough to impress anyone. And though I had a great memory for detail, it was never the kind needed to memorize passages from books. There'd been nothing I could have learned in ten days that could have put me on the weakest girl's level.

Even if there had been, I'd been too distracted by my mission to commit to it, anyway.

"If you don't know what you're supposed to do, let alone what you can do, then there's no chance you have any quality to offer the prince or the kingdom," Loujaïne stated bluntly. "But I thank you for making our job easier."

Farouk's disappointment felt personal—like I had let him down—as he glowered at me and called out, "Next!"

I walked off the stage and blew past the other girls, my own heartbeat and breathing becoming the loudest things in the world, roaring in my ears.

Cherine caught me by the arm, pulling on it like a demanding child. "Where are you going?"

"To pack."

"But you can't leave."

I limply wiped my eyes. "I can't stay, either."

Cherine stomped her feet. "This isn't fair! We have to find a loophole of some sort. Arts, music and crafts—that can't be the end of it, there have to be other ways—"

"It's too late for that now!" It came out harsher than I meant it to, taking her by surprise.

Her face fell for seconds before it was reanimated again, this time with excitement. "You can stay with me, as my companion. Fairuza is allowed her handmaidens, I better be allowed to keep you. I'm Cyaxares's cousin too!"

That sounded like a lifeline. If I could stay…

No, I couldn't. I was an idiot to consider it. These people stuck by their rules rigidly and any hope they'd let me stay was a false one. I had to hurry, make use of the time I had left around here.

I pulled my arm free from her grip. "I came here to compete and I lost. They won't let me stay. Now let me go."

"No! You can't leave me now."

"Why not? This helps you move forward."

"Not like this. We were supposed to make it to the final week together, where we attend dinners and balls, where I can introduce you to my family."

"Cherine, you're making this worse."

She pulled harder on my arm. "No! This is not how this is supposed to go. I already planned everything. You can't go!"

Her intensity bewildered me, made me stop resisting her. "Why do you suddenly care so much?"

"Because you're the only friend I have!" she shouted shrilly in my face, her lower lip trembling, her hazel eyes brimming with tears. "I am to marry the prince and you are to marry my brother, and we'll be sisters."

That hit me like a kick in the teeth.

It hadn't occurred to me that she liked me, let alone enough to want to be my sister-in-law. Only one person had thought of me this fondly since my mother.

For a second, through blurry, tear-filled eyes I saw her small form, defiant expression and round face become that of Bonnie Fairborn, the only friend *I* had. Or at least hoped I *still* had.

I pried her fingers off my arm. "I'm sorry, Cherine, but I have to leave."

She burst into loud, gasping sobs as her grip slid off my arm, her hand remaining outstretched, reaching for me as I backed away.

I couldn't bear looking at her, not without envisioning Bonnie. Or worse, seeing her as the friend I now knew her to be, the one I had to leave behind.

I ran out of the gardens, hurtled up every set of stairs and sprinted towards our chambers. I couldn't waste one more second.

Before I could reach the door, my midsection collided with something hard and flexible. An arm.

Cyrus!

He caught me by the waist like he'd done in the tunnels, stopping and steadying me, crowding me back into a hidden corner. "Where are you going?"

The storm of despair, stress, exhaustion and sadness overwhelmed me. Unable to get a word out through my gasping and sobbing, I went straight into hyperventilating.

He bent to bring his eyes level with mine, worry swirling in their depths. He cradled my head in his long fingers, my jaw in his large palms, calloused thumbs stroking the tears off my cheeks.

This should have been a sweet, soothing moment. One

that was self-contained in its closeness, and the gentle intimacy of him comfortingly touching my face. One I'd always treasure. But my mood was too dark to see even this moment through a rosy tint. In fact, it was a cruelly tantalizing taste of something I was about to lose forever.

"What is it?" he whispered, deep voice vibrating with urgency. "What happened?"

"Please," I gasped. "You have to help me now. I don't have much time left."

"What are you talking about?"

"I'm getting sent home tomorrow."

His head moved back away from mine, his thumbs continued rubbing smooth circles on my face, moving upwards like he meant to massage away my headache. "You scared me. I thought they'd discovered you were missing this morning and were going to punish you."

"I would take that over being sent home right now."

"What's wrong with going home?"

"Because there's no one to go back to!" I cried. "Not if I don't have that stupid lamp!"

"How? I swear I will help you find it if you just tell me what it's for."

"That's the thing. I don't know what it's for. I just know I have to get it."

"You make no sense. Nothing about you makes any sense."

Nothing about me?

I moved out of his reach, the tinge of suspicion in his eyes proving enough of a distraction to halt my tears. "What does that mean?"

He shook his head, appeared to be wrestling with his own thoughts. Then he finally pinned me in a pensive gaze. "It's for a god, isn't it? The lamp?"

That had come out of left field. “W-what do you mean?”

“That’s the only way this makes sense,” he said. “That it’s a sacred lamp for the shrine of a god. I know that in some cultures, major gods have extravagant temples equipped with ceremonial articles and that it’s considered sacrilege to remove them from the hallowed grounds, as that’s equal to stealing from a god. But that’s never stopped thieves, has it? Was that lamp stolen from your god’s shrine?”

If Nariman turned out to be a goddess I was going to fling myself off the mountain.

But, if that explanation would get him to stop looking at me like I’d grown a second head and help me, then I was going with it.

“Testy minor goddess might be a more appropriate title,” I admitted, putting as much truth as I could in the lie to make him believe me. “As for the thievery, would that make it harder or easier to find?”

“Depends on who took it.”

According to Our Lady of Merciless Threats, the king himself had taken it from her. Didn’t bother to explain how, or why, or even when that had happened.

“Someone who lives in this palace, that’s for sure,” I dodged.

He raised one eyebrow. “That’s all you know?”

At my nod, he gave me a long, hard look then stepped away, his expression solemn as he waved one hand in invitation. “We’ll start by searching the shrines on the eastern tower.”

I was trembling so hard I could barely put one foot in front of the other. “You’ll search with me?”

He nodded. “And I’ll search for you as you sleep tonight if it will help.”

"You don't have to..."

"I want to," he assured me firmly, looking deeply into my eyes, before turning his ahead as we started walking.

I was so touched my tears started falling again. But I didn't know how to express my gratitude beyond a shy brush on his arm and a strained thank-you. I had a feeling I would be thanking him for his invaluable help so much that all words and gestures of thanks in the world would lose their meaning.

We walked in a tense silence full of stolen glances. I didn't know where we were going but for a while, nothing mattered but being with him, feeling him beside me. I found myself lagging behind him as I marveled at all the shades of brown and bronze in his hair, at every detail of his powerful body and every assured, graceful move he made.

On our way to the tower, we passed by eyebrow windows that looked down on the gardens. I spotted the girls still lined up below, the presentations ongoing as a girl in a yellow dress played the fiddle. Out of another window, I saw the garden wall that overlooked the very edge of the mountain. The dismissed girls were now making their way up to the palace through the sloping path.

As the line turned the corner, reaching the highest point of the border wall, I saw Cora retreating as another girl advanced on her. It was Fairuza, hard to miss in her turquoise dress, the silver in her hair reflecting sunlight blindingly. Cherine cut through the line and squeezed herself between Cora and Fairuza, stopping everyone's ascension. Then everyone joined in on what appeared to be a heated argument.

From that distance, I could only hear wisps of their shrill voices. Then as the girls behind them decided to cluster around the trio, I could no longer see them, either.

Suddenly, I heard a familiar blood-curdling scream.

All the girls stopped moving for moments then surged as one, crowding at the edge of the low wall. Their voices were so loud now I could make out what they were saying.

They were screaming for help.

Someone had fallen over the wall.

CHAPTER TWENTY

Every ounce of nerves and exhaustion were blown away as I blasted past Cyrus. And that was before another scream exploded in my head. Cora's.

"Cherine!"

Cherine was the one who'd fallen over the edge.

No. No, no, *no*!

I no longer felt the ground beneath me as I hurtled down the spiraling stairs, heart stampeding, following the commotion until I found a balcony that directly overlooked the wall where the girls crowded. But I was still one level up, still too far away.

Palace guards had arrived, some were interrogating the girls, some looking over the side of the wall, yelling. Yelling down. It seemed they were talking to someone.

It had to be to Cherine. Which meant she hadn't fallen off to the bottom of the mountain.

Yet.

Why weren't they doing anything to help her? Why were they just standing there?

Cyrus caught up with me, panting, alarmed. "What happened? Did someone fall over the wall?"

I only nodded as I pounced on him in my urgency. "Where can I get a rope? And a hook?"

He blinked. "From the armory." Which was across the palace. "Why?"

Mind going a mile a minute, teeth chattering, I didn't have the words, or the time, to explain. All my energy crammed into the need to save Cherine.

"Forget it."

I grabbed the balcony's curtains, yanking on them desperately.

Cyrus joined me, and being much taller, he managed to pull the long curtains with their rod down for me. "What are you planning exactly?"

"Anything that can help her! She's still hanging on!"

I threw the rod with its curtains over the balcony ledge. As I swung my legs in the massive skirt over it, Cyrus leaped over the ledge and down what had to be at least ten feet. He landed on bent knees, beating me to the ground.

He stood up, held his arms up.

Without a second's hesitation, I let go of the balustrade and fell into his arms.

The impact emptied both of our lungs. But there wasn't a moment to lose, not by regaining our breath, or registering the moment of closeness.

He set me on my feet at once. "Now what?"

Without answering, I knelt, slid one set of curtains off the rod and tightly knotted their ends. Then bundling it up and holding the rod up like a flagpole, I leaped to my feet. "Follow me."

I ran toward the clucking crowd, tore through them,

knocking them out of my way with my improvised spear to reach the ledge. The sight below froze my blood.

At least fifty feet above the narrow mountain plateau—and thirty feet beneath us—Cherine was hanging onto a gargoyle, hair blowing in the wind, legs kicking in the air.

"Help!" Her pleading scream cracked, lodging like an arrow in my heart.

"Hold on until we get a net below you," a guard yelled down at her.

"No!" she shrieked, terror turning her eyes rabid. "It's too high."

It *was* too high. Falling on a net from that height wouldn't make much of a difference. She'd still impact the ground hard enough to shatter every bone in her body. Or they might not be able to catch her at all.

I elbowed the guard. "Out of my way!"

"Get back upstairs," the guard ordered, sticking an arm out to block me. "All of you go to your quarters and let us work."

Dread and anger burst like lava from my gut and I screamed shrilly in his face, jamming the end of the rod in his side. "You're not doing anything, so either help or *get out of my way!*"

"Miss, he told you to step aside," another guard said. "You're holding up the rescue."

"What rescue?" Cyrus shoved the first guard away from me while Cora did the same to the other one. "Go get a rope so we can pull her up."

As soon as the guards ran away, I immediately threw the curtains over the edge, holding the rod by the middle. Cyrus and Cora at once rushed to my side, each holding an end.

"Cherine! Grab on!" I yelled.

She opened her eyes, arms trembling over the gargoyle's

neck. The end of the curtains was over two feet above her head.

"I can't!" she whimpered.

She was losing her strength, and despair was starting to eat at her will to hang on.

The best way would have been to loop a rope around her. But by the time they fetched one, she would have slipped. Our only hope was dragging her up by those curtains.

"Yes, you can!" I tried to sound as certain as I could. "Just reach up!"

Shaking, she stuck her feet on the wall and unwrapped an arm to reach up and —

She slipped, slamming her chin down onto the head of the gargoyle, and ended up hooking her arm tighter around it, clinging for dear life, sobbing, "It's too high!"

My heart shivered in my chest, shaking my voice as I hissed to Cyrus and Cora, "We need to hang it lower."

"How can we do that?" Cora asked, peeking over the edge, face pale as ashes.

There *was* no way we could. Any lower and we'd go over the edge ourselves. There was only one thing to do now.

I had to climb down to her.

I'd climbed up and down walls before, but they were the facades of houses or the fences of gardens, not hundred-feet-high palace walls. That, and I always climbed up with an empty backpack and down with loot small enough to tuck in it. Now I'd have to climb up with an armful of wriggling, panicked girl.

But if I didn't do it, Cherine would fall to her death.

I turned to Cyrus, found him watching me, his anxiety evident despite trying to keep a blank face. Cora had let go of her end of the rod, her hands over her heart and her eyes aimed up, as if hoping for a solution to fall out of the sky.

Since I knew none would, I tore off my dress. The billowing skirt would not only hamper me, it would fill with wind like a sail and tear me away.

Before either of them could vocalize their surprise, I'd stripped down to my pant-like undergarments and shoved the rod back firmly into their hands. "Hold this. Tight."

Cora's eyebrows met her parted bangs. "Ada, what are you doing?"

"Exactly what it looks like." I grabbed the curtain and jumped on the ledge, swinging my legs over the wall and sliding down the curtain, pulling them both by the rod so their waists lodged against it.

"Get back over here!" Cyrus ordered, pulling on the rod with one hand, trying to grab me with the other.

I evaded his grasp, tightened mine on the curtain as I started climbing down. "I have to get to her."

"No, you don't! I'll do it!"

"You're too heavy for Cora and me, and even if we manage to hold you up, the rod might bend under your weight and Cherine's. And I'm already halfway down."

"No, you're not!" he shouted angrily as he tried to lunge for me again.

No, I wasn't. I was still practically at the top, just barely ducking out of his reach.

I gulped down a bracing breath, tore my eyes away from his horrified ones. Then, not looking down, looking straight at the curtain, I held it tighter and started walking down the wall.

"W-what are you doing?" Cherine's hysterical shout

signaled that I was right above her. "You're going to fall on me!"

"Thanks for the vote of confidence." I removed one hand from the curtain, wiping my sweaty palm over the wall before reaching it down. "Grab hold of my ar—*aah*!"

Vertigo hit me like a punch to the head. My world swayed and my sight blurred and blacked out on and off between blinks.

This height—it made the house walls I'd scaled to squat in or steal from look like mere hurdles. From this perspective I realized the palace wall was at the very ridge of the summit the palace sat on. The ledge the guards had proposed catching Cherine on looked like a measly strip. From this protrusion and in this wind, if we fell, we'd probably miss it.

We'd plunge deep down the side of the mile-high mountain.

From that daunting height, the city stretched out below us, buildings looking like matchboxes and people like ants.

Exhaling the dread, I swallowed my nausea, contorted around the curtain and stretched my hand down lower. "Grab. My. Arm."

Her teary gaze goggled at me as she stuttered, "Th-this i-isn't a g-good idea."

"Do you have a better one?" I panted.

She shut her eyes tightly, squeezing out terrified tears. Visibly trembling all over, she removed one hand from the gargoyle. Clinging to the curtain with both legs, I lunged down and caught her arm in the hook of mine. I pulled her up till she was on my level, thanking the terrible fates that it was her and not Cora. I wouldn't have been able to pull up anyone heavier.

"N-now what?" she clung to me as she breathed in my

face, cheeks shuddering and eyes swimming.

"You climb up the curtain."

"Over you?" Confusion seemed to crash into her fear, stalling it. "But—but you could fall!"

Every inch of me was starting to burn. "Climb up or we'll both fall!"

"But—" she stuttered looking absolutely panic-stricken.

The muscles in the arm holding her up stiffened and shook, and the hand holding us both slid a bit down the curtain, chafing my aching palm. "Move! *Now!*"

She reached overhead for the curtain and tried to pull herself up. It felt like forever until she managed to climb above me. But the moment she pressed her feet down on my shoulders, I skidded down hard, making the curtain swing and Cherine slide down. She screamed along with Cora and Cyrus, who were now almost spilling over the wall.

As soon as the mad pendulum of the curtain stilled, I panted, "Hold still. I'm coming up."

"Th-then what?"

"Then you get on my back."

"H-how is that d-different from standing on your sh-shoulder?"

I gritted my teeth, feeling my heart bursting and my breath tearing through my lungs.

I still tried to infuse my voice with an assurance that was the last thing I felt. "I'm ready this time. And we'll be one mass, instead of two pulling in different directions."

Bracing myself with all I had, I climbed back up, avoiding looking below me and focusing on the world above. Cyrus was twisted into a weird angle to hold us up, taking most of our weight, his muscles bulging, his eyes blazing with a dozen fierce emotions, his hair rioting in the wind. The sunlight fighting the shadows on his face added atmospheric depth to his features, making him look like an otherworldly being.

Struggling to breathe past the heart booming in my throat, I focused on him, just him.

I soldiered up, trying to block the pain screaming in my every cell. Once I was directly below her, Cherine lifted her legs from the wall. I dragged myself up so she could latch onto my back. I wrapped what remained of the curtain below us tightly around one leg.

"Ready?" I panted.

She squeaked. I took that as a "Yes."

My arms were on fire, my wrists felt like they'd snap off. The soles of my shoes had little traction. But I poured all my strength and agility into my hold on the curtain. I somehow managed to keep it firm as I climbed up, with Cherine clamped tight around me like a very heavy octopus.

Once I got close to the wall's edge, Cora and Cyrus heaved back with enough force to yank us up and over it. Cherine immediately crawled over me and landed on the ground, practically hugging it as she heaved deeply, her sharp pants punctuated by relieved sobs.

Cora knelt by Cherine, stroking her back and murmuring reassuring words to her.

Cyrus hauled me to my feet and herded me away from the wall, hands tight on my arms, eyes wide and pupils dilated as he searched my face feverishly.

He finally shouted, "Are you insane?"

Head spinning, I swayed in his grip, my voice slurring. "Been debating that for weeks."

His teeth gnashed together. "You could have fallen and died."

"So c-could have Cherine," I hiccupped.

"Better her than you."

I stopped swaying, squinted up at him disapprovingly.

His grip loosened but he kept stroking my arms softly, almost lovingly. "I was just mad with worry about you. That was a very reckless decision. It could have cost you your life."

I leaned back into his hold, trembling. This whole thing would sink in later. For now, I felt almost drunk with relief. "But I'm still here."

"Yes, you are, and for that, I am endlessly grateful."

Princess Loujaïne burst through the crowd of girls and onlookers, followed by Mistress Asena and Master Farouk, all looking pale with panic.

"What happened?" Loujaïne demanded as she reached us. Noticing Cyrus, she glared at him until he reluctantly moved away from me, hands turned up in resignation.

Her glare darkened as it left him for me before landing on Cherine, who was still on her knees, clinging to Cora and weeping. "I said what happened here?"

It was Fairuza who answered her, voice higher than usual. "She fell over the wall."

Suddenly, I was certain of one thing, instant fury evaporating all exhaustion and disorientation. "*You* pushed her over the wall."

Fairuza, lips trembling, gave me a downcast glare identical to Loujaïne's. "She *fell.*"

Hot rage engulfed my every sense, scorching my face, drying my tongue and numbing my fingers as frustrated tears sprang out of my eyes.

I was out of the competition, out of time to save Bonnie, and Cherine had almost died.

Reservations and inhibitions going up in smoke, I slammed my fist into Fairuza's face.

CHAPTER TWENTY-ONE

"Before you go, I just want you to know that you are my hero," Princess Ariane of Tritonia told me gleefully, holding out a tray of multicolored sweets.

I managed a spastic half-smile as I accepted the tray. "Thanks, Princess."

Ariane curtsied, auburn hair almost falling over from its conical hairstyle. "Truly, that was the best thing I have ever seen."

It was only then I realized she wasn't talking about me saving Cherine. That malicious gleam in her eyes was all about the black eye I'd given Fairuza.

If catfights were this sorely lacking in the royal world, then they'd enjoy the outlet of the aggressive commoner privileges I had experienced in schoolyards or on the job.

We were in the top floor's waiting area. Yesterday, after the spectacle the Blue Opal tenants had caused, we'd been separated, with Cherine and Fairuza both staying overnight in the nursing wing. Cora and I had been the only ones left in our chamber. She was packed and ready to go home, while I, aside from failing, was probably going to jail for attacking a princess. The prince's cousin, no less.

Surprisingly, since last night Cora had said nothing to me. Even now, she remained in her own head as she attacked Ariane's gift as soon as she walked away, gnawing on sliced gelatinous rolls, picking the ones filled with pistachios rather than walnuts.

After a period of silent chewing, she suddenly blurted out, "That servant boy, the one who helped me hold you up, who was he?"

I tried to play dumb. "Servant boy?"

"I saw you talking to him at our first test."

"I was getting juice."

"You talked to him for a good while."

Why was I being interrogated? I'd suspected she knew I'd been lying about everything I was since day one. But now she gave me that look that made me feel she could read my mind. As if she knew why I was here, and what Cyrus was helping me with.

"Am I not allowed to make friends?" The neckline and sleeves of my dress tightened, suffocating me with trapped heat beneath the cotton under her shrewd gaze. "Anyway, I was just asking him questions about the palace and life here and then I asked him to help me with Cherine. If I hadn't, you would have been left holding us both since none of the other cows in this competition bothered to help. Probably hoping to take her spot in the line."

She cringed, curling her bottom lip in an exaggerated grimace. "You're not wrong."

It seemed my defense worked since she let it go and continued eating. Minutes later, another ten girls joined us in the waiting room. Among them were Cherine—looking smaller than usual, still shaken and pale—and Fairuza, equally sallow, her left eye swollen shut and purple with the edges of her brow and cheekbone a dark red.

Did I regret socking her in the eye? No. Did I dread the punishment for it? Yes.

Fairuza spotted me. Channeling her anger through her clenched teeth and one good eye, she made a furious beeline towards me.

Cora stuck out her long leg and tripped her before she could reach my seat, sending her flying face-down on the carpet. I tapped her arm warningly.

Cora shrugged, uncaring. "What? I'm going home either way."

Laughter broke out, spreading like fire, only to be extinguished by Fairuza rearing up to her knees and sweeping a glare around the room. Her handmaidens rushed over to her sides but she slapped them away from her and lunged at me, hands on my neck.

An expert in fighting dirty from my years on the street, I bent her middle finger back, weakening her grip while squeezing her other wrist viciously until she yelped and let go.

"I'm not in the mood," I drawled.

Ripping her hands out of mine, she swung one back in a hard slap that knocked me sideways.

All the girls but Cora gave us a wide berth, close enough to observe but far enough to not get reeled in.

I set myself back upright, rubbing my cheek as I stared at her blankly. My face throbbed and I knew I was going to bruise, thanks to her silver rings. But I couldn't feel bad about it, not when I could see her state. Fairuza wasn't as regal with her hair spilling messily from its updo and her attire in disarray from her fall. And with one of her enviable turquoise eyes bruised shut, that docked a few more pretty points.

"Is that the best you've got?" I taunted, straightening to my full height.

"You wouldn't believe the trouble you've marked yourself with," she hissed, wincing after trying to stare at me menacingly, her bruised eye cracking open before sealing back shut.

"What?" I sneered. "Are you going to throw me over the wall, too?"

Hushed comments went through the room like a lit fuse, just as Cherine burst through the onlookers with sharp elbows.

She didn't say a word. She just hurtled toward us, lunged with her arms outstretched and going straight for Fairuza's neck. Fairuza caught her wrists, digging her heels in to prevent another fall, sticking both of them in a stalemate of wrestling and stomping.

"Get her off me!" Fairuza shouted.

Agnë and Meira rushed to the rescue, one lifting Cherine by the belt of her dress and the other trying to peel her hands off Fairuza. Cherine jostled one hand free and slammed her elbow into Meira's throat before pulling it forwards to rap her knuckles against Fairuza's teeth.

Seeming to have had enough, Cora grabbed each girl by her updo and ripped them apart in one yank. Crying out in pain, their furious struggle turned into failed attempts to wrestle their hair from her grip.

The handmaidens tried to gang up on Cora when Fairuza's attempts to scratch her way to freedom failed. Cora merely looked down at them, stony-faced and almost a whole foot taller than the tallest among them. "Can I help you?"

"Uh. Um. Release the princess?" Meira choked.

Cora swung her arm, tossing Fairuza right at her handmaidens, knocking them all down like dominos. She dragged Cherine to her couch and plopped back down beside her, resuming her snacking on Ariane's sweets.

New rule: never anger a farm girl who wrestles wolves off her livestock.

Flustered, Fairuza retreated to the end of the room, with Meira rearranging her hair and Agnë fawning over her, asking if she needed anything. Both got shoved aside for their troubles.

The prince was going to have his hands full with her. I sure hoped they had good nannies and decent tutors to do the childrearing for them since a nation ruled by their obnoxious spawn would be ripe for a revolution.

Speaking of the prince, twenty days here and we never got to see the reason for all this. Not a mention by the palace dwellers to tell us what he was like or even a single portrait of him hanging in the halls. It was weird that neither King nor Crown Prince seemed to have any presence in the palace. Where were they hiding, and why?

Not that it mattered to me. Nothing mattered but my impending elimination…or imprisonment.

Cherine left her seat next to Cora and came to drop next to me, pearled hairpins between her teeth as she rearranged her hairstyle. She mumbled word by word as she removed them from her mouth. "Why. Did. You. Do. That?"

"She came at me first."

"I meant yesterday," she said quietly, nothing like her usual animation, feeling her hair for imperfections. "When I fell off the wall. Why did you do it?"

"Punch her?"

"Save me."

Dumbfounded, I ran all possible meanings through my mind. Why would she even ask something like that? Shouldn't she just thank me and go back to being a fussy handful?

"You were in trouble, so I had to help."

"But everyone else just stood there, even the guards didn't do much. I would have already fallen by the time they did something." She looked at me directly, searching my face with earnest intensity. "You could have fallen, too."

I shuddered as I remembered those terrible moments hanging over the void. "I know."

"But you still came for me."

"I did."

"But I'm your competition."

"Not anymore you're not." I nudged her lightly, not really attempting humor.

Cherine sniffled and threw herself at me, trapping my arms against my sides and pressing her cheek against my neck. It was the clumsiest hug I had ever experienced, a sincere thanks from someone who never learned how to say thank you.

"Please stay with me after this," she gasped between sobs. "I can send you to Anbur with an envoy. Stay with my family, get to know them. My brother would love you."

I softened in her grip, slipping out an arm to wrap around her, resting my cheek on the top of her head. This exact position with this same size difference took me back to the times Bonnie had latched onto me to sway me, begging me to move in.

If I couldn't get my old life back, there might be a chance for a new one here if I took Cherine up on her offer. A part of me wanted it, to just go to a nobleman's mansion and marry a man who felt indebted to me, on the demand of his fussy sister. I would be a true lady, safe, cared for, rich and possibly loved.

It was so tempting, so freeing. But it would make me no better than the girls who'd watched Cherine dangle moments away from death. I couldn't think of my own future when Bonnie's was on the line. If I couldn't save her and her father…

Unable to complete that thought, I shook my head. "I'm sorry, Cherine."

She sobbed and held on tighter. All her strength wouldn't be enough to hold me if I wanted to end her embrace. But her hold did add more cracks to my breaking heart.

Princess Loujaïne and the judges arrived, walking into a suddenly silent room.

Her silvery eyes flashed a frosty look towards us then narrowed in a glare at Fairuza's end of the line. I had expected a much worse reaction towards me, something that may have involved spitting or cursing, but that was probably way beneath her gilded upbringing.

"In you go," Mistress Asena ushered us into the next room. I could tell which of her girls were going home by how she avoided them.

I rose, my hands held out behind me. Cherine grabbed the left and Cora grasped the right and we made our way in, avoiding eye contact with Loujaïne. Master Farouk gave me a curt nod of acknowledgment as I passed him. We took our seats closer to him in the middle row.

"Fifteen of you will go home today," Loujaïne announced, looking as if she was focusing on something beyond our rows.

Discreetly, I checked the room for Cyrus. Having him here would have made this easier. I could request him to escort me to the chambers and "help with the luggage." If we managed to be alone, we could slip through the trapdoor again, check every possible direction the tunnels took, check the shrines in the palace and city.

I also wanted more time with him. I wanted a last chance to brand his face in my mind. Enough to last me the rest of my life. He would be another fixed point in my timeline, a base of what-ifs I could touch on whenever I needed a mental escape.

But what I truly wanted was to ask him to pack up all his loot and come with me.

He wasn't in the room. And I had missed the first three names called during my search for him. The girls stood and left, one with upturned eyes who looked about sixteen, another who resembled Ariane with knee-length red hair, and a third with dark, shiny skin and silvery tattoos.

The next four were from the same region, all in pretty much the same type of colorful outfit that must be what passed as fancy there. The next three that left made Asena cover her eyes in shame. The last of her girls, apart from Princess Ariane, it seemed.

That left five. I squeezed Cherine's hand one last time and let go, readying myself to get up and leave quietly. The less of a reaction I exhibited, the less noticeable I became. Hopefully, it would make escaping punishment for Fairuza's black eye more likely.

"Lady Isgerda of Avongart. Miss Merlisa of Cöll," Loujaïne continued. "Duchess Ethelstine of Wisterna."

Fairuza turned, baring her teeth at me in a grim cross between a snarl and a smile.

The finality misplaced my heartbeat, sending it up to my throat then between my ears, making Loujaïne's voice hard to hear as she read out the last two names.

"Lady Ad—" I inhaled and squeezed my eyes shut. "—ina of Lorthos and Lady Raena of Galantis,"

Then Loujaïne was finished and wrapping up her scroll.

Cora slouched forwards, gawking ahead.

Cherine let out a squeal of delight and hugged me frantically again.

I almost fainted with shock and the violent drain of tension.

Fairuza jumped up and pointed at me, her voice shrill. "Why is *she* still here?"

Good question.

CHAPTER TWENTY-TWO

I felt like I was watching the scene before me unfold from underwater.

Everything was muffled, dimmed, blurred in the tears frozen in my eyes. Yet I could see and hear everything, my thoughts rushing in almost painful speed and clarity. One thing reverberated over everything else.

I wasn't going home.

I had more time to find the lamp, to save Bonnie and Mr. Fairborn.

I had more time with Cyrus.

"I assume you know how these competitions work, Princess," Master Farouk said calmly, readjusting his fez. "You are given a task in your test, you pass it and you move on to the next."

"But she failed!" Fairuza yelled. "She failed the worst out of everyone! She has no skill, no talent, no hint of culture or artistry in her—"

"Who said it was a talent show?" Loujaïne glared at her, mouth tight with displeasure.

Fairuza dropped her accusing finger, blinking in stunned silence before getting riled up again. "What else could 'quality' mean?"

"Your quality as a person is the value you can have in other people's lives," Farouk said, smoothing the flared sleeves of his patterned robe. "It has nothing to do with mastering a demanding aria or reciting complex archaic poetry. As for your question about why Lady Ada remains among you, despite displaying no artistic talent..."

Loujaïne cut him off, livid. "You almost killed your own cousin over a petty argument."

Fairuza had the nerve to look shocked. "What are you talking about?"

"You pushed me over the wall!" Cherine screamed, getting to her feet, for once towering over half the room. "The real question is what are *you* still doing here, you murderous hag!"

Fairuza turned on her, shock evaporating, fury replacing it on her spectacular face. "Because I gave, by far, the best performance, you subpar, forgettable runt!"

"Then why did you try to murder me if you didn't feel threatened by me!"

The argument escalated into an incoherent frenzy. Traumatized, shaking rage from Cherine, scandalized, restrained rumbles from Loujaïne and defensive, tearful screeching from Fairuza.

I only wished I could slip away without anyone noticing and use the time they would waste at each other's throats to find Cyrus and resume my search.

All I could do was remain glued to my seat with my shocking reprieve and watch members of the royal family shriek fancy insults at each other.

Who knew there were so many tasteful alternatives to common name calling?

Suddenly, an ear-splitting whistle cut through the noise.

Master Farouk was now at the podium, fingers still poised near his mouth, his thick brows flat over his dark eyes, accentuating his ire. "Your Highness, forgive me, but we aren't finished here. You can resume this family matter on your own time later."

Color rose to Loujaïne's cheeks as she held Farouk's reprimanding gaze for a moment too long. Then clearing her throat, she turned to us. "To you who remain, congratulations. You are moving to the penultimate round. Within the next ten days you will have more chances to prove, not just your general worth, but how you can conduct yourself in various situations in and out of the palace."

"You will meet the prince in the final round," Farouk reminded us. "So, keep that in mind and think critically about your task."

"Which is?" Fairuza growled, a very uncouth, unladylike noise. "You didn't even explain what it was last time, or how that would lead to these two..." She pointed at Cora and me, "...somehow winning another round of the competition."

Farouk suddenly looked exhausted. I could see the color fleeing his face as Fairuza attempted to drag him back into an argument. "It's not the judges' fault that you couldn't tell the difference between a rehearsed skill and someone's worth as a person."

I swear I felt the anger radiating off her in waves all the way across the room. She crowded him, delicate, manicured fingers curling into claws as she continued to point at me. "And what exactly is her worth, especially after she proved herself vulgar and hostile?"

I thought it wasn't disappointment that dropped his shoulders and hollowed out his gaze, it was something worse. Disgust. "If you think blackening your eye is on par with *attempted murder,* Princess, then I have nothing more to say to you."

"What do you all keep talking about?" Fairuza exclaimed. "I did no such thing. There were so many girls crowding a narrow path when that commotion started, and as she tried to jump up to attack me, she was pushed by the collective and fell off the wall. That's what anyone but her delusional self and her ugly, useless, low-class friends will tell you."

"It was *you* who pushed me," Cherine screeched. "We all know you pushed me."

The frenzied gleam of a trapped animal entered Fairuza's eyes. "You're still here, aren't you? If I had pushed you, I'd have only done you a favor. It made you the center of attention for a few hours, something you could never achieve on your own."

I finally found my voice. "So, you admit it?"

The bitterness in Fairuza's tone was so strong I could taste it in the air as she turned to me. "Shame it wasn't you. A few might have mourned little Cherine for her family's sake, but you would have just been dumped over yet another wall into the river with the rest of the trash on the garbage barge."

I jumped up and crossed to the first row, fist poised. "How about I make your eyes match?"

Loujaïne stepped between us, glowering down at her niece. "You're dismissed."

"You can't dismiss me, this isn't tutoring hours," Fairuza cried out.

Loujaïne split her aggravation between us. "Yes, I can. You can all go now."

Cherine at once hooked her arm through mine and dragged me out.

Cora followed us, shuffling her feet as she groaned mournfully, "I want to go home."

Cherine stared back at her. "I really can't understand why you do!"

"Because it's agony for me here," Cora complained. "The weather is too hot and dry even up here, and we don't do anything all day. I'm bored. When I'm home, I get a dozen things done each day. My knees are starting to creak like a crone's from sitting around!"

I couldn't fight the upward curve of my mouth. "You miss doing chores?"

Cora slouched forwards, swaying on ambling feet. "I miss being able to do what I want, wherever I want, in work and between working hours. I miss my farm, which is mine, where I follow my own rules. I don't have to be trapped in rooms all day in a land where little grows."

Halfway to the dining hall, I spotted a flash of white hair. Ayman!

In a few steps I could see his red-purple eyes watching us from the shadowy curve of a tower stairwell. Following his line of sight, I realized he was watching Cherine, not me, with a mix of fascination and longing.

My heart resumed its thunderous pounding, hoping Cyrus wasn't far behind.

He wasn't. Cyrus appeared behind him, hastily tying a sash around his waist. They must have been up all night, sneaking and stealing.

Even looking disheveled and tired, Cyrus was still mesmerizing. He was the kind of attractive that would look good covered in mud and wearing a potato sack.

From across the room, his face lit up with that slow, teasing spread of his lips as his gaze fell on me, a careful and steady exposure as to not blind anyone with his smile. The light, bright green of his eyes were the closest to the sea this city would ever come.

"I need to go to the bathroom." I unhooked Cherine's arm from mine. "I'll meet you later."

"Ada, not now," Cherine whined.

"Yes now. Nature calls." I slipped past her and Cora and rushed away in the direction of the public bathrooms. I made sure I was out of sight before ducking into a detour to meet Cyrus and Ayman by the staircase.

"You're still here," he greeted, his bewitching eyes twinkling with a mixture of relief and elation.

I could feel how glad he was to see me, how relieved that I was still here.

"Can't get rid of me that easily," I said in what should have been a cocky rejoinder, accompanied by a confident wink, but my weak throat betrayed me, cracking my voice.

"I wouldn't dream of it," he whispered, taking a step closer.

Ayman rolled his eyes and stepped between us. "We think we may know where your lamp is."

I jerked with a brutal surge of hope. "Where?"

"It's not precisely one place but a few interconnected spots," Cyrus explained. "Knowing a minor goddess sent you here to retrieve it got us thinking. According to legend, this very mountain is the heart of an earth goddess and her veins spread through the city, the holiest spots holding temples. Where there are temples, there are shrines. And where there are shrines—"

"There are lamps!" I finished for him.

If Nariman's lamp were such a thing, then naturally the king would have taken it to offer to his patron god or goddess.

I turned my eyes up to Cyrus, my heart trembling with a mixture of anxiety and anticipation, and the thrill of being near him again. "Where do we start? I have nine days till the next test. So how can I sneak out every night into the city to search the shrines, and come back by morning? Can I use the tunnels? Do you have a map for them?"

He grinned at me, those jewel-like eyes gleaming in the shadows. "They didn't tell you about the schedule for those nine days, did they?"

I blinked. "No. Why?"

He grinned. "Because you're going everywhere now, to every major spot in the city, including the shrines."

After a moment of digesting this, I slowly said, "A kind of a pilgrimage?"

He shook his head. "More of an investigation. What do you do when you want to find out what someone is truly like? You throw them in an unfamiliar and trying situation and watch how they behave and what they do with their new surroundings and circumstances."

And that summed up my situation in a nutshell since Nariman had dragged me into this world.

I didn't know what the trials and adversity were revealing of my true self. I only had to make sure whatever they unearthed didn't crack under the pressure. Not before I fulfilled my mission.

CHAPTER TWENTY-THREE

The descent down the mountain reminded me of the first time I rode a horse. Full of expectant worry and a heavy feeling weighing down my lower gut, making my organs vibrate and squeeze against my spine.

Once again, the girls and I were in our own compartment. From time to time I could see Cyrus passing through the hallway, acting as security. He always caught my eyes through the door's window, instilling a much-needed ease within me.

I still hadn't asked him to run away with me to Arbore. The thought was becoming less stupid and more plausible the longer I stayed in Sunstone Palace.

"Cherine," Cora lisped her name around the wand of licorice she was gnawing on. "What does the prince look like?"

Cherine, staring blankly out the window, hummed but said nothing.

"The prince," Cora persisted. "We haven't seen any paintings of him, let alone one of the king. What do they look like?"

Still looking lost in thought, Cherine said, "King Darius resembles the portrait of King Xerxes we pass on the second-floor staircase. But I believe his eyes are grey."

The portrait of King Xerxes was of a man in his late-forties, with thick, jaw-length, dark hair and greying temples. I remembered he had a prominent brow, deep-set green eyes, and a short, pointed nose and high, square cheekbones like Loujaïne and possibly Fairuza. I envisioned Darius to be the same, but with his sister's eyes.

"And the prince?" I nudged her. "The same as his old man?"

She shrugged as we entered the tunnel behind the waterfall. "I said I haven't seen him since I was five. I was born at court before Xerxes died and Darius ascended as king. Cyaxares must have been about eight or nine at the time, the age where princes and sons of lords are passed around to squire for other royals and nobles. Even before that he didn't live at the palace."

"So you saw him when?" I asked.

"During the time between Xerxes death and Darius's coronation. I haven't been back to Sunstone since," she said, running her hand over her diamond-studded citrine rings. "I've kept in touch with letters through the years, like I do with all of my royal or noble relatives. But I haven't seen him since he officially returned to Cahraman as crown prince."

"Where was he before?"

"A nearby principality, can't remember which."

Without missing a beat, Cora said, "He's hideous, isn't he?"

Cherine spun away from the window, jangling the chains and coins in her bronze necklace loudly. "No, he is not! Why would you say that?"

"Why else would he be hiding? That's why we can't see him until there are too few of us and it's too late to turn back."

"I didn't think milkmaids had room to be judgmental, or even picky," Cherine sniped.

Cora glowered. "I'm not a milkmaid."

"You're not a noblewoman, either, so where do you get the gall to call him ugly?"

"Gee, I didn't know you had to be of a certain rank to have eyes." Cora imitated her in a vapid, high-pitched voice, fluttering her lashes in hilarious wide-eyed wonder.

Cherine harrumphed at her and turned her attention back outside the window.

In spite of all the tension and uncertainty storming inside me, I found my lips twitching.

Seven more days with these idiots. I was so going to miss them and every bit of their antics. But at least their swipes at each other never posed an actual danger, unlike Fairuza's.

Speaking of her, after Elimination Day, Fairuza had put her foot down and insisted on getting her own suite. Princess privilege—what had saved her from being eliminated based on the rule against "dishonorable activities"—had pulled those strings, leaving the three of us alone in the Blue Opal chambers, with no risk of Meira shredding our belongings or Agnë cutting off our hair as we slept.

It figured that the only people who could stand to be around her would be paid to do so. Annoying as Cherine could be, and despite her being the sort to make ambitious connections rather than friendships, I knew she liked me for *me*. And I actually liked her, more every day, for everything that made her *her*.

Cyrus passed our compartment again, pushing a trolley. He winked at me before he moved on, singing quietly.

"What are you smiling at?" Cora asked, leafy-green eyes contemplating me.

I forced a neutral expression onto my face. "Nothing?"

Her gaze intensified, making me feel scrutinized.

"What?" I couldn't help sounding defensive. "Can't I smile when I feel like it? Lots of people are just smiley."

"But you're not. You hardly ever smile."

"Neither do you."

"Because I'm—"

"Bored. Yes. We *know*," Cherine finished for her, crabbily.

"Homesick," Cora stressed. "I miss my dogs, cats, land and home. I miss my mother."

Cherine laughed humorlessly. "I don't."

After that, we fell back into idle silence. Cherine seemed to be fixated on watching every detail we passed on our way down. Cora crossed her arms and lolled her head back as she napped. I split my attention between the compartment's windows, catching glimpses of the city below on one side, and of Cyrus whenever he passed again on the other.

After two hours, the train came to a creaking halt, on the edge of the marketplace near the town square. We were hustled out and arranged into lines, each walking behind their handler.

Compared to the interior of the train, and the cooler temperature at the palace elevation, the heat felt like a stinging slap to the face. It was the peak of midday, with the merciless sun beating down on the paved streets and reflecting blindingly off bronze domes, whitewashed buildings and stained-glass windowpanes.

As we walked into the city, people hustled and bustled

around us in the bazaar, chattering and shouting and bargaining. Merchants called out singsong slogans, advertising their goods from their counters, carts or windows among the cramped view of the ever-changing crowds. Rectangular buildings hovered above us, with spiraling stairs, flat steps and dovecot roofs. Some houses even had what looked like pigeonholes for windows. We were close enough to the river to feel the humidity and hear the barges and boats passing by, carrying merchandise for the market and people to the focal points of the city.

In another circumstance, I would have loved to explore every nook and cranny of those amazing attractions and comb over the stalls and shops. But now, all I could think of was how I was going to slip away, rendezvous with Cyrus and start our search.

"What is this place?" a girl from Master Zuhaïr's line asked.

"The downtown of our capital, Sunstone," Loujaïne said, opening a parasol. "We're going to take a detour through the city to our destination."

"You mean we are to *walk* there?" a girl from Ariane's line gasped.

"I am not walking through this place." Fairuza flung her hand toward the market.

"You will walk," Loujaïne snapped. Then without giving anyone else a chance to utter another word, she linked arms with Mistress Asena and they walked ahead.

"I hate to admit it," Cherine whispered. "But she's right. I don't want to walk here. Common people are dangerous. They might rob us or kidnap us for ransom"

Cora rolled her eyes. "You can always go back to hang out with the ghoul in our room."

A squeal ripped out of Cherine. "No!"

Not in the mood for another session of bickering, I held out my elbows to them. "Alright then, hop on and off we go."

Cora roughly linked her arm with mine and shaded her eyes as she looked around. Cherine held onto the crook of my other elbow and bunched her skirt up as we hopped over a puddle where a merchant was washing his fruit pyramid with a hose.

As we waded through the crowds, most of the girls fussed, complained and expressed hyperbolic disgust. I didn't know if they were genuinely that sheltered or if they were trying to outdo each other on the uppity front. One thing was for sure: Cora and I wanted to punch them all because it wasn't even that bad. I'd slept on the ground of far, far worse places.

After a lot of huffing, puffing, whining and stumbling, our little field trip ended at the ornate gates of a lofty one-level building. Its huge, shimmering façade was a mosaic made up of octagonal tiles of blue and opalescent marble and too many columns to count. To complete the stunning picture, there were peacocks strutting across the front yard.

"Oh, look at that one!" Cherine cooed, pointing at the end of the porch as we climbed up.

A peacock, white as snow, sat on the porch steps, its tail folded into a train behind it. At the approach of a peahen, it unfurled its tail and shook it at her and at us while cawing loudly. It was beautiful.

Speaking of beautiful, I again wondered where Cyrus was. I was burning with anxiety, anticipating his appearance, and how we'd begin our sweep of the city's shrines.

Cherine looked mesmerized by the snowy peacock. "How is it that color? I didn't know they came in that color."

"Everything can come without color," I said. "There are people who are like that."

She jumped around with a gasp. "Really? Have you seen one?"

"Yep," I said, holding back the "So have you" part of the answer.

"I've been dreaming of a man with silver hair and snow-white skin, whiter than the people in the Northland Kingdoms. Do you think I should visit a priestess while we're here, have her interpret my dreams?"

I didn't know what to make of her fascination with Ayman, as she had both wonderful dreams and terrible nightmares about him, each starring a different aspect of him.

I finally shrugged. "Sure, why not?"

Cherine ran off to find a map of the city and Cora started roaming the place like it was a museum, checking every statue and decorated wall. As I started to snoop around, too, many of the trinkets on display beckoned me to swipe. Then I remembered what Cyrus had said about angry gods and stealing from temples and focused on the actual reason I was here.

The building was a cross between a courthouse and a temple. Along with sculpted altars and their ancient, preserved shrines, there were alcoves and podiums for priests or judges. It was clear this was where many came to get married, as a line of couples stood in wait, some in full ceremonial garb, others just in their best clothes. All outfits were gorgeous, their complex patterns combining with lush materials, rich dyes and multi-layered jewelry to create a sumptuous whole.

What did the weddings themselves look like if the bride and groom were that festive and extravagant on their own?

Cyrus appeared behind me as I was sizing up an incense burner, whispered in my ear, "Find anything?"

The feeling of his warm breath on my skin was like a charge, raising every hair on my body in an intense shudder and almost making me drop what I was holding.

Gulping down my haywire reaction, I turned to him, handing him the burner. "This isn't gold, is it?"

He tilted the incense burner, checked its corners. "It's rusting around the bottom, so, definitely not."

He offered it back to me with a bow of his head. My fingertips brushed over his as it passed from his grasp to mine, sparking a jolt of awareness up my arm.

Trying to steady my jangling nerves, I pretended to examine the burner, feeling the vine-like etchings in the metal and smelling the burnt remains of myrrh. But all I could really feel was Cyrus standing so close, his warmth radiating over me.

As I placed it back in its nook, he said, "I've already checked the place. Nothing gold in here save for the rings."

It took me a second to get that he meant wedding rings. I swallowed.

"Would you like me to show you around?"

I wanted to blurt out "I would like anything as long as you're involved."

Thankfully, I only nodded.

As he held out his arm, I saw Cora watching us from across the room, expressionless save for the quirked brow. I swallowed again, ignoring his arm and moving ahead, hoping she'd take that as him giving me directions.

We moved past the entrance columns and into a darker hall where newlyweds lit candles below shrines.

"This is the House of Love," he suddenly whispered close

to my ear, his voice zapping through me all over again. "Primarily a temple to the water goddess Anaïta, where the lovers come to commit themselves forever in her presence and where the lonely ask for her help in finding their mates."

In the center of a stone fountain with floating lanterns at its periphery stood a life-size sculpture of a woman who held out her hands with a slight, comforting smile. Her hair tumbled down around her body and she wore a headdress that arced over her head like the spread tail of a peacock. As we approached I could see her round cheeks, full lips and down-turned eyes and that...

...she had the exact same face as that of Jumana Morvarid in the vault!

I turned to Cyrus to ask if he too thought so and found his mouth dropped open at the sight of her. That was answer enough for me.

But if he was surprised by the perfect resemblance between the two statues, did that mean he'd never been in here before?

As I started to ask, he hushed me with a gentle finger on my lips. A couple was ascending past us to the statue. Each slipped a hand into one of Anaïta's and placed lilies over the floating flames, burning the petals and reciting an oath over their smoke.

The air got heavier with the hot perfumes. It became stifling with the bittersweet tension of Cyrus hovering closer over me as we watched the union of the couple before us.

My every nerve crackled as the back of his hand brushed mine. They almost combusted when his fingers traced across my palm to wrap around it. I didn't know if I should return his grasp. I didn't even know if I could, if my hand would obey me if I tried. I hadn't held hands with a boy since I was twelve, and it surely had felt absolutely nothing like it did now.

No one's touch had ever affected me like this before.

His thumb brushed the back of my hand in soothing strokes, applying a light pressure to my veins. I hoped he couldn't pick up a pulse, or he'd know he had my heartbeat stampeding.

"Does everyone go through this ritual?" I whispered, voice raspy and alien in my ears.

He nodded, turning to gaze deeply into my eyes. "Getting married in the eyes of love herself is a must before doing so in front of the law of the land. You have to appease her first or else she might feel slighted and curse your marriage."

"Goddess of love, indeed," I said, attempting a sarcastic tone. I only sounded breathless. As I was.

"Is she any worse than your goddess who's threatening you with severe consequences if she doesn't get her lamp back?"

His probing gaze told me he believed I was still holding out on him, was hoping I'd give him more specifics.

Since I couldn't do that, I shook my head. "So, one shrine down. What next?"

A disappointed look flitted over his face before he hid it in a smile and said, "We go shopping."

CHAPTER TWENTY-FOUR

"Why are we here again? What is the point of this?"

At Cherine's loud, approaching moan, Cyrus squeezed my hand, whispered he'd see me later and slipped away.

Still trembling, I tried to compose myself as I turned to her. "Think they're showing us what to expect of living here."

That or they were gauging our reactions to the idea. Judging by most of the group, they didn't like the heat, humidity, markets, stray dogs or even people because they kept cringing away from anyone who brushed past them. Oddly enough, Fairuza was the only one not overreacting. Her complaints were limited to the heat, the distances we walked and the wet potholes drenching the bottom of her skirt. All of which were, admittedly, reasonable.

I let Cherine drag me back to the entrance where Cora was waiting with the others. In five minutes, we had exited the temple and were walking back to the market. Seemed we really were going shopping.

I lagged behind as we snaked through the fresh produce

corner of the market. Everything was under a wide, continuous roof supported by arches and columns, and surrounded by huge blocks of ice that didn't melt, cooling the passage considerably. I kept looking back for Cyrus, but he remained far behind. Seemed he had to play security officer for now.

Giving up, I caught up with the rest as we stopped near a stand with buckets of blooming flowers, clay pots of herbs and spices and multi-sized satchels of seeds.

"What flowers would you have in your bouquet?" I heard Asena ask.

"Silver roses from the forests of Rosemead," Fairuza answered automatically.

"Blue water lilies from Rhakotis," said Ariane.

"Whatever doesn't smell like dog piss," Cora grumbled under her breath.

I thought those sparkly lilies in that stand would be lovely.

Cherine outdid all the answers. "Primroses for eternal love, yellow poppies for wealth, white heather for health and ivy for faithfulness."

"I hope it's poison ivy," Fairuza sneered.

"I hope your beast brother ate all the silver roses."

Loujaïne shut down the brewing fight. "What would you serve at the wedding?"

They fought over who could yell their answer the loudest. I caught "Roasted alligator!" and "Shark fin soup!" and "Stewed prunes!" among other weirder options.

If I ever got married, I would just host our wedding guests in the backyard of our house with food I knew how to cook well. I would serve cakes people would actually like to eat, because in my experience, wedding cakes were just pretty. Pretty inedible, that was.

Anyway, I didn't know how to make anything that wasn't pub food.

Then again, people generally loved pub food.

Mistress Asena's voice rose over the cacophony. "What desserts would you offer?"

The responses got even more enthusiastic and competitive.

Farouk pushed through the clucking girls and came to stand between Loujaïne and Asena. Seemed he'd decided they'd had enough unruliness. "Here's your task. You are to search the marketplace for elements of those three items and you are to cook and arrange them for us by the end of this week."

So, that was the shopping Cyrus had talked about.

Farouk made a dramatic pause, before he added, "That is when you will meet the prince."

The girls erupted in excited chatter, deluging our quintet of judges with questions about the prince, what our task had to do with him and why he'd be there before the penultimate elimination.

"Now!" Loujaïne's shout ended their clamoring. "You have three hours."

The group clashed like a gaggle of headless chickens, going in random directions then stopping to complain and yell questions. Some even refused to go anywhere without our handlers and their handmaidens.

Cora wandered off somewhere to sample the local produce, and Cherine was swept away with the crowd. Relieved that I wouldn't have company, I looked around to see if Cyrus would catch up with me as he'd promised.

He was nowhere to be found.

But I had a deadline and couldn't afford to waste a second.

I had to get this done without him. I also had to secure something first.

I stepped back and took note of what was where before circumventing the flailing bodies of the group. Too engaged in the argument, Meira didn't notice as I pretended to bump into her and carefully lifted one of Fairuza's coin pouches. I knew it contained a hefty sum of silver and bronze. I had money, but why spend mine when I could spend Fairuza's? With that amount, I could probably get myself a few of those sparkly flowers along with everything I had to buy.

That was nowhere near a big enough price for flipping a girl to her bone-crushing death. But there would be time for vengeful robbery of something of real value to her later. For now, I had some serious shopping to do.

With the coin pouch shoved down my décolletage, I zipped around the town square, a mental shopping list getting longer with each consideration.

I soon had to stop in a shady corner. The sun beating down on me was overheating my brain and soaking me in sweat. But I couldn't stay long. The clock was ticking.

As I stepped back into the street, another shadow came over me.

"A bit hot, isn't it?" Cyrus's voice drenched me in its cool drawl.

I spun around to find him holding up a parasol big enough to cover three.

My heart did its usual jig inside my chest at his sight. "Scorching."

And I didn't mean the weather.

His smile rivaled the sun as he came forwards, shielding me in the protection of his aura and the shade. "The dog days are by far the worst part of the year, but cooler weather is due by the time the competition is over."

I smirked. "So we go home when it gets good. Typical."

"Who said anything about you going home?"

"Let's be honest, there's no way I'm staying."

"Who knows what will happen."

I did. Though I'd thought I did twice before, I was certain there was no way I was staying this time.

I shrugged. "Anyway, no use focusing on anything but the matter at hand. Any idea what I'm supposed to get? A few things and get the rest from the palace, or the whole ingredient list?"

"Depends on what you intend to make. I assume you have a plan?"

Not exactly, but if there was anything I had learned from pub and tavern food, it was that you could never go wrong with potatoes. They were cheap, enduring, satiating, and you could slice them, dice them, boil, broil, mash or fry them and they would be good in any way. I could just make a whole set of potato dishes and pretend that I was so varied and clever.

"Do you have potatoes in Cahraman?"

From the way his brows rose, that was the last thing he'd expected me to ask. "We do."

"Good, I'll need about ten dozen."

"Then you'll have them." He grinned as he offered me his hand.

At first, I thought he was handing me the parasol and set my hand over his, fingertips on his knuckles, waiting for them to slide out and leave the handle in my grasp. Instead, he bent his arm so my hand was on the crook of his elbow in a light ladylike hold on an escort's arm.

I flashed back to the moment in the temple when he'd

held my hand. I hoped to pass my blush off as the result of the heat rather than his closeness and the memory of his touch.

He led me to a stall stacked with potatoes, sweet and regular, along with other root vegetables; onions, beets and carrots. It was the front of a shop that sold grains, dried fruit and spices. He picked up a bag of potatoes before we went into the shop, where we checked every colorful barrel and sniffed every aromatic pile.

Though he was playing escort seamlessly, I couldn't shake the feeling that this exploration was as new to him as it was to me.

"You don't do you this often, do you?" I asked. "Go on errands for the palace?"

He sighed. "No, I was never allowed to go out much. My father thought I had better things to do indoors. Seeing nothing but those walls and those people all the time is suffocating."

My heart clenched at the melancholy in his voice. He felt trapped. The idea of begging him to escape with me became an almost unstoppable compulsion.

If he came back with me to Ericura, he could achieve his freedom and shirk all that bound him to this place. And he'd be with me. I wouldn't be so focused on Bonnie as I was before, wouldn't risk suffocating her if I split my love and attention between them. Together we could set up a new life completely detached from our old ones, where we wouldn't have to be thieves, and I would never fear being alone in the world again.

But I couldn't ask him now. Not yet. All I could do was try to lift him out of his slump.

To do that, I had to draw on my experience with homelessness, relive the anxiety and sometimes terror of not knowing what the next moment would bring.

This time I put my hand on his, felt the currents that flowed between us getting stronger. "But at least it's safe and clean, not to mention constant. You know where you'll sleep, where you'll wake up, how you'll get your next meal. And knowing who's around all the time is far better than repeatedly starting over with people you don't know. There's no worry or risk in your future when you know where you're going, right?"

"But what if you don't like where you are going and the people you're with?" He sounded and looked forlorn as he reached up to pick me a bottle of vinegar off the shelf. "What if you have no choice because there are no other places or people that you've experienced?"

"Then I would go look around, but still come home, not keep moving around forever. It's exhausting." I avoided the questions in his eyes by checking out a jar of pickled pearl onions.

He exhaled. "So is being limited and held back, especially after you realize that there are other ways to go about everything. What if you want to see what your other options are in the world rather than succumb to the fates and take what you're given?"

"What if you find out there are no possibilities but the ones you already see?"

"Then I would have at least gotten that answer."

He *wanted* to leave. He wanted to see new places and people and have choice and adventure. I so wanted to give him everything he wanted.

Without even intending to, I blurted out, "You can come with me."

He stopped weighing the potatoes. "What do you mean?"

"You want to leave, and I'm going to be sent off next week."

"Why are you so sure about that?" He slammed the vegetables in the cart he pushed around the stacks.

"Because I've survived this long only because others fared worse than me. The ones who remain are better than I am in just about everything."

"They're certainly no such thing!"

He actually sounded offended. On my behalf. That felt... good. The best thing I remembered feeling in a long, long time.

Fighting the urge to hug him for it, I shrugged. "Whatever, I'll end up leaving. But if you come with me, you can explore your other options, like you said, and achieve the peace of knowing what's out there and what you want for certain. The prince himself got us all here because he wanted the peace of mind of seeing if he had options beyond the obvious ones." His gaze grew more intense until I rushed to lighten the mood. "Not that the brat even came to see said options for himself. He sent his auntie to sort them out for him."

His face suddenly grew emotionless, his tone flattening. "Right."

I sighed. "Wish I had some of that peace as well."

He turned me to him, looking earnest. "You will. As you saw in the temple, it is always best to appease the goddess first before moving forwards, and I'm going to help you do that."

If only Nariman were a goddess to be appeased as easily as Anaïta was.

"Think you can appease Anaïta with me?"

He almost slammed the cart into the people ahead of us.

Realizing I had said that out loud, the blood drained out of my face and shot straight towards my bubbling stomach.

"Joking!" I tried to laugh it off, but my giggle came out a bit hysterical as I pushed him along to the checkout station.

"So, you don't want to propose to me?" he teased, letting me herd him.

"Uh...sorry, no. Don't have a ring for you today."

"What if I had one for you?"

It was my turn to halt and slam into the one behind me.

As the man grumbled, Cyrus laughed. It was a clear, joyous sound that turned my knees to jelly, threatening to buckle my legs out from under me.

Unaware of my messy state, Cyrus pushed our cart ahead when the customers ahead vacated their spot.

The vendor checked our purchases calmly. "That will be thirteen *oksokos*."

Fingers buzzing like a thousand ants were marching through them, I took the pouch out of my bra and peeked at the silver and bronze coins. Even if I had I known what each was worth, in this moment when I was in danger of forgetting my own name, I wouldn't have remembered.

"Er...which ones are those osk—oks—?"

"May I?" Cyrus took the pouch from my numb fingers, making sure to brush my fingertips. Then still grinning widely, he picked out thirteen hexagonal bronze coins and handed them over.

"Foreign wife, huh?" The vendor gave him a knowing nod. "I have one of those, from The Granary. Took her ages to understand our money. They still mostly barter over there."

I spluttered, words breaking apart on my tongue.

Cyrus took our bags and nudged me ahead without

correcting the vendor. "She's only been here three weeks, so we'll see how she adapts. She's doing great so far."

We left the shop with me clutching the smaller bag as if it would stop me from flying away.

"You were saying?" he asked innocently as he reopened the parasol.

I shook my head dazedly. "I forgot."

"I didn't." His gaze on my upturned face felt like a caress. "You can have whichever ring you want from the vault."

"How about the one you said grants wishes?" I choked. "I could really use some wishes coming true right now."

"To find that lamp?"

And everything else I wanted to come true, including a peaceful life with him. "Among other things."

For endless moments, I felt as if the marketplace disappeared around us as our eyes locked. There was nothing left in the world but his eyes and my thundering heartbeat. Then he finally nodded, as if deciding something.

Before I could even think what that could mean, he offered me his arm again. "Where to now, my lady?"

I vaguely remembered what we were doing there, and what I needed to do next. Dessert. I needed to go where I could pick what I needed for the dessert.

Back on Ericura, there hadn't been places that had trusted me to make more than simple dishes and portion and serve already-made pies and cakes. But my mother had been a good baker, so I was bound to remember a few things.

I took his arm, no longer pretending he was my escort, clinging to him for the sheer pleasure of it. "To wherever they sell nuts and flour. I'm making a walnut-raisin cake."

"To the fruit section we go, then," he said jovially, steering me down another road.

We eventually found ourselves behind a group of the potential future queens. They were rushing in a loud, lost hurry. I caught the loudest of their complaints.

"What is the point of this stupid trip?"

"We have chefs and cooks and bakers and such, why in the world would *we* need to make our own food?"

"I can't believe I have come here to be treated like a common maid!"

"How is this meant to be a test? They should be assessing if we're to be good hostesses, not errand boys!"

"The nerve of those people, dragging us down here and leaving us to fend for ourselves. I was raised better than that!"

I knew being dragged around the market in this heat was tiring and inconvenient but, by the level of disgust, you'd think they had been asked to dig up a grave for a necromancy ritual.

"What giant children." Cyrus huffed. "They expect to help rule a kingdom when they can't manage to get their own food?"

"They're rich girls. They don't need to do anything, things are done for them. It's all in one's expectations."

He didn't comment.

We reached our next stop. As I was sampling raisins from different barrels, I spotted a woman digging through her bag at checkout. Holding onto her skirt was a little girl, staring at the floor guiltily, a bitten apple in her hand.

"You bite it you buy it," the vendor told the woman crankily. "No excuses for anyone, including children."

"But we've done our shopping and our budget is used up. I came to this part of the market by mistake. I wouldn't have risked it if I knew the products were imports."

The begging mother was still young, a little younger than

my own mother when I'd last seen her. But her exhaustion made her look ten years older, with dark circles under her eyes and hair sticking out of her bun, adding to her dishevelment. Her impoverished state seemed to be new. She wasn't used to her daily grind yet.

She must be a widow. Young and with a girl who couldn't be more than five, and they were about to get shaken down, all for one lousy apple.

"Then return something and pay for the apple," the vendor insisted.

"But I need everything. My family—we can't—" the woman spluttered, desperate.

"Then you should have thought about that before you brought one of them with you."

I left Cyrus, who was busy checking walnuts for me, and headed toward them, shaking the coin pouch. "Hey, how much is a bag of these apples?"

The vendor immediately put on a friendlier face for me, bowing and presenting a box of pink apples. "These go for twenty-two *oksokos* a pack."

A dozen apples for almost double the price as all the spices, herbs and vegetables I got? This was why I had never been able to afford the finer things. It had been either the good chocolate or dozens of potatoes I could live on for days.

"They'll take one," I said.

The woman stopped digging in her bag, unsure if she'd heard me right.

The man got a sack, filled it with the pink apples and handed it to me. I took out one apple and tossed it to him. "To replace the one that means so much to you."

I then knelt by the girl and offered her the sack. "Think you can carry this for your mommy? My mother always made me carry the bags if I embarrassed her in the market. It made her less mad at me later."

Hesitant at first, the girl cracked a wide smile and took the sack, almost dropping it at first, before raising it stoically.

The mother just watched, mouth open as I started counting the hexagonal coins.

"The—the round ones count as thirty of those," the woman said, her voice shaking like she was about to cry. "He can give you change for it."

"Oh, there it is." I fished out one round bronze coin and gave it to the man. "We good?"

When he gave me back eight pieces, I eyed my remaining coins. I probably wouldn't have enough to buy the rest of the stuff I needed. But no matter, what was important was that I—

Before I could finish that thought, the woman tackled me with a hug. It was more shock rather than the impact of the hug itself that almost sent me tipping over.

"Thank you," she sobbed, sounding like her heart was breaking with relief.

Sharp sadness tightened my throat. I wrapped my arms around her shoulder, resisting the nostalgic urge to set my head there and pretend she was my mother.

"You're welcome," I choked.

Giving me one last squeeze, she stepped back and took her daughter's hand, leading her away. The girl slipped her hand out of her mother's grip to reposition the sack and wave at me happily.

I waved back, fighting back the tears that threatened to pop out of my eyes.

On my way back to Cyrus, I swiped two apples from the stack and stuck one in my mouth. A trade-off for the vendor being an uncompromising jerk. There was no way he could sell all those apples before they spoiled. He could have given the girl one before it did, at least let it slide when she took one herself. But he hadn't.

As I stepped back under the parasol, biting my apple, I handed Cyrus the other apple and he stared at me blankly.

I let my apple fall out of my mouth into my hand. "What's the matter?"

"Why did you do that?"

I slowed my chewing. "Hey, you steal priceless objects, so don't get holier-than-thou with me about a couple of apples."

"I'm not talking about the apples you stole, but the ones you bought for that woman."

"What kind of question is that?" I crunched another huge bite, talking with my mouth full. Cherine would be *so* disappointed. "That man was giving her a hard time just because her daughter wanted to try one. She needed help and I could offer it, so I did. It's something I wished happened to me when I was younger. Maybe they'll pay it forward someday."

He suddenly dragged me towards him, bent and pressed a lingering kiss on my cheek, before whispering against it, "You just have to keep surprising me, don't you?"

I would have answered him, but I was too busy trying not to choke on my apple and my heart—or to spontaneously combust.

I'D FINALLY UNDERSTOOD what the phrase "walking on air" meant.

I'd barely felt the ground beneath my feet as we'd continued our shopping and our hunt for the lamp.

Purchases-wise, I'd gotten everything—well, almost everything. I'd budgeted the money to cover it all with Cyrus's help, but there hadn't been enough left to buy any of those extravagant, sparkly lilies. He'd wanted to get them for me, but I'd declined, suspecting they wouldn't last till the end of the week anyway. No wedding bouquet for me. Not that I'd cared as I'd treaded the clouds of bliss with him by my side.

But by the time Master Farouk blew the whistle that ended the shopping field trip, I'd landed back to the ground of grim reality with a thud.

Cyrus and I had checked every nearby temple's altar and every closet in their priests' quarters, and it seemed there was no such thing as a golden lamp.

Lamps were oily, smelly objects that were expected to crack after a few years of use or at least oxidize and turn an irreversible black with soot. While a gold one would be more durable, it was still something only the obscenely wealthy would commission. Which brought the question of why King Darius would take Nariman's lamp rather than make his own? He had mountains of gold in his own vault, lying untouched for decades.

None of this made sense. There had to be something very special about that one specific lamp. The problem was, I couldn't begin to guess what it could be. And I was nearing my wit's end with this dead-end quest I was on.

Everyone had regrouped at the starting point, chattering up a storm as they checked each others' acquisitions. Fairuza, having lots of money and seeming unaware of her missing sack, had Agnë and Meira carrying more flowers than produce. Cherine mostly had flowers, too, and said she'd ordered sweets to be delivered to the palace. Cora had only a satchel with corn ears sticking out of it.

We returned to the train and Cyrus slinked back to the service area before I could talk to him again. And I wanted to talk to him. I wanted to do nothing but talk to him. Even when I knew I'd sound like a giddy girl. I *was* a giddy girl.

He'd kissed me.

On the cheek, sure, but he'd still kissed me.

I kept trying to catch any glimpse of him as our purchases were taken from us to be inspected and, somehow, graded. I had no luck again during the trip up the mountain. It was even more pensive and quieter than the one down, for which I was thankful. I couldn't get my mind off Cyrus enough to talk about anything else.

The one thing that pulled me out of my thoughts was when I saw Ayman's eyes watching us through the clear spaces in the compartment window. Going outside would have been painful for him, so why had he tagged along if it meant he'd stay on the train?

By the third time he passed, I became certain it was only Cherine he had eyes for.

His fixation with her was making me feel worse for him. She considered him a monster.

But—she also believed her memories of him to be such intensely romantic dreams. Maybe if she officially met him, talked to him, something could work out.

I turned to her, aiming to find out what his chances were. "Cherine, what would you do if you lost the competition?"

She started from admiring her magnificent bouquet. "Blacken Fairuza's other eye."

I sat forward. "I'm being serious. Do you have any plans for what you'd do if you lose?"

She set the bouquet down, toying with a few petals,

looking more crestfallen than I'd ever seen her. "Probably marry some other member of the family."

"What if you met someone you fell in love with and wanted to marry him?"

Cherine's eyes rounded as if she'd never considered the possibility of marrying for love.

Before the answer trembling on her lips left them, Cora broke the moment, deviously suggesting, "You could get shipped off to marry Fairuza's brother. Then you'd be sisters."

Cherine shuddered, sticking her tongue out and crossing her eyes in disgust. "If she's the one chosen, I'll tip her out the tower and marry the prince myself."

"Will you be hauled off to princess jail before or after the wedding?" Cora wiggled her eyebrows. "And who knows? Arbore could even go to war with Cahraman over it."

Cherine sat back, sighing wistfully. "Imagine a war breaking out, just over you."

Cora's eyes bulged with disbelief.

With the moment to probe Cherine's feelings gone, my companions resumed their squabbling. I sat back, my mind paused at their blithe mention of war, especially Cherine's glamorous view of it.

While I was agonizing over actions that, if worse came to worst, would cost only three people their lives, she romanticized being the cause of a war.

I failed to imagine what it would be like if anything I did led to anything as catastrophic.

CHAPTER TWENTY-FIVE

The next days passed in a blur.

The ball Loujaïne had mentioned wasn't going to be held for us. Instead, we had to arrange it ourselves. We were going to be judged on our contributions, not individually, but as a group.

I didn't understand how this was going to work. Anyone who'd ever done group work in school knew that one person did all the work, another delivered a sloppy ten to twenty percent and the rest sat around doing nothing until they took the credit.

Unsurprisingly, this was exactly what happened during our arrangement of the ballroom, our preparation of the meals and the baking of the desserts.

Cyrus hadn't shown himself all since the ride back to the palace. I feared it might be out of regret. He'd held my hand, offered to get me a ring and kissed my cheek and now didn't know what to do about it.

Or it might have been me proposing for him to come with me.

Or proposing in general.

I might have scared him off.

I tried to take into consideration that the cause of his disappearance might not have been that serious, but with no leads to go on, I could only guess and obsess in total futility.

I knew I couldn't afford to be on edge about him, even when I couldn't help it. I had two days left and still no lamp. I had run out of places to look. It wasn't in the palace or in the temples in the city. I had wasted four weeks chasing my tail. And when I went back to Nariman empty-handed...

I couldn't bear thinking about what would happen then.

Now I was fifteen feet up in the air, nailing Princess Ariane's banner to the wall. She was quite handy with craft-work, but I was the only one who'd had experience with heights higher than three-feet, so I was tasked with hanging duty.

"You don't look too good."

The deep, raspy voice felt as if it was projected from nowhere. It startled me so much I dropped my hammer and nail and flew back with a shout. Before gravity could slam me down with its grasp, I latched onto my ladder and threw my weight forwards, steadying its legs.

A shadow separated from the corner of the ballroom. Ayman!

For a terrible moment there, I'd thought it was something else.

Since that day in the market, I could have sworn I'd been feeling...something watching me. I couldn't tell if there really was something or if it was my morbid imagination.

Trying to steady my trembling hands, I scowled down at him. "Just because you look like a ghost, doesn't mean you have to creep around like one."

He chuckled softly. "The reason I creep around is because I look like a ghost."

"Right. Forgot. Sorry."

"You *forgot?*" That seemed to stun him.

I shrugged. "Once I got a good look at you, I thought the difference in your coloring only makes you more interesting than regular folks, almost magical. But if it really bothers you, and limits your life, you could easily blend in if you wanted to. I personally think it would be a shame, but you could dye your hair with henna, like greying staff here do, and maybe shade in your brows. People would think you're a really fair foreigner."

Judging by his dumbfounded expression, he hadn't thought he could do any of that.

"Also, can I have my hammer and nail back?"

After making sure the ballroom was empty, he lifted the hood of his cloak and left the shadows to return my things. He stabilized the ladder for me as I hammered the banner in place.

When my feet touched down on the floor, he repeated, "You don't look too good."

"Yes. Thank you. I know."

"Why?"

I didn't answer him as I strode to the door, peeked outside to check the corridor. Finding no one, with all the girls escaping their chores, I slipped out of the room, heading to the kitchen on this level. He tailed me, as soundless as a shadow, and repeated his question.

I turned my face to him as he fell in step beside me. "I'm under a lot of stress here."

"You seem to know what you're doing."

"Not about my potato festival. The lamp."

"I'm still not clear on that part."

It seemed Ayman hadn't bought my story like Cyrus had.

I shrugged. "Well, neither am I."

We arrived at the kitchen and found it mostly empty. A few bakers were at the far end by the stone oven with six girls, watching their efforts to make bread by the looks of it. As I crept in with Ayman behind me, exclamations of distress and disgust reached us across the massive space as the girls' fingers stuck to a too-wet dough or their handful became rock hard.

I was tempted to go over and show them how to knead the dough in flour to make it less sticky or keep wetting their hands to make it more malleable. The bakers must have instructed them at first, but were now content to watch them struggle unaided.

But my time was almost up and I had to focus on trying to find a way out of my own mess. I couldn't waste even more time helping others in this stupid competition to marry the elusive and probably grotesque prince.

Speaking of grotesque, the rumors about Fairuza's brother had been escalating. It made me wonder; what if it was hereditary? What if both her brother and cousin had a sort of disease that ran in their family that made them look like monsters to the superstitious, and that's why no one ever saw them?

Shaking my head at the turn my thoughts had taken, I exited the kitchen with Ayman on my heels.

Once we reached the alcoves by the tower's staircase, secure that we could have a conversation unseen, I turned to him. "Why are you here again?"

"Cyrus has been busy this week. He wanted you to know that."

So, he wasn't avoiding me?

Relief drenched me like a midsummer torrent.

"And he said I should keep an eye on you for him."

I exhaled raggedly. "Because?"

"Because he can't do it himself. Princess Loujaïne has noticed how...friendly you two were being in the city."

I gulped. "He's not in trouble, is he?"

"He will be if he's caught alone with you again before the verdict is made."

We definitely had to leave soon. We needed to find the stupid piece of junk, hand it to Nariman, get the Fairborns, go home, and get Cyrus and Ayman to adjust and find jobs on Ericura. And, if Ayman liked tiny, bossy girls that much, I could set him up with Bonnie.

That sounded like such a perfect plan. What were the odds any of it would come to pass?

With my luck, none.

I inhaled, trembling. "Is there any other place where that lamp could possibly be?"

He regarded me thoughtfully for a long moment as if debating what to tell me.

Then he finally exhaled. "The king has a safe in his own quarters. That's the last possible place it could be that we haven't searched."

The king's quarters themselves.

Now that I thought of it, it was probably the first place I should have considered. And the last place in this world we could possibly sneak into.

This just kept getting better and better.

LATER THAT NIGHT, the feeling of being watched proved to be more than I could dismiss, or bear.

Cora and Cherine, my only company now, were both deep in dreamland. But with this unsettling feeling, sleep eluded me, even harder and longer than usual. Knowing I wouldn't be able to sleep, I got up, unlocked the balcony doors and stepped out into the night.

The city in the distance was a dark pit of inactivity and the palace gardens were quiet and still. The only movement was the clouds' reflections gliding off the glass domes and the breeze sifting through the trees swaying below me. I breathed in the rare moment of peace.

"Your time is almost up."

Heart almost exploding with fright, I jolted with a shout that blasted its echoes through the night. Spots of yellow light flared all around the gardens like massive fireflies, as the night watchmen snapped up the intensity of their lanterns.

As I stumbled back out of their sight, a faded apparition in the form of Nariman appeared before me.

Her face was frightening in its see-through pallor, her hair undulating like dark flames past her shoulders and the snake staff clutched in her hand seemed alive.

Her disembodied hiss zapped my every nerve again. "Have you found it yet?"

"How—how are you here?" My voice shook with my shivering.

"A mere projection." Her image distorted sideways. "And not a strong one. The city wards interrupt my magic. It has been hard enough trying to monitor you from afar the past few days."

So, it hadn't been just my imagination. She'd been watching me.

I tentatively reached out and poked her midsection. My finger went right through her but a painful buzz discharged through my fingers. I snapped my stinging hand back.

She stalked closer, half of her washing out, the anger in her expression and voice made more menacing by the warping in her apparition. "Well? Did you find it?"

I wanted to retort that if she'd been watching me then she should know I hadn't. But then she'd said she'd been "trying" to monitor me, implying that she'd failed. I also didn't want to be shocked again.

"I…uh…might know where it is now."

For a moment, her image seemed to solidify, coming to life with vibrant color as if she was right before me. "You might? It's been nearly a month. What have you been doing all this time? Every time I managed to get an eye on you, you seemed to be lounging around."

"Yes. Lounging around. In between risking being thrown into the dungeons for sneaking around looking for your lamp, and struggling through this ridiculous contest trying to buy myself more time to continue searching!"

She retreated, the intensity of her colors fading. "Where have you searched?"

"Vaults, temples, shrines, silverware cabinets, staff and servants' quarters and storage rooms. Literally everywhere."

"Then where is this place you now think it might be?"

"The king's quarters."

She seemed to freeze, a hand hovering over her heart.

I huffed. "Didn't think of that, did you?"

"Of course, I did." Her image brightened again. Fury did a lot for her complexion, it seemed. "But I hoped he kept it somewhere else. The king's quarters are guarded all day and all night, with no way to reach them except through the front door." She paused a moment before floating nearer like a menacing ghost, almost making my heart catapult from my mouth. "But this is where your special skills come in."

Her image fizzled again, becoming cloudy with silvery fog before it swirled into a revolving circle, becoming a window into another place.

Within the fog, a complex image formed and began to move, the figures within it becoming clearer, familiar.

In a dungeon with craggy, stone walls, a shackled greying man was slumped to the side on a patch of hay. A girl in a cornflower-blue dress rushed over to him, lifting his face and yelling in distress and desperation.

Bonnie! Mr. Fairborn!

A monstrous shadow crept over her and she turned with a scream, spreading out her arms to shield her father, horror written all over her face.

The shadow of the beast covered her and the window vanished in wisps of smoke, thickening back into the fog and reforming again as the washed-out form of Nariman.

"The beast has finally found its latest offerings. You should hurry before it rips her and her father to shreds."

"B-but if it already found them..."

"I can still hold it off."

I swallowed, my tongue as dry as sandpaper. "How long do I have?"

"You've already wasted a month."

"Because you sent me here with no instructions about what I was getting into, didn't tell me where to look, and because what I'm looking for doesn't seem to exist. An oil lamp made of gold isn't even a concept here."

"Of course, it's not. That's why it's unique. It had to be

pure gold, or else no one would have been able to lure the thing into it!"

My mind screeched to a halt. "Thing? What thing?"

Nariman's wavering image suddenly became completely still.

When she finally spoke again, her voice was an ominous echo that froze me down to my marrow. "The girl who wins the competition will be invited to the king's quarters to be presented with Queen Zafira's tiara. I will hold the beast off until they announce the winner. After that, it will be over for your friends. And it will be your fault."

Then she blinked out of existence.

CHAPTER TWENTY-SIX

"You nervous, honey?" Princess Ariane asked me, setting her hands on my arms, startling me out of my fretful daze. I realized I had been biting my lip tight enough to draw blood. "You don't have to worry that much, not like some of the others. Your food looks great, and it smells amazing too. Where did you learn to cook?"

My practiced answer of "Our mansion cook" or "My lady mother" couldn't form on my tongue or get past my grinding teeth.

I felt if I opened my mouth I'd rave and rant my real feelings to the whole palace; that I cared about this petty competition and this whole pointless world only because I wanted to get the mad witch her lamp and save my friends.

Nariman had implied that only winning this competition would get me into the King's quarters, when she expected me to use my "special skills" to swipe the lamp.

But winning was impossible, and she must know it. I would be eliminated tonight. Her extension was pointless, just the cruel clemency of an unhinged woman. Then, like she'd said, it would be all over. She'd unleash the beast on Bonnie and Mr. Fairborn.

This meant one thing. Now I knew where the lamp was, I had one last chance to acquire it. Tonight, while everyone was preoccupied with the prince's arrival.

I'd been waiting all day for Cyrus to show himself during the ball's preparations so I'd ask him to do whatever it took to get me into the King's quarters. But he hadn't appeared. And every minute that passed sent me farther out of my mind.

It all felt even worse now I realized there was more to this than I'd thought. Nariman's slip-of-the-tongue last night had felt like a mallet to my temple, still reverberated its confusion and dread in my head.

What thing had been lured into that lamp?

Everything was like those riddles of the Simurgh of Alabasta. But unlike Esfandiar of Gypsum, I had no clever answers. I had only more questions that tangled and compromised my sanity further by the second.

"Isn't this the same dress you wore the first week?" Unable to drag my thoughts to the one-sided, mundane conversation with Ariane, I stared at her blankly. She smoothed the complex, glossy braids crowning her head and elaborated, "Don't you have anything else of the same caliber?"

I did. My magical *qarin* had conjured more clothes and accessories for me, but this was the same turquoise dress I'd worn on the first test. I'd needed some sense of familiarity to keep me grounded, some illusion of good luck to keep my wits about me.

Not that it was working. I started to chew on my nails.

Ariane tutted and removed my hand from my mouth.

"Don't do that. Even if you don't get picked, you still have other options. You have quite the reputation now."

Her last words snapped me out of my fugue. A reputation? Did they know I'd stolen the jewelry from the vault and Fairuza's coin pouch?

I was going to get thrown in prison before I could even try robbing the king's safe.

"You're a hero!" I gaped at Ariane, sluggishly realizing she'd meant the opposite of what I'd feared. She rubbed up and down my arms, and that affability she exuded somehow managed to calm me down a bit. "You punched Fairuza in the face and ruined her week." I blinked at her again, and she snorted a small laugh, shaking her elegant head. "You saved Cherine. Really, I have never seen anyone act that selflessly. I didn't think anyone like us had it in them."

"Like us?"

"People who are used to being helped, not helping. You know, now that I know what kind of person you are—" She pretended to dust my shoulders and adjust my necklace. "—once the prince picks me, my family will come for the wedding."

I continued to stare at her. Was there a point to all this?

"I have three—uh, actually two brothers. The eldest is the heir and expected to marry from a neighboring kingdom. But it's no issue. You can have your pick of the other two."

It took me a long moment before her meaning sank in. And if I could feel anything besides gnawing, debilitating anxiety, I would have laughed.

I couldn't believe it. Another girl offering to set me up with her brother.

And not any brother, but a prince. Many steps up from Cherine's lord of a brother.

Not that this offer mattered to me in any way. Such a royal alliance would have been tempting only if it could help me save Bonnie and Mr. Fairborn.

But with every second that passed, I feared nothing could. Nothing except something just as magical as Nariman was. If I needed anything in this world, I needed that ring that granted wishes.

And I needed Cyrus.

And not only because he was the one who could help me.

At Ariane's prodding, mind swirling with desperation, I dully said, "Cherine already offered me her brother."

Ariane crinkled her nose at me. "I know she's your friend, but let's be honest here. Her brother is probably just as insufferable as she is." She paused, as if waiting for my input. I couldn't utter another word, so she went on. "And he's a distant member of the royal family. My brothers are princes. You came for a prince and you'll get one. Just a different one." She smiled cheerily. "So it wouldn't be like you've come here for nothing."

It had better not be for nothing.

But it would come to nothing, on every front, if I couldn't find Cyrus.

Where was he? He should be catering this ball!

As if on cue, Ariane dragged me after her, deeper into the ballroom.

We had decorated it as part of our test, and our collective efforts ended up being haphazard. Mismatched furniture and silverware stocked the room, along with bowls of questionable punch, rock-hard bread and dishes that were half-cooked or overcooked. It was like a birthday party set up by a bunch of eight-year-olds.

Ariane and I parted ways at my table. I gazed down at my

potato festival, my stomach churning. It was cold and getting leathery, but at least it was edible and cohesive. Ariane, the only one apart from Cora who had practical skills, had made most of the decorations hanging on the wall and adorning the tables. Cora had, once again, gone to the orchards and picked colorful vegetables for an arrangement in a hand-made bowl rather than a basket this time. All that effort and it was still her version of trudging through the assignment.

The guests had started pouring in an hour ago. The governors of each Cahramani city, the mayors of each town, the heads of ministries, the nobles and elite of the merchant class all mingled. Many sampled my offerings as they passed by. Most found the pan-fried and mashed potatoes the most fascinating, and asked me about them. I was too caught up in my own distress to answer them properly.

I stared at them in their multi-layered silk outfits, their extravagant jewelry, and their utter lack of worry as they puttered around and a sudden surge of self-pity and loathing swamped me.

I hated it here. I hated everything about these gilded chickens and their obliviousness and selfishness. I hated the king for banishing Nariman to protect his palace and city, instead of imprisoning her so she couldn't play havoc with the lives of those beyond them. Like she was doing with the Fairborns. For that alone, he deserved that I break into his quarters and steal the lamp, along with any irreplaceable items I could safely carry.

I looked around for Cyrus again. He was still nowhere to be found.

My frustrated gaze fell on Cherine beside me, who was being judged by a group that included Asena, Loujaïne and Farouk. The guests were sampling her food—stewed chickpeas in spicy soup, and a colorful fruit salad on frothy yoghurt. They questioned her on everything from why she chose that menu, how she prepared it, to again why she was here.

Across from me, Cora was serving samples of the corn she'd boiled and spread with butter with all the enthusiasm of a barmaid during happy hour. But those who tried it seemed to love it.

A bell rang and the groups switched tables, moving on to other girls. Mine moved on to Fairuza. The only thing that could possibly cheer me up right now would be the judges tearing into her offerings.

Eight people grouped around me. Loujaïne, Asena, Farouk and five guests; a noblewoman, a merchant, a mayor, a governor and one of the cooks from the kitchen.

"Present yourself, your dishes and bouquet arrangement," said Farouk, clearly a bit tipsy and failing to keep himself from looking Loujaïne's way. I wondered what that was about.

I forced myself into customer-service mode, plastering on a big smile that felt like it might crack my face as I curtsied. "I am Ada of Rose Isle and I have six potato-based dishes: mashed potatoes, potato skins, baked potatoes, julienne fries, creamy potato soup and wedges. For dessert, I have made a carrot cake with walnuts and raisins."

At my mention of carrot along with cake, every eyebrow shot up. Seemed they'd never heard of the combination.

After I handed out the potato sampler plates, I kept checking for Cyrus through the gaps between them as they chewed and made thoughtful noises.

If only I knew where he and Ayman holed up during the night, I might have been able to go to them myself. Cyrus hadn't told me much about himself beyond what had slipped out during our conversations. I never found out who his father was and where he worked exactly, or really, anything else about his life.

It didn't matter. I might not know much about him, but I knew *him*. He was clever, funny, gentle and considerate. He'd more than helped me for no reason at all, listened to me, thought of solutions for me, and searched with and for me all over the city. He seemed to…care about me. If anything, it was I who should be telling him the truth.

Yes. When he finally showed up tonight, I was telling him everything. Once he learned what was at stake, he'd realize the urgency of it all. There had to be a tunnel to the king's quarters; some escape route for him and his heir and advisors in case of an attack or siege. If there was one, Cyrus, with his extensive knowledge of the palace and its hidden pathways probably knew of it, or could at least find it. I'd ask him to come with me when we accomplished the mission. Once we found the lamp in that safe, we could take off into the night.

"Why all the potatoes?" Loujaïne asked, poking the mashed potatoes with suspicion.

They're good to live off if you're constantly struggling to find your next meal didn't sound like an answer I could use. Neither did *they're the simplest thing I could safely cook while driven to distraction.*

Instead I said, "Potatoes are the most practical food. I used them in a variety of dishes to prove how versatile they are. They're abundant, they taste good in every form, and they have all you need to survive on should you ever suffer a food shortage. That's something a desert kingdom needs to take into account, if anything ever were to happen to your imports from farmlands. The problem of having nothing else to eat can be made easier if you know how to enjoy what you have in many ways."

They all took time to process my answer—which was

based on stories I had heard about a period of famine in the South of Ericura—while eating everything on their plates. It was either that good or they were starving because every other presentation was inedible.

Maybe I should open a restaurant once we got back to Ericura. Cyrus and I could sell our loot, buy a place where I could be the head chef and he'd run the place and charm everyone into becoming regular customers, with Bonnie as our bookkeeper and Ayman our guard. It would be a struggle, but it would be a good life. A steady life with a family that would never leave me.

And I was daydreaming again.

"You have put some good thought into this," Farouk said, seeming much steadier now, setting his empty plate down and dabbing his mustache with a napkin. "It is also well-made. Who taught you to cook?"

I offered him a piece of cake. "My mother."

He took the plate with a gracious bow of his head. "I should very much like to meet your lady mother. She raised a formidable young woman, very brave and capable."

How I wished he could do that, too.

I murmured that she'd passed and received the appropriate condolences from everyone. Loujaïne, who'd commiserated with me on my first night here, said nothing this time.

I was explaining my cheap bouquet arrangement–a collection of goldenrod and cattails I'd gathered from the garden our dorm overlooked—when I spotted Cyrus. At the sight of him, my heart fluttered chaotically, circulating a surge of scalding heat to my numb face and extremities.

His hair was styled differently today, combed flat from a side parting, making it look darker. His servant's uniform of a buttoned, patterned kaftan and belted sash had been traded for an open, mid-thigh, deep-blue satin coat, with its edges embroidered in a metallic teal paisley pattern. Beneath it was a white, silk shirt, silver sash that topped slate-grey pants tucked into below-knee, polished, black leather boots.

He looked as stunning as ever, if far more put-together and formal. But most importantly, he looked perfectly fine. Nothing bad had happened to him like Ayman had made me fear.

The bell rang again and all the judges and guests moved away from the tables, retreating to the center of the ballroom, where an ensemble of musicians now started playing a sedate melody and all the attendees paired up to dance.

Some judges and guests asked the girls to dance, probably another test to gauge their grace and character. Most girls looked pleased for being chosen and hopped to it as the music sped up to a danceable tempo, with the string, wind and brass sections playing an exotic, quarter-toned tune to the accompaniment of the percussion section's lively rhythm.

Cyrus moved around the room with the other servants, who were dressed nothing like him, maybe denoting his rank among them. I tried to catch his eye and failed as he moved behind everyone as if avoiding attention.

Master Farouk returned to my side, bowing as he offered me his hand. "Would you care to dance, Lady Ada?"

An impulsive, frustrated 'No!' collided with my clenched teeth.

Knowing I could do nothing else, I silently gave him my hand.

He set my hand on his shoulder, held the other and kept his other hand low on my back. I let him lead entirely as I kept trying to catch Cyrus's attention with subtle if desperate gestures over Farouk's shoulder.

"Forgive me for saying, but your hands are quite rough," Farouk said, dragging my attention back to him. "Did you do all the preparation and cooking yourself?"

"How else was I supposed to get everything done?"

He chuckled lightly, pulling back to twirl me. "The cooks were there for a reason, to help."

"I thought they were supervision, in case someone fell into a boiling pot or cut off their own fingertips along with the carrots."

His chuckles rose. "They were that as well, but you didn't have to damage your hands."

"They were rough already."

His eyebrows rose. "Do you cook often, then?"

"You could say that."

"Interesting. You also do your own shopping, and interact with vendors in the market? I believe I saw you bargaining for the raisins."

"I wasn't going to get a tiny bag of wrinkled grapes for the same price as a sack of potatoes."

He raised a hand at my defensive tone. "I know. It was a good call. I'm just curious, where did you learn any of this?"

"Experience?"

"Yes, but how did you gain that?" he pried. "What exactly is a nobleman's daughter doing going to the market and cooking her own food?" He slowed down to peer into my eyes. "Where did you say Rose Isle was again? I don't remember sending an invitation further than Eglantine in Arbore."

My train of thought came to a screeching halt before it was derailed altogether.

He was onto me.

The music shifted to another rhythm as sweat sprouted all over me, sticking my dress to my back. My heart boomed as I searched every corner of my mind for my once-effortless ability to spout convincing lies. But it had slipped out from under me, sending me facedown into the grave I had been digging all month.

"Lady Ada?" His dark eyes searched my face as he nudged me to move to the new tune. "Are you ill today?"

I opened my mouth, but nothing came out. I couldn't even latch onto that excuse. I—

"May I cut in?"

Before I could process what was happening, Farouk had stepped aside with a gallant gesture and Cyrus had taken hold of me and spun us further into the dance floor among the other couples, turning heads and sparking whispers in a line of wildfire.

I snapped out of my cornered daze. "Cyrus! What are you *doing?*"

"Dancing with you, my lady?" he said cheerily, stepping back and spinning me away, still holding my hand.

"Are you crazy? You can't be seen dancing with me," I hissed, trying to pull my hand from his grip.

He only tugged me back into his hold. "Why not?"

"You'll get in trouble," I spluttered. "And you're drawing attention to us. This is the last thing we need right now."

"Ah, are you that worried to be seen with me?"

"If you mean afraid people will notice us and remember us when we go missing, then yes."

"Go missing where?"

"I told you I wanted you to come with me once I got eliminated, remember?"

"You are too certain about the negative outcomes in your life. It can't be healthy." His eyes gleamed with mischief as he twirled me between two couples who gaped at us open-mouthed.

What was going on? Was he drunk? I hoped not, since I had to tell him about the king's safe now, not later. I couldn't wait until I got eliminated. We had to leave while everyone was busy here waiting for the prince to show himself.

I also had to tell him the entire truth, about who I was and what I needed to do.

"Cyrus, I have to tell you something—" I started urgently when he gathered me back in his arms.

"So do I." He pressed closer, raising our clasped hands to his heart, whispering, "You're not going home tomorrow."

I stopped trying to match his pace, my mind and body no longer able to coordinate. "How could you possibly know that? Only the prince can know that now."

"Haven't you figured it out yet, my dearest Lady Ada?" He laughed, a free, heart-fluttering sound, his eyes merry and mesmerizing. "I *am* Prince Cyaxares."

CHAPTER TWENTY-SEVEN

Realization hit me like a lightning bolt.

Stiffening with the enervating blow, I stumbled in his grasp. He steadied me, seemingly unaware of my condition, continuing to swing me around the room, lifting my feet off the floor and whirling my full, layered skirt. Everything revolved right along in a tornado of shock.

The prince.

The prince was Cyrus.

Cyrus was the prince.

Time slowed down as the last month flew past my eyes, unfolding across my stunned mind as it feverishly upturned every word and glance and incident, searching for hidden hints or blatant signs I had missed. I couldn't see anything, couldn't understand anything. Nothing but that I had more or less blackmailed the Prince of Cahraman into helping me in my quest, had been running around with him for weeks, sneaking through the palace's secret underbelly, robbing the vault of the royal family—

His family.

I'd been about to ask the Prince of Cahraman to rob his own father and run away with me.

The implications of who he truly was were an avalanche, burying me beneath them.

He was the prince and everything was lost—my dreams of being with him, and every possibility of saving the Fairborns.

He slowed down, his grin shrinking into an uncertain smile. "Ada, are you alright?"

"D-do I look alright?" I choked, trying to draw a full breath and failing. I could feel the air being sucked out from the whole world, leaving me to suffocate. "Why-why didn't you tell me this before?"

He brought our dance almost to a stop. The music followed suit, as if tied to his every movement. As it probably was. He was the *prince*, and everything here, in this palace, in this kingdom, happened because of and for him.

Now every person around slowed down to accommodate him, and the music became a distorted, discordant background noise in my thundering head.

His hold on my hand tightened, thumb pressing gently on my knuckles, his gaze intense and his smile coaxing. "This wasn't all a game to me, as you once suggested. I needed to see you all for myself as you truly are."

He made no sense. Nothing made any sense anymore. I could only shake my head, staring up at him helplessly in growing horror.

He pressed my closer. "Do you think any of you would have shown me your true selves if you had known I was the prince?"

I'd been about to. But he was right. I would have shown my true self to Cyrus. To *Cyaxares*, I could no longer do that. And I couldn't ask him to rob his own father for me. Or to leave with me either. I had pinned all my hopes for the future, for even having a future, on him. Now they were all over.

I had one remaining night to try to fix everything alone. And if I get caught breaking into the King's safe—make that when—it would be far worse than punching a princess or being caught stealing from the vault. It would be treason. Without Cyrus all I could do with Nariman's extension was out myself as a spy and have my neck put on the chopping block.

But maybe that wouldn't be such a terrible fate. It would probably be better than whatever torture Nariman had in store for me if and when I failed. It killed me to remember the glimpse Nariman had shown me of the horrifying threat to the Fairborns. Imagining it had been bad enough, but seeing it for myself—seeing Mr. Fairborn's vulnerability and Bonnie's desperation—tore me apart. If they were to die because of my failure...maybe it was better to die, too, with the swift blade of an executioner.

"I hope you're not too upset with me," he said, squeezing my limp, trembling hand before pressing it to his chest. "But we'll have all of next week for me to explain."

"W-what do you mean?"

He flashed me a dazzling smile, before letting go of me. "Let me show you what I mean."

Without his support, I almost dropped to the floor as he bowed to me before striding across the dance floor and heading up toward the stage.

Every eye turned to him with rapt attention. Cora and Cherine left their partners and rushed to huddle by my side, asking me what was going on.

"Ladies and gentlemen, I thank you very much for attending today," Cyrus began, projecting his deep, powerful voice across the vast room. "I also thank those who have helped me with the search for a new princess. Your hard work is close to paying off."

Laughter from the palace staff among us stirred the expectant silence. My gaze swept around aimlessly, numbly registering Princess Loujaïne shaking her head at him with a resigned half-smile. Aunt. She was his aunt.

Cyrus's smile seemed to become tinged with apology as he nodded at her, and he continued addressing the crowd. "After a month of observation, and the evaluations of tests both known and unknown, we have now chosen the Final Five in our Bride Search."

Cherine clutched my arm so hard it hurt. Cora gaped at me then at him, speechless.

"That's Cyaxares?" Cherine said, for once too shocked to emote.

"He's the prince," I said, to make myself believe it, heard my voice as if coming from the end of a tunnel.

"Our final five are—" He paused to beckon to a waiter, picked a golden wine glass off his tray, raising it as if to toast the selected ones. "Princess Ariane of Tritonia."

Ariane floated forwards, full of grace and assurance, bowing to the thunderous applause.

"Princess Fairuza of Arbore."

Fairuza joined her, no less majestic, but to less enthusiastic cheers, her eye still bruised but her pride untouched as she curtsied with a flourish in her glorious silver dress.

He turned in our direction, gorgeous green eyes sparkling with eagerness.

It would have been too easy to get lost in him in that moment, just the sight of him, if not for the crushing realization of who he was and what that meant for me.

He seemed proud of this endeavor. Proud that he hadn't just accepted whatever bride they'd shoved on him. He was picking his own future, as much as he could, based on his own set of rules. From his excitement, it seemed to be working, and would end up giving him the peace of mind we'd spoken of in the market.

I would have been happy for him. If I could feel anything at all besides desperation.

"Lady Cherine Nazaryan of Anbur!"

Cherine squealed and shook my arm with her as she bounced happily. She checked her hair and dress before rushing through the crowd, elbowing her way to the front in an excited frenzy, bumping Ariane out of the way as she took her spot below the band.

"Miss Cora Greenshoot of the Granary."

"What?" Cora blurted out. "*Why?*"

Mistress Asena rushed to herd her to the front, ignoring her incessant questions of how she could possibly still be chosen and why.

"And last, but not least, our fifth of the Final Five…" He looked right at me, his heart-melting smile reaching his eyes as he raised his glass, "Lady Ada of Rose Isle."

Air rushed into my lungs under pressure as a cacophony of congratulations submerged me, and urgent hands pushed me forward in a wave through the sea of curious onlookers and envious girls.

I stepped up beside the other four girls, unable to feel anything over my internal chaos.

Cyrus raised his glass to the room and they all did the same. "To the future Queen of Cahraman."

"To the future Queen of Cahraman!" They rejoiced.

As the cheers and chatter surrounded me, the last rational

corner of my mind shouted for me to snap out of it now fate had thrown me a lifeline.

As massive a shock as all of this was, it was as huge a reprieve. I was officially part of the Final Five with both of my friends, and had one last week here. One last chance to get things right, save the Fairborns and get out alive. That was far more than I had been hoping for.

But my hopes had also included Cyrus joining me in both the heist and the great escape.

Now he was not Cyrus—my Cyrus—but Prince Cyaxares.

It was strangely ironic, how we were both playing the same elusive game. He was a prince who had been playing the role of a servant in his search for a bride, while I was a thief in the role of a prospective bride in my search for salvation.

It sounded like a situation straight out of a folktale, one a playwright would fictionalize as a comedy of errors. One underscored in tragedy and could very well end in one.

He was the Prince of Cahraman. And this changed everything.

I would have taken great joy in sharing my secrets with Cyrus, but I couldn't afford to reveal my true self to Prince Cyaxares. Probably not ever.

I needed to get into his father's vault. And I couldn't enlist his help.

That left one way. That single opportunity when I could be invited into the king's domain.

This meant that, to save our futures and very lives, I had to continue as Lady Ada of Rose Isle not Adelaide of Ericura.

And as such, I needed to play this game to win.

I needed to win the Prince of Cahraman.

NOTE FROM THE AUTHOR

I hope you've enjoyed the first installment in the *Cahraman Trilogy!*

If you did, please help me spread the word! Reviews are everything to indie authors, and even a line would make a world of difference on Amazon, and also on Goodreads and Bookbub.

Ada's adventures continue as the competition takes a perilous turn and shocking secrets are uncovered in *PRINCE OF CAHRAMAN.* Her epic adventure concludes in the emotional and heart-pounding *QUEEN OF CAHRAMAN.*

FAIRYTALES OF FOLKSHORE continues with Bonnie's story in BEAST OF ROSEMEAD and BEAUTY OF ROSEMEAD, and Ella's story in PRINCESS OF MIDNIGHT.

For news and updates and special offers and content, please sign up to my VIP mailing list at www.lucytempest.com

I love to hear from my readers, so please contact me at lucytempestauthor@gmail.com

Thank you for reading!

Lucy

PRONUNCIATION GUIDE

— People

- Ariane: Aa-ree-ann
- Cherine: Sheh-reen
- Cyaxares: Sigh-ak-sa-reez
- Esfandiar: Ess-fun-dee-yuhr
- Etheline: Eth-ell-leen
- Fairuza: Fey-roo-zah
- Farouk: Fah-rooq
- Jumana: Zhoo-mah-nah
- Loujaïne: Loo-zhaiy-enn
- Nariman: Nah-ree-mann
- Ornella: Ore-nell-ah

— Places:

- Almaskham: Ul-maz-kham
- Cahraman: Quh-rah-maahn

- Campania: Kaam-pahn-yuh
- Ericura: Air-ree-cue-ruh
- Tritonia: Try-tone-yaa

ABOUT THE AUTHOR

With one foot in reality and the other one lodged firmly in fantasy, Lucy Tempest has been spinning tales since she learned how to speak. Now, as an author, people can experience the worlds she creates for themselves.

Lucy lives in Southern California with her family and two spoiled cats, who would make terrible familiars.

Her young adult fantasy series FAIRYTALES OF FOLKSHORE is a collection of interconnected fairytale retellings, each with a unique twist on a beloved, timeless tale.

Visit her and sign up to her VIP mailing list at www.lucytempest.com

And follow her on Amazon amazon.com/author/lucytempest, Goodreads goodreads.com/lucy_tempest, Bookbub bookbub.com/authors/lucy-tempest Facebook facebook.com/lucytempestauthor, Twitter twitter.com/lucy_tempest, Instagram instagram.com/lucytempestauthor

facebook.com/lucytempestauthor
twitter.com/lucy_tempest
instagram.com/lucytempestauthor
amazon.com/author/lucytempest
bookbub.com/authors/lucy-tempest
goodreads.com/lucy_tempest